"What do you need scarves for?" he asked.

"Well, you said you couldn't find your hand-cuffs. . . ." She paused for effect, encircling one of her wrists with the fingers of the other hand, then whispered, "But I've always preferred scarves anyway. I seem to remember you do, too. . . ."

"Jesus, Cahill," he groaned, "you're killing me."

"Maybe so, but at least you'll die with a smile on your face. . . ."

He could feel her smile through the dark, and he laughed, then sat up and grabbed her around the waist, pulling her onto the floor next to him.

"Pillow," she muttered.

He reached for the one she'd been using and slid it under her head, then pulled her closer.

She snuggled into him.

For a moment, he just enjoyed the sensation of having her this close again.

"Stay," she whispered. "Stay this time."

She was reaching her arms up to draw him close when his phone began to ring.

"Don't answer it," she protested. "Any time the phone rings at two o'clock in the morning, it's not going to be good news. . . ."

By Mariah Stewart
Published by The Random House Publishing Group:

DEAD EVEN
DEAD CERTAIN
DEAD WRONG
UNTIL DARK
THE PRESIDENT'S DAUGHTER

MARIAH STEWART

DEAD EVEN

BALLANTINE BOOKS • NEW YORK

A Ballantine Book
Published by The Random House Publishing Group

www.ballantinebooks.com

ISBN 0-345-46394-3

Manufactured in the United States of America

OPM   9   8   7   6   5   4   3   2   1

First Edition: August 2004

For our darling Katie,
with love and pride, as you graduate from
college—from Mom, who wonders
where the years have gone

The belief in a supernatural source of evil is not necessary; men alone are quite capable of every wickedness.

—JOSEPH CONRAD, *Under Western Eyes*

PROLOGUE

February 2004

THE RIDE FROM THE PRISON HAD BEEN TENSE AND gloomy in the narrow van. The storm had started around midnight, pelting the roads with a steady rain that turned to sleet just before the dark, gray dawn. To compensate for the slick film beneath the tires, the driver had kept one foot on the brake almost all the way to the county courthouse, where he would deliver his six passengers: four prisoners, two armed guards.

Archer Lowell—nineteen years old, thin and pimply-faced, with soft features and soft hands—sat in a seat on the right side of the van by himself—all the prisoners sat alone—and worried about his upcoming trial. His court-appointed lawyer hadn't had much good news for him when they'd spoken the day before. The D.A. had several witnesses lined up who would testify that he, Archer, had indeed stalked and harassed Amanda Crosby for several months, and, as a result of his obsession with her, had beaten her following her last rebuke of his declaration of undying love. He'd also threatened to kill her business partner and one of her friends.

Things weren't looking so good, his attorney had told him as he urged Archer to accept the deal the ADA was offering.

Bullshit. It was all bullshit. Amanda knows I love her. And as for that asshole guy, Derek what's-his-name, that guy who was hanging around her all the time, I know what he was trying to do. Trying to take her away from me. He must think I'm stupid or something, like I couldn't see what he was up to. I'd like to show him who's stupid. Yeah. Someday, I will show him. . . .

The van pulled to the rear of the courthouse and stopped near a ramp leading from the ground level to the first floor. Lowell watched as the other three prisoners were led off, then stood and followed obediently when the guard released the lock that secured him to his seat and motioned him forward.

He ducked his head as he stepped through the door, took the big step down in a quick hop, and waited for the brown-clad deputy sheriff to take custody of him. He followed his guard up the ramp, cursing the leg shackles that prevented him from making a speedier move into the building, hating the icy needles of sleet that peppered his head and slid down the back of his neck. Once inside, he shook it off as best he could, and allowed himself to be led to the anteroom where, a picture of studied calm and infinite cooperation, he'd wait for his lawyer.

In his head, he imagined the judge interrogating his guard.

And what was Mr. Lowell's demeanor while in your custody, Deputy?

He was totally cooperative, Your Honor. A true gentleman.

The sort who'd stalk and harass a lady like Amanda . . . ?

Oh, no, Your Honor. He was gentle as a lamb.

I have no choice but to dismiss the case against Mr. Lowell, and offer our apologies for any inconvenience.

Apology accepted, Your Honor, he'd say with a shy smile. *Oh, and thank you.*

Yeah, sure. It could go down like that. . . .

The opening of the door snapped him out of his reverie, and he looked up, expecting to see his lawyer. Instead, a second deputy sheriff had poked his head in, just far enough to whisper something unintelligible into the ear of Lowell's guard.

"We're going to ask you to step into the room next door," the deputy announced.

Through the doorway, Lowell could see into the hall, where the second deputy stood, his hand on his gun in a casual, almost unconscious gesture. Puzzled, Lowell stood as the cuff that secured him to his chair was released, and he shuffled toward the open door.

"Why?" Archer asked.

"Just come with me now." The deputy gestured with his left hand, his right still resting atop his holster.

"What about my lawyer?" Archer stood uncertainly. "He's going to be here any minute."

"When he gets here, we'll let him know where to

find you." The deputy stepped aside and waited for Lowell to move into the room next door.

The hall was crawling with law enforcement types, local uniforms as well as state police and the ever present county deputy sheriffs. Some were running, some gathering in small excited groups. Lowell looked over his shoulder, trying to gauge what could create such a buzz, but he was shoved forward before he could get a handle on what was going on.

The new room was wider than the one he'd just left, with two long windows and eight or ten chairs, one of which was occupied by another of the prisoners who'd shared the ride in from the prison that morning. His was the only face that had looked even vaguely familiar to Lowell, though Archer couldn't quite place him. The man was stocky, like a prizefighter, his arms and face freckled, and his eyes golden brown. His red hair—faded a bit with age, but red nonetheless—came as a surprise.

Where had Lowell seen him before? He didn't recall having seen him out at High Meadow, but there was something about him. . . .

The sound of running feet in the hallway broke his concentration. There was a bit of shouting, and by craning his neck, Lowell could see that activity just outside the door was increasing.

"What do you think is going on out there?" he asked his companion.

"What *is* going on out there?" the man asked, and Lowell realized that from his seat, his companion was unable to see the glass window in the door.

"Lots of cops. *Lots* of cops. Several different departments and some state police. People running every which way." Lowell stretched his neck farther to get a better look.

"My guess is that someone might have escaped from custody."

"Really? You think someone's on the run?" Lowell felt a thrill of excitement. "Someone from High Meadow?"

"You were in the van from High Meadow this morning," the red-haired man noted.

Lowell nodded, more interested in what was going on outside.

"Me, too," the man continued, "me and Waldo, the guy who, I suspect, is on the fly out there. There was a rumor he might decide to take off."

Lowell stared at the man who sat, shackled, at the opposite side of the room.

The man smiled, a don't-mess-with-me-smile that Lowell knew instinctively had nothing to do with wanting to reassure him.

Lowell cleared his throat and pretended that he was not intimidated. "You think he'll get away with it?"

Before he could answer, the door opened to allow another prisoner to join them. He, too, had been in the van that morning. He was tall and thin, and he moved in a way that made Lowell think the man was more muscle than one might immediately suspect. His hair was short, light brown, and his eyes were deep set and murky gray.

For reasons that Lowell could not explain, he recoiled slightly. The man had an air of the sinister about him, though from outward appearances, he gave the impression of being more amused than deadly.

The deputy took a moment to remind his prisoners that there was a guard right outside the door, "armed, and he won't hesitate for one minute to bring you down if you so much as move."

"A bit heavy-handed, wouldn't you say?" The new man grinned slightly and looked directly at Lowell.

"He's just trying to scare us." The red-haired man shrugged. "They ain't really that good."

"What d'ya suppose they're doing out there?" Lowell squirmed in his seat. Something about this new guy made him nervous.

"They're playing 'Where's Waldo.' Waldo Scott." The redhead turned to the newcomer to explain. "He was in the van with us on the way in this morning. He got himself free somehow and took off. Get it? 'Where's Waldo'?"

"No." Lowell told them, and the other two explained about the children's book where one searched each page to find a certain character, Waldo, throughout the book.

Lowell, who hadn't spent much time reading as a kid, thought it sounded stupid.

Waldo's attempted escape—and the odds of his succeeding—was discussed in low voices, and the consensus seemed to be that the three men were placed together temporarily to free up two of the deputies who would be in on the hunt for the escapee. Since all three prisoners in the room were shackled to their seats, the chance that any one of them would join Waldo in his quest for freedom was unlikely.

"What're you in for?" the red-haired man asked the newcomer.

"I was stopped for going through a stop sign, and it turns out there was an outstanding warrant for a guy with the same name," he responded, and ignored the redhead's subsequent sarcastic comment about "manly crimes." "You?"

"I'm in here pending appeal of a conviction," the redhead replied.

"For what?" Lowell heard himself ask.

"A domestic dispute."

"Oh." Lowell studied the man carefully. That he had seen his face before was a certainty, but he just couldn't remember where. "I'm supposed to have my trial today. I hope they find Waldo in time to get started. I want to get it over with."

"What are the charges?" the man nearest the window asked.

"Well, see," Lowell was eager to explain, just as he would once he got into that courtroom, "they're saying that I stalked this girl. But I didn't stalk nobody. She was my girl, you know? They got the whole thing wrong."

"She must have complained about something, for them to charge you with stalking," the red-haired man noted. "What did she tell the police?"

"She was confused. The cops made her lie," Archer said. An edginess began to move over him, and he felt it spread through his body.

"What's your name, son?" the man with the buzz cut was asking.

"Archer Lowell."

"I'm Curtis Channing," the man told him.

"Well, Archie . . ." the other occupant of the room began.

Archer saw red.

"Don't call me Archie. Do not ever call me Archie."

"Whoa, buddy. Chill. No offense." He offered what for him must have been an apology. "No need to get all upset."

"I hate the name Archie."

Hey, Archie! Cartoon boy! Where's Veronica? The childhood taunt echoed in his ears.

"Okay, then, you're Archer, and I'm Vince Giordano." The third member introduced himself. "Named for my uncle, but we don't talk no more. Bastard testified against me in court. So much for blood being thicker than water."

It was then that Lowell recognized him, and it took a major effort on his part not to shrink back. Vince Giordano—the man who had murdered his own children rather than lose custody of them, before turning the gun on his wife—had been very big news locally over the past two years.

"I know who you are. I saw you on all the news channels. I saw when you were arrested . . ." Lowell heard himself saying. He wished his buddy Glenn—small-time con man that he was—could see him now, rubbing elbows with the most notorious killer the county had ever seen. That would show him a thing or two, wouldn't it?

"Yeah, well, I got a lot of press. The trial got a lot of airtime," Giordano said.

It appeared to Lowell that, rather than ask about that, Channing chose to change the subject back to the lockdown and the number of media types outside the courthouse.

Archer could not have cared less. The important thing to him was what was *not* happening *inside* the courthouse.

"I don't think it's fair that I should miss my trial just because they lost someone and can't find him."

"Yeah, well, tell it to the judge," Giordano snapped. "I ain't too happy about the delay myself. We had a big day planned here. My attorney thinks he can get my conviction overturned."

"What were you convicted of?" Channing asked.

Lowell, who knew all too well what Giordano had done, turned to see just what the man would admit to.

"Shooting my wife, among other things."

It was the other things that had bothered Lowell. What kind of a person could put a gun to the head of a little boy who was sleeping in his bed, and pull the trigger? And hadn't it been two little boys . . . ?

The thought made his stomach hurt.

Archer looked up just in time to see some sort of odd exchange between Channing and Giordano. Though no words were spoken, there had been something there, and Lowell wondered if the men were telepathic. He'd heard about such things, about people who could read other people's minds. He watched the two men warily. The whole idea gave him the creeps.

"Did you?" Channing was asking Giordano.

Uh-oh, Lowell thought. Obviously Channing had absolutely no idea who Giordano was. Otherwise he wouldn't be asking a convicted murderer—*a child killer, for Christ's sake*—if he did it. He held his breath, waiting to see what Giordano would do.

Giordano smirked.

"Then why would they overturn your conviction?" Channing asked, as if his question had been answered in the affirmative.

That telepathic stuff again? Lowell wondered.

Giordano began to explain how all of the evidence presented against him at trial had been fabricated by one of the cops, and that his lawyer was going to prove it.

"They can let you off for that?" Lowell was drawn back into the conversation. "If somebody lies?"

"Yup," Giordano said smugly.

"But don't they just try you all over again?" Lowell began to ponder the possibility of getting someone to lie at his upcoming trial.

"Nope," Giordano was telling him. "My lawyer says they can't do it. First time around, the D.A., he was out to get me. Loaded the charges, every fucking thing he could think of." Giordano chuckled. "Imagine his surprise when he found out that the cop he'd built his case around had lied from day one."

"How do they know for sure he lied?" Archer asked.

"Because he shot his mouth off, admitted that he'd lied about seeing me running from the house that day, lied about everything. Wanted to make sure the charges stuck, he said. Now he's facing perjury charges. Guess crime doesn't pay, huh?"

"What's the first thing you're gonna do when you get out, Vince?" Lowell couldn't help but admire Giordano in a perverse sort of way. Here he was, a convicted killer of three innocent people, and he was apparently about to walk. What was not to admire in being able to beat a rap like *that*?

"Depends on whether or not I'd get caught."

"What if you wouldn't?" Lowell said.

"What, wouldn't get caught?"

"Yeah. What if you could do anything—anything at all—and not get caught?"

"Gotta think on that a minute." Giordano appeared to be giving the question some heavy consideration before lowering his voice. "If I could get away with it, I'd put a bullet through the head of my former mother-in-law." His face began to darken. "And then I'd do that woman—the advocate—who worked for the courts and told the judge to take my kids away from me. And then the judge who said I couldn't see my kids no more."

Lowell shifted nervously in his seat and prayed that Giordano wouldn't wig out, the way he looked like he was about to do, and bring half the sheriff's department into the room.

"Where are your kids now?" Channing asked.

"They're with their mother," Giordano said, looking Channing directly in the eye. After a long moment of staring coldly, he turned to Archer and asked, "How 'bout you? What would you do, if you could do anything and not get caught doing it?"

"I don't know," Lowell said, surprised to have the question turned back on him. He hadn't given it any thought until that very moment. "Maybe . . . maybe that guy, that guy who kept bothering my girl. Maybe him, if he's still around. And maybe that friend of hers, the nosy bitch . . ."

Archer Lowell felt a burning build within, slowly at first, as he thought about the woman who owned the antique shop across from Amanda's. The one who called the police every time she saw Archer in the neighborhood. What business was it of hers if he'd wanted to wait outside Amanda's shop at any time of day, whether first thing in the morning, before she opened, or late in the day, at closing time. It was still a free country, wasn't it? Besides, he had a right to know what she was doing, didn't he? How else would he have known about that other guy, the one who was there all day, every day?

"What about your girl?" Giordano was smirking again. "Seems like she's the real problem here. I'll bet she's the one who pressed charges, right? Seems to me that you'd want to call on her. I know I would, if it was me."

"Oh, I'm gonna call on her, all right. I'm gonna call on her first thing, I get outta here." Lowell's jaw tightened, and his palms began to sweat at the thought of seeing Amanda again.

"What 'bout you, Channing?" Giordano turned his attention to the third member of the group. "Anyone you gonna go see?"

"Don't know."

"Oh, come on now." Giordano lowered his voice a little more. "We're just bullshitting here. There has to be someone, someplace, that you'd like to show a thing or two."

Once again, Lowell thought there'd been some silent exchange between the two older men, and while he couldn't quite put his finger on it, something about the wordless communication made him uncomfortable. That woo-woo shit spooked him.

"Well," Channing began slowly, "if I were to pay a visit to someone in my past, I guess I'd look up my mother's old boyfriend."

"That can't be all." Giordano encouraged him to continue.

"And there's this writer I wouldn't mind having a chat with."

"That's only two," Lowell reminded him. "You got one more."

"Well, there's a cute little FBI agent I'd like to see again. Just to see if the chemistry is still the same."

Confusing, Lowell thought, his eyebrows knitting together. His mother's old boyfriend, a writer, and an FBI agent? What the hell is that all about? Channing probably doesn't understand what we're doing here. He must think we're talking about *visiting*.

But me and Giordano, we know what's going on.

He felt a sudden kinship with the convicted murderer, and a sudden need to try to enlighten Channing as to the nature of their theoretical "visits."

" 'Course, if we really did these things, if we really did go see 'em and . . . well, you know, did *stuff*, it isn't like the cops wouldn't know who to look for, you know?" He met Channing's eyes, trying to convey his meaning without words, but the older man's expression never changed. So much for being subtle.

He tried again.

"Like Vince, they find your mother-in-law with a bullet in her head after you get out, the cops'll be like, *duh. Wonder who did her?*"

Lowell continued to watch Channing's face.

"Well, it was just talk. Didn't mean nothing." Giordano brushed it all aside and stared at the door as if he was afraid to have been overheard.

"Unless we like, you know, switch our people," Lowell heard himself saying.

"What d'ya mean, switch our people?" Giordano asked suspiciously.

"You know, like that movie." Lowell felt himself growing excited. "The one on the train, where these two guys meet and they each agree to whack someone that the other wants—"

"Whoa, buddy." Giordano interrupted him brusquely. "This was just idle talk. That's all. Just idle talk."

Lowell felt the color rise in his face. Giordano was looking at him as if he were stupid or something.

"Sure. I know that." Lowell defended himself. "But it doesn't hurt to pretend. We got nothing else to do in here right now. No TV, no VCR. Gotta think about something."

"How old are you, Lowell?" Giordano asked.

"I'm nineteen."

"That explains it." Giordano was wearing that

smug look again. Lowell knew he could learn to hate him for that.

"Explains what?"

"Your loose mouth, that's what."

"No, come on." Lowell tried to ignore that snotty tone in Giordano's voice, that Lowell-you're-nothing-but-a-dumb-shit tone that he'd heard from everyone all his life. "It's just a game. A game, that's all."

"You ever kill anyone, Lowell?" Giordano's voice dropped yet again.

Lowell shook his head.

"You, Channing?" Giordano turned suddenly.

Channing didn't respond, and Lowell thought it best to ignore the noncommittal stare Giordano had earned in return for his question.

"If we were going to play the game, then we would each have a list, and we would each promise to do the other's list, right?" Lowell said, as much to break the tension as anything else.

"Boy, you don't give up, do you?" Giordano laughed for the first time that Lowell could remember.

"First we'd have to decide how to figure out who would, you know, do whose people."

After a moment during which he'd thought this over, Lowell brightened. "I know. We could each pick a number between one and thirty and guess which number the other guy is thinking of."

Lowell thought this made him appear clever, to have come up with the method of choosing, but Giordano was laughing again, as if the whole thing was a big joke. Which, of course, it was.

"Okay, Channing, you go first. Think of a number between one and thirty, and me and Vince will see if we can guess. Whoever comes closest to your number, gets your list."

"Why don't we just keep this simple," Channing suggested. "Archer takes my list, I'll take yours, Giordano, and you'll take Archer's."

"Cool." Lowell nodded, pleased that his new friends were apparently beginning to get into the spirit of things.

"It's just a game, Archer. Just a game." Giordano was back to that annoying tone of his.

Lowell shot him a look that said, *Of course it is,* then turned to Channing, who was being much more fun than Giordano was.

"Okay, so who's on your list, Channing? Who would I be going to see?"

"I think we should lower our voices," Giordano insisted. "Just in case someone is listening. Even though it's just a game . . . and none of this is ever going to happen."

"Right, right, sure." Lowell nodded with mounting enthusiasm. "Sure. None of this is going to really happen. It's just a game. I know that. Just a game."

Yet even as he spoke, there was a keen sense of conspiracy in the air, and he couldn't help but wonder what it would be like to play the game for real. What it would be like to put his hands around the throat of a stranger, and squeeze until there was no reason left to keep on squeezing. Or to pull the trigger of a gun, and watch a man fall, his life spreading around him in a thin red pool.

He sneaked a side glance at his companions. *They* knew what it was like, both of them. He'd bet his life on it.

But he'd never really know, he reminded himself. After all, it was just pretend.

CHAPTER ONE

FINGERTIPS TAPPED LIGHTLY ON EITHER SIDE OF THE rim of the steering wheel, a quiet expression of annoyance favored by FBI Special Agent Miranda Cahill when faced with a vexing situation over which she had no control. The current immovable object was the rental car that had buzzed along nicely from the Natrona County Airport just a short hop from Casper, Wyoming, where she had picked it up, to the spot where it had sputtered unceremoniously to a stop some fifteen miles from Pine Tree Junction.

At least, that was where the last road sign had placed her, but that had been close to half an hour ago. She wondered if perhaps somehow she'd taken a wrong turn. Tough to do, she thought wryly, when there had been so few turns to be taken.

She turned the key in the ignition one more time, praying for a smooth start. Her prayers were answered with the clack-clack-clack of an engine that steadfastly refused to turn over. Battery, maybe. Or perhaps the starter. Either way, the Taurus was dead. And that meant she would be walking the rest of the way to Linden, however far that might be, if she was going to get there today.

Cursing aloud, she got out of the car.

"I should leave you unlocked, you know that?" She spoke aloud to the car, pausing with the key in her right hand. "Let's see how you like being abandoned out here in the middle of nowhere, all alone. Defenseless. May you be pilfered and vandalized."

She locked it anyway, tossed her large brown tote bag over her shoulder, and set off on foot toward her destination. Hardly defenseless herself, she slipped her Sig Sauer into the holster that rode on her hip, just in case a mean-spirited rattlesnake or equally ornery cowboy crossed her path.

While she walked along the narrow shoulder of the road, she fiddled with her phone, found the autodial number she wanted, and hit Send. When there was no answer, she dialed a second number, never missing a stride.

"Please leave a message for John Mancini. . . ."

"Damn," she grumbled. "I hate voice mail."

She blew out a heavily agitated breath.

"John, it's Miranda Cahill. I'm currently hoofing it up what I believe is still Route 387, but since there are no signs out here in the middle of No Where, Wyoming, that's just a guess on my part. I'm due in Linden in twenty minutes for the meeting, but that looks way optimistic right now. I tried calling Aidan, but he didn't pick up. If you or someone else could reach him, please let him know I'm going to be a little late. If he'd like to come and pick me up, even better. I'll be the one walking along wearing a tan suede jacket and a we-are-not-amused expression."

She ended the call, slipped the phone into her

pocket, and hitched the bag a little higher. Her long legs ate up lengths of the road at a healthy clip despite the high-heeled boots, partly because her natural pace was quick, partly because the temperature was barely thirty degrees and certain to be dropping as the day began to fade. She was determined to reach Linden before that happened. If there was one thing she hated more than anything, it was the cold.

"Jamaica," she mumbled under her breath. "Bahamas. Acapulco. Bermuda. The Keys . . ."

She tried to recall the words to some of the old Beach Boys surfer songs they played on the local oldies station, but the only song that came to mind was "Kokomo," so she sang those few words she knew over and over—"Bermuda, Bahama, come on, pretty mama, to Key Largo, Montego, baby why don't we go"—hoping to mentally transport herself to some warm clime. But the wind began to pick up and blew her dark hair around her head, and the soft sands and blue waters faded away. She stopped, rummaged in her bag for an elastic, then pulled her hair back into a ponytail before moving on. She walked for nearly forty minutes before the outline of a building appeared in the distance.

"Please be Linden. Please please please . . ."

Ten minutes later, she found the building to be a gas station attached to the small diner that was her destination. She walked across the parking lot, which was little more than one large pothole, and smiled through a grimy window at the man who sat behind an old metal desk on the other side of the glass.

She opened the door and took a half step inside. "Hi. I don't suppose you have a tow truck?"

The old man at the desk shook his head, struck dumb, no doubt, at the sight of the tall, willowy beauty who'd appeared literally out of nowhere.

"I was afraid of that." She nodded and let the door swing closed behind her.

She walked a dozen more steps and entered the diner, pausing momentarily to look around. There were only two customers. Fortunately, they were the two people she'd come to see.

"Hey, Aidan." She greeted fellow agent Aidan Shields with a pat on the back, then dropped her bag onto the floor before reaching out to hug his companion. "Mara, it's good to see you."

"Good to see you, too." Mara Douglas stood and embraced her friend. "I couldn't believe it when Aidan said you were on your way out here. It must be something really important."

Mara's eyes were shining with hope.

"It is, but I'm afraid it's not what you want to hear, honey." Miranda pulled a chair over from a nearby table and sat down. "I'm sorry, Mara, I wish I could tell you that we've been able to confirm that your daughter and your ex-husband are part of the group out at the Valley of the Angels, but they are not."

"But we—Aidan and I—have tracked them here. Jules is here; he's got Julianne here with him." Mara's eyes widened. "We had a credible tip—Aidan, tell her. . . ."

"We did have a credible tip." Aidan Shields nodded

slowly. "But, Mara, I told you that we weren't sure how old that information was."

"But . . ."

"Miranda, why don't you tell us what you've heard?" Aidan covered one of Mara's hands with his own.

"Jules is working with Reverend Prescott in some executive capacity, we do know this. He's apparently involved with their finances, but right now, we're not sure exactly where he is. He has been here, at some time, but I'm afraid that neither Jules nor your daughter is with the movement here in Wyoming."

"How do you know?" Mara fought to control her emotions. "How can you be certain?"

"All I can tell you at this time is that the Bureau has someone inside the compound. She has confirmed that they are no longer here. Unfortunately, she hasn't been able to find out where they went when they left, but she's still working on that. She has asked that you and Aidan leave the area. The interest you've shown in the movement, the questions you've been asking of the members when they come into town . . . it's been noticed. Our agent is afraid you'll call unnecessary attention to the group and, sooner or later, to her."

Mara looked at her blankly.

"In other words, back off, because we could jeopardize the life of our agent." Aidan summed it up.

"That's exactly right." Miranda nodded. "I'm sorry, Mara, I know how hard this has been for you—"

"No. No, you do not." Mara pushed herself away from the table slowly. "With all due respect, Miranda, you have no idea how hard this has been. If you'll excuse me for a minute . . ."

When Mara passed through the door to the restroom, Aidan turned to Miranda and said, "Who's inside?"

"Genna Snow."

"The boss sent his *wife*?" Aidan's brows lifted in surprise.

"Who better to look into a phony religious movement led by a bunch of self-appointed apostles who seem to be attracting a lot of runaways and street kids? All adolescent girls, many of whom seem to have disappeared into thin air?" Both agents knew Genna Snow's story. As a child, she'd been abused by a pedophile who masqueraded as a man of the cloth. Twenty years later, he'd been released from prison and had tracked her down. She'd taken him out with one shot through the heart, but not before he'd engaged in a bloody business that had left few survivors. "We think some of these kids are being sold over the Internet. It's a very ugly business they're running out there. Valley of the Angels, my ass. More like the Valley of Lost Souls."

"Why don't we just go in and shut it down?"

"So far, the Bureau is apparently long on suspicion and short on facts. We've been trying to get into their computers, but someone inside has been remarkably good at erecting firewalls around firewalls." She toyed with her hair. "Funny, but we originally started looking at Prescott because we'd traced Jules Douglas to him in Colorado. Then, the agent who went in noticed all of these messed-up young girls coming in, staying for a while, getting their acts cleaned up, then just disappearing. When he asked, the only thing he was told was that the girls had been 'cleansed' and sent on their missions."

"Cleansed?"

"A lot of them come in drugged up, dirty, sick, right off the streets. The movement promises them a new life, new hope. They get them clean, perhaps brainwash them a bit, then sell them to willing buyers." She made a face that spoke volumes of her disgust. "God only knows what happens to them after that. It's no secret that there's a huge market for underage kids. From your basic pedophile to the porn industry, there's a long line of hungry buyers just waiting for the right girl to come along. Reverend Prescott is getting very, very rich making sure that everyone finds the right girl to suit his—or her—needs."

"Genna's found Jules and Julianne in there?"

"Are you sure you want to know?" Miranda raised one eyebrow. "Could you know and not tell her if she asks?"

Aidan mulled the question over.

"I knew as soon as I got the call that you were on your way that we must be very close this time."

"Closer than you know, pal." Miranda leaned back in her chair and watched his face.

He sighed deeply.

"It's been more than seven years since Mara's ex-husband took their daughter and disappeared with her. It's ripped her apart. She won't stop searching for Julianne until she finds her. I promised I'd follow every lead with her, do whatever it took to find her daughter and bring her home. I didn't figure on having to withhold information from her."

"How do you feel about outright lying to her? If she asks you point-blank if you believe that Julianne is not in the compound, what will you say?"

"I don't like the idea of lying to her. I hope it doesn't come to that. I don't know if I could do it. On the other hand, if she knew for a certainty that Julianne was in there, she'd walk right into the compound herself."

"That is precisely what we're afraid of."

"Let me ask you this. How much danger is Julianne in?"

"My guess is that her daddy has been able to shield her so far. Which makes me think that old Jules is performing some big service to Prescott. We suspect he's found a way to launder some of those dirty dollars," Miranda said softly, even as she smiled gently at Mara's approach, "But we're still trying to build the case."

"Hungry?" Miranda asked as Mara sat back down.

"Not really." She shrugged.

"Well, I am ravenous." Miranda caught the eye of the tall blonde waitress who was leaning against the counter, watching them. "As long as we're here, we might as well eat. Then, if it's okay with you, I'll hitch a ride to the airport with you."

"We'll need to check on a flight, I suppose," Mara said, grim defeat drawing down the corners of her mouth.

"Taken care of." Miranda patted her bag. "Compliments of the federal government."

"You knew we'd leave with you?" Mara asked suspiciously. Her sister was a profiler with the FBI, and Mara knew sometimes things weren't exactly as they seemed.

"I picked them up when I made my own flight arrangements. I figured . . ." Miranda paused and smiled as the waitress approached, paper menus in hand, which she distributed silently.

"Thanks, Jayne," Miranda said, noting the waitress's name tag. "We'll let you know when we're ready to order."

"Not very friendly, is she?" Mara frowned when the waitress had disappeared into the kitchen.

"Oh, I'm sure she has her good points." Miranda skimmed over the menu. "Anyway, as I was saying, I figured you'd be wanting to go back east. I mean, why waste precious vacation time on a dead lead, when a live one might pop up later on?"

Mara pondered the logic. It did make sense.

"Okay, if you're sure." Mara turned to Aidan. "You're sure, right? That it's the right thing to do? You're convinced that Julianne is not with Reverend Prescott's group?"

"I am absolutely convinced it's the right thing to do," he told her, choosing his words carefully. "Miranda wouldn't have come all this way to turn us in the wrong direction."

"Okay." Mara sighed, shaking her head slowly. "You know, I felt so sure this time—"

"I know, baby." Aidan rubbed her shoulders. "Maybe next time."

"It's been *maybe next time* for seven years now," she reminded him.

Aidan looked at Miranda through guilty eyes, and appeared about to say something when Miranda's phone began to ring.

"Cahill."

"Cahill, it's John. Sorry I didn't get back to you sooner. I just got out of a meeting and heard your message." John Mancini, head of a special crimes unit within the FBI, sounded uncharacteristically tense. "Are you still—what was the phrase you used—hoofing it down Route 387?"

"No, right now I'm sitting in Ye Old Bumfuck Falls Café with Aidan and Mara, about to order lunch. Then, because my car rolled over and played dead about six miles back, I'll be getting a ride to the airport with them. You might want to have someone pick up the car and return it, by the way. It's charged to the Bureau."

"Mara's agreed to leave?"

"Not a problem." Miranda studied the chipped polish on one of her fingernails.

"Have you told Shields the truth?"

"I didn't have to." She rested the phone on her shoulder and motioned to Aidan to order her a roast beef sandwich by pointing to the specials board. The sandwich was the only special.

"Good, good. Well, try not to miss your flight, Cahill. You need to be in Fleming, Pennsylvania, by noon tomorrow."

"What's in Fleming?"

"An old friend of yours was just released from prison."

"Old friend of mine?" She frowned.

"Archer Lowell. Ring a bell?"

"Sure. Amanda Crosby's stalker. What's he up to?"

"That's what you're going to find out."

CHAPTER TWO

AT PRECISELY THE STROKE OF NOON, THE LITTLE RED sports car pulled into the first available parking spot accompanied by a flourish of pebbles kicked up by braking hard on the gravel surface. The driver's door opened even as the engine shut down, and Miranda Cahill stepped out, pausing to take in the surroundings. The old hotel on the edge of town was just this side of shabby. Paint a few years past its prime. Shutters a wee bit crooked. Even the sign that hung from the wooden post out near the edge of the parking lot—THE FLEMING INN ~ EST. 1741—needed a sprucing up. But in spite of its obvious need of updating, the place did possess a certain charm. There were pumpkins marching along the hand railing at the front steps and clay pots holding an abundance of brightly colored chrysanthemums nestled in a corner of the porch.

On the whole, it wasn't bad for a hole-in-the-wall town like Fleming, Pennsylvania, she nodded. Not bad at all.

She checked the other cars in the lot. As she'd expected, the compact belonging to Bureau profiler Anne Marie McCall was already there. Next to Anne Marie's car sat a dark blue Passat with D.C. tags. No idea who that belonged to. An SUV with Pennsylvania tags, again, no clue. Five other cars, all with Pennsylvania license plates, were parked at the far side of the lot. Maybe staff, Miranda thought as she slammed the car door and headed up the cobbled walk to the front door, which she found standing open.

She stepped into an entry that was decorated somewhat prematurely for both Halloween and Thanksgiving, with a cornucopia on a wide sideboard and several more mums in huge pots at the base of a wide staircase, and a wooden bowl filled with candy corn on the receptionist's desk. Small fabric ghosts and orange pumpkin lights draped the newel post.

"Hi." Miranda greeted the middle-aged woman who appeared from the room on her right. "I'm to meet some friends here."

"Ms. McCall's group?" The blonde woman asked.

"Yes."

"Right this way. Your group is meeting in a small side room so you can have some privacy. Not," she grinned wryly, "that we're overcrowded here for lunch today. But Ms. McCall did say that privacy would be appreciated."

The woman led Miranda through a large dining room on their right to a smaller room beyond. Only three of the eight chairs that flanked the long refectory table were occupied. A warm fire glowed from a small corner fireplace, and lace curtains hung from the two windows. An oddly genteel place, Miranda mused, for a discussion such as the one they were about to have.

"Sorry I'm a little late," she apologized as she removed her jacket. She draped it over the chair next to that of the only other woman in the room and sat down.

"You're right on time. We were just sitting here, enjoying the atmosphere before we have to get down to business," Anne Marie told her. "Besides, we still have one yet to arrive, so let me pour you a cup of this excellent coffee"—she did so as she spoke—"and you can just have a minute or two to relax."

"Evan, it's good to see you again." Miranda sat and accepted the cup Anne Marie offered her.

"Always a pleasure." Evan Crosby, a detective from nearby Avon County with whom Miranda had worked on several cases over the past year, greeted her with a smile.

"And Jared, I'm guessing you're the man in charge here today?" Miranda leaned forward to address the man on Evan's left.

"Just standing in for John." Jared Slater sipped at his coffee. "He had a previous commitment. Since Philly is the closest field office, I got the call."

"I spoke with John briefly yesterday." Miranda's eyes met Evan's from across the table. "He mentioned that an old friend of ours is no longer a guest of the commonwealth."

"Footloose and fancy free, as of Monday." Evan nodded.

"How'd he get out so soon?" Miranda frowned.

"First offense plus good behavior equals a light sentence. Eight months in the county prison, three years probation."

"And he is where now?"

"In a trailer park about four miles from here."

"Really?" She mulled this over. "Explains why we're meeting in beautiful downtown Fleming."

"Never could put a thing past you, Cahill."

Miranda's cup froze momentarily midway between her mouth and the saucer. She'd know that voice anywhere.

Shit.

"Hello, Will," she said to the newcomer without looking up. "I wasn't aware you'd be in on this pow-wow."

"We've invited Will to join us because of his computer skills as well as his insightful investigative ability," Jared explained.

"My charm, wit, and dashing personality had nothing to do with it." Will Fletcher took the seat next to Evan, seemingly oblivious to the flash of annoyance that crossed Miranda's face.

"Aren't you lucky to have those computer skills to fall back on," she murmured.

"How about if we get Mrs. Duffy back and put in our order for lunch so we can get started." Jared went off in search of the owner.

"You're looking well, Cahill." Will faced Miranda from the opposite side of the table.

"Thank you." She chose not to return the compliment, though he did, in fact, look pretty good. He always did. Dark hair, dark eyes. Great body.

Forget it, she cautioned herself. That game has been played out.

"I can take your orders if you're ready." The

blonde woman Miranda met out front had followed Jared back into the narrow room.

"Let's make this quick." Jared trailed after her. "We have a lot to cover today."

Orders were hastily placed, glasses of water replenished by a young man wearing a white buttoned-down shirt and khakis, and the door separating the small dining room from the larger one was pulled partially closed.

"Alrighty, then, folks." Jared removed a folder from the briefcase that rested on the vacant chair next to the one in which he sat. "Time to get down to business. If I recall correctly, everyone here—except for Agent Fletcher and me—has had some contact—direct or indirect—with our subject, Archer Lowell."

Anne Marie, Evan, and Miranda all nodded.

"Archer Lowell, age twenty years, ten months, first child and only son of Lionel and Sissy Lowell. Father left home when the boy was three. Graduated from Fleming Regional High in 2001, ranked three hundred twenty out of three hundred seventy-three students. Worked as a driver for All-County Auctions from June of 2001, until he was arrested for stalking and assaulting Amanda Crosby in 2002." Jared looked up from the sheet of paper that lay before him on the table. "Your sister, Detective."

"Correct." Evan's jaw tightened.

"He entered a plea, accepted a reduced sentence at the strong urging of his lawyer." Jared folded the sheet of paper neatly in half. "So much for past history."

"So what's he done since he's been released?" Will asked.

"Nothing yet. At least, nothing that we know of," Jared said.

"It's what he's expected to do that's the problem," Miranda told him.

"What's he expected to do?" Will frowned.

"Murder three people," Anne Marie replied.

"Who is he going to murder?"

"If we knew that, Will, we wouldn't be having this meeting," Jared said, holding up a hand to stop the conversation while the young male waiter returned to serve their lunch.

"Anyone need anything else?" the waiter asked. Assured that no one did, the young man left the room, and once again closed the door.

"Somehow I get the feeling that I'm the only person in this room who doesn't quite know what's going on." Will's gaze went from one face to the next, stopping when he reached Miranda.

"That must be a first," she murmured as she picked a slice of tomato from her sandwich.

Ignoring her, he turned to Jared.

"How 'bout you bring me up to speed?"

Jared nodded and finished chewing a mouthful of sandwich.

"Several months ago, there was a series of murders in Lyndon, a community about thirty-five miles from here. All women whose names were listed in the phone book as Mary Douglas or M. Douglas."

"Wait, I heard about this. Mara Douglas, your sister, was the intended victim," Will addressed Anne Marie.

"That's right. That's how the Bureau became involved in the first place. I called in Aidan Shields from medical leave to work with us."

Will turned to Miranda.

"You called me during that investigation. You wanted information on an old case from Ohio. The victim was Jenny Green. . . ."

"Proving that the rumors about Will are all true." Miranda glanced at the others. "He never forgets a damned thing."

He continued, "You wanted copies of the statements of a suspect you'd interviewed at the time. He'd been let go."

"Right again." Miranda nodded. "Here's the story in a nutshell. We had several victims here in eastern Pennsylvania. Evan was the lead detective on these cases because, at the time, he was with the Lyndon Police Department. Something about the crime scenes reminded me of a case I'd worked on about six years earlier. That Ohio case was the first time I'd worked in the field, so everything was memorable. I remembered wanting to reinterview a suspect who'd just flat-out disappeared. I called Will to look up the file, get the name of the suspect for me. Once we had that, and a little information on him, Aidan followed that thread to a man named Curtis Alan Channing."

She paused to sip at her water.

"Channing was a serial killer who'd been a real busy boy over the years. But he'd flown so far under the radar that his prints weren't even on file any-where."

"If he was under the radar, how do you know he was a serial killer?" Will asked.

"The Bureau has been running his DNA through the data banks," Miranda explained. "So far, we've had hits on old, unsolved cases in Ohio, Indiana, and Kentucky. He was not only busy, he was clever. He could have gone on for years."

"Then a few months back, he ran a stop sign in my town." Evan picked up the story. "The officer who stopped him found an outstanding warrant for an-other Curtis A. Channing, and over Channing's pro-tests that they had the wrong man, he was hauled out to the county prison, since the arrest had been made on a Saturday night." Evan leaned back in his chair. "The following Monday, when the courthouse opened, Channing went before a judge, proved his identity, and was released."

"And he then proceeded to murder how many women?" Jared shuffled through the stack of notes he'd made the night before.

"Three women named Mary Douglas," Anne spoke softly, "and two other women. My sister, Mara, would have been his sixth victim, if he'd had his way."

"Where is he now?" Will asked.

"In hell, where he belongs," Anne Marie replied.

"So what's this got to do with this Archer Lowell?" Will asked.

"All of the victims—including his intended victim, Mara Douglas—had a connection to a man named Vincent Giordano. He killed his family in cold blood, and was convicted and sentenced to several life sentences," Evan told Will. "Sentences he'll never serve, because the evidence used to convict him was all tainted, all fabricated. They had to let him go."

Will whistled long and low. "That had to hurt."

"More than you could imagine." Evan grimaced.

"How were Channing's victims connected to Giordano?" Will pushed his plate aside and rested his arms on the table.

"Mara was the child advocate who recommended that the court terminate Giordano's parental rights to his sons," Evan said. "One of the other victims was the judge who ordered that termination; the other was Giordano's former mother-in-law. The other three Douglas women were killed by mistake. Channing hadn't done his homework too well at first. He'd been a little sloppy there in the beginning."

"So you were able to put Giordano back into prison as Channing's accomplice?" Will surmised.

"No. Not only was Giordano still behind bars while the killing was going on, we have not been able to positively establish that the two men ever met. Giordano, of course, swears he never met Channing and has no idea who he is."

"I'm confused. I don't understand what this has to do with this other guy, this Archer Lowell."

"Shortly after Giordano was released from the county prison, my sister Amanda's business partner was found with a bullet through his head." Evan spoke levelly. "Not long after that, another close friend of Amanda's was found murdered."

"And Lowell, who had been convicted of stalking

and assaulting your sister . . ." Will's fingers began to beat softly upon the table.

"Was still in prison," Evan told him.

"And your sister?" Will asked tentatively.

"Is alive and well because of Miranda and the local chief of police," Evan said. "Giordano came after her."

"But what was the connection between your sister's partner and her friend—the two deceased—and Giordano?" Will accurately followed the sequence.

"There was none to Giordano," Evan said, "but they were both people who had pissed off Archer Lowell. Both had given statements to the police about Lowell's actions; both had made it very clear they were going to testify against him at his trial. Their testimony was the main reason Lowell's attorney insisted that he accept the plea offered by the D.A."

"*Strangers on a Train,*" Will murmured. "You do mine, I'll do yours. . . ."

"Exactly." Miranda nodded, then added grudgingly, "You figured that out a lot faster than we did."

"Channing offed people who had connections to Giordano, Giordano took out people who had connections to Lowell. So if the pattern holds, we could expect Lowell to be going after people who have ties to Channing," Will said.

"That's the way we see it." Miranda munched a potato chip.

"So, if we're correct in assuming that Channing got the names of his victims from Giordano," Will continued, "and Giordano got the names of his victims from Lowell, we have to figure out whose names

Channing gave to Lowell. Who, over the course of his life, pissed off Channing sufficiently that he'd want them dead."

"Unfortunately," Miranda reminded him, "Channing himself is now dead."

"Guess we won't be getting much help from him," Will muttered.

"So the question is, who is Lowell going to go after, now that he's out of prison, and how do we get to them before he does?" Jared stated the obvious.

"Why don't we just ask him?"

Four heads swung in Will's direction.

"Why don't we ask him?" Will repeated.

"I doubt he's going to admit that he's part of a conspiracy to commit murder," Jared said dryly.

"One of two things will happen." Will's fingers were all now drumming on the table. "He'll either tell us the truth, or he won't. Either way, he'll know that we know. It might be a deterrent, if in fact he was planning something."

"Will has a point," Anne Marie said. "At the very least, he'll know that someone will be watching him. Of course, he won't tell the truth. . . ."

"Why not?" Will turned to her. "Who is there for him to be afraid of? Channing's dead, and Giordano is back in prison, right?"

"He won't admit to the conspiracy." Evan shook his head. "He's out, he's going to want to stay out. Why should he implicate himself in anything?"

"Maybe, if he thought he could get immunity, he'd tell the truth," Will suggested.

"I know this guy," Evan told him. "He'll smirk and

he'll lie, but he'll never admit to knowing either of the others. As a matter of fact, he's already denied ever having met them. Believe me, I've asked."

"What's his incentive?" Will persisted. "There's no one to make him follow through."

"We don't know what his intentions are," Anne Marie agreed, "but I think, knowing what we know, we have to proceed as if he is planning on playing this out. Several lives could be at stake."

"Then we really have nothing to lose by confronting him." Jared turned to Miranda. "Since you were involved in the other two cases and know some of the players, I'd like you to take the lead here. Pay him a visit, have a little chat with him."

"My pleasure." Miranda smiled. She'd expected this.

"You, Fletcher." Jared directed his gaze to the opposite side of the table. "You'll go along. I want him to know that the Bureau is very, very serious about this. Two agents will make a stronger impression than one."

"But what about Annie and Evan?" Miranda frowned. "Evan's dealt with Lowell before, and Annie's insights into his personality would be invaluable. I'd think either of them would be better suited to the assignment than Will."

"Annie is headed back to Quantico for a lecture she's giving tomorrow, and Detective Crosby—who, may I remind you, does not work for the Bureau—is heading back to his classes at the National Academy. John asked them here today strictly for their input." Jared closed his folder and slipped it back into his briefcase. "The case is all yours, Agent Cahill. Yours, and Agent Fletcher's. Visit Archer Lowell. Find out what he's up to. Put the fear of God into him. Any questions?"

He looked from Miranda to Will, then back again. They both shook their heads no. No questions.

"Good." Jared grinned amicably as he stood. "Now, let's see if I can find Mrs. Duffy. Anyone else want dessert?"

____ CHAPTER ____
THREE

"WHAT A GREAT WAY TO START OFF A NEW WEEK," Miranda grumbled under her breath as she hung her clothes in the small closet of her room at the Fleming Inn. Just peachy.

Under ordinary circumstances, she'd live out of her suitcase rather than take time from a job to unpack. But these circumstances were not the norm, and she needed a little bit of a break between finding out with whom she'd been partnered on this assignment, and actually forging ahead. It wasn't that she had doubts about Will's abilities. On the contrary, he had an unfailingly accurate mind for facts and dates. Unfailing, and highly annoying, as far as she was concerned. The man had a mind like a steel trap. He never forgot a damned thing.

Except the things that might have mattered most.

"*Might* have is the key here," she murmured to herself. "Apparently, some things mattered only to me."

Let it go. That was then; this is now. You're a professional. He's a professional. You have a job to do. Several innocent lives may very well depend on how well you do it.

"Right," she muttered aloud as she debated a change in clothing. The red jacket and short black skirt had been fine for the meeting, but now she was going into the field. She decided to change.

"Absolutely right. Focus on Will Fletcher, federal agent, and stuff Will Fletcher, the man I once thought I was in love with, into some dark, subterranean place where he belongs."

She traded the short skirt for tailored black pants, the white sweater for a crisp white shirt, all the while mentally toying with the image of Will Fletcher being physically stuffed into a dark place. Dark and dank. One filled with spiders.

Picturing Will with big black spiders crawling on him somehow cheered her.

"There. I feel better already." She switched jackets and closed the closet door.

She turned off the light and left the room, her leather bag swinging from her right shoulder, her key chain in her hand. She marched down the steps to the first floor.

"Well, you're in a better frame of mind," Will observed from the bottom of the steps, where he leaned upon the newel post.

"Must have been the chocolate mousse."

"I must say I'm a bit disappointed, Cahill." He eyed her as they went out the front door.

"Oh? In what?"

"In the wardrobe change. How many of those black suits do you own, anyway?"

"I have closets full of boring black suits, Fletcher."

"Seriously, what's with that?"

"When I'm in the field, I want to fade as much into the background as possible. I don't want my clothes to be an issue."

"Well, I hate to be the one to break it to you, Cahill, but it would take a hell of a lot more than a black suit for you to fade into the background." He glanced at her sideways, saw her jaw clench.

"Thank you. I think." She shifted her bag a little higher on her shoulder. "Can we get back to the case now?"

"Whatever you say. You ready to take on old Archer?"

"Piece o' cake." She walked past him and took the path that forked to the right.

"My car is over here." He stopped midway down the walk.

"Well, mine is over here." She called back without turning around. "Don't make me remind you who is the lead on this case."

"That entitles you to drive?"

"Absolutely."

"Do I have to ride with you in that?"

She laughed. "Chicken?"

"Just try to keep it under seventy when you go through town. I hear the police in these little hamlets get a wee bit testy about—" He had barely gotten in and closed the door before she put the car in reverse. "Shit, Cahill . . ."

"Hey, I thought you liked a little speed."

"I love speed. I love a fast car. When I'm behind the wheel."

She smiled to herself. It still pleased her to get a rise

out of him. She understood it was childish and accepted that.

"Do you know where you're going?" he asked, as he snapped on his seat belt.

"The directions to Archer's mother's place were in the packet Jared gave me. I'm assuming you had the same info in yours."

"I assumed we'd be leaving right away. Had I known you were going to take twenty minutes to carry your suitcase up to your room, I'd have read through it."

She responded by pushing a little harder on the gas pedal.

"Jesus, Cahill." He blew out a long exasperated breath.

Miranda laughed and cut back on the gas just enough to let him know it had been deliberate.

"Three miles down Pine Top Road—which we are on—we will come to a fork. We will take the road on the left—that will be Edgemont Road—for another mile, until we come to the Pine Top Trailer Park. The Lowells' trailer is on Oak View Lane, number seventeen." She recited without taking her eyes from the road. "Also found in Jared's packet was Mrs. Lowell's work schedule for the next three weeks. She left the trailer at seven this morning, won't be back until five-thirty this afternoon. Gives us almost three hours with him."

"How do you want to play it?"

"Chat him up a bit, make him wonder why the FBI is looking for him. He's young and he's very stupid, according to the file and Anne Marie's notes. I think I can make him nervous."

"God knows you make me nervous," Will said under his breath.

"What?" she asked.

"Nothing."

"Anyway, I think we can play with him a bit, then we'll bring up Giordano."

"Anyone ask Giordano about Lowell or Channing?"

"You're kidding, right?" She frowned. "Of course he was asked. Read the damned file, Fletcher. He denied ever hearing their names before."

"So we have denial all around." He ignored her jab. She knew he wouldn't have had time to look through the file. She also knew that by the time he had, he'd be as familiar with the case as she now was.

"As deep as it gets."

"If Lowell is as dumb as everyone thinks he is, maybe we can convince him that Giordano gave him up."

"That's part of the plan, Stan." Miranda pulled off the main road into the trailer park, and slowed when she saw the number of small children who were out playing on this late October afternoon.

She stopped in front of the last trailer on the left.

"This is it," she announced as she turned off the engine.

The trailer was small but neat, with checked curtains hanging in all the windows and some seasonal decorations—a few hardy purple cabbages and a wooden barrel of purple pansies—near the painted door.

"Mrs. Lowell keeps a tidy house. At least on the outside," Miranda observed.

"Let's see what's going on inside." Will stepped forward and knocked on the door.

From inside, they could hear the jingle for an allergy medication commercial.

"Someone's catching a little daytime TV," Miranda noted.

The door opened partway, and a sleepy-faced Archer Lowell looked down at Will.

"Whatcha want?" he mumbled.

"Just a word or two." Will smiled and placed his hand on the door just as Archer's eyes shifted to Miranda, who was holding up her FBI credentials.

"Oh, no. Uh-uh." He tried to shut the door, but his best efforts were no match for Will. "I didn't do nothin'. I swear. I served my time. I'm done. You get off my property. I don't have nothin' to say to you."

"Of course, you do, Archer." Miranda smiled and stepped in front of Will to push her way into the trailer, Will following closely behind. With every step she took forward, Archer took one back. "We have lots to talk about. We have so many acquaintances in common."

"I don't know what you're talking about." He stopped when he found himself backed into the counter that separated the kitchen from the living area.

"Why, sure you do. Now, I was just talking to Detective Crosby this morning—I know you remember

Detective Crosby—and he was telling me how you were out and about. Well, here I was, so close by, I figured I should stop and say hi." She never took her eyes from his face. As if fascinated by her, Archer could not look away.

"What do you want?" He forced himself to look elsewhere.

"Well, first I wanted you to meet my good buddy Agent Fletcher. Say hello to Agent Fletcher, Archer."

"Hello. Why are you here?"

"We just stopped by to check out something that Detective Crosby mentioned. About Vincent Giordano."

"Who?"

"Oh, Archer, don't play that game with me. Please. We all know about the favors you and Vince and Curtis Channing agreed to do for one another."

"I don't know what you're talking about. I don't know no one named Vince or Curtis."

"That's funny. 'Cause Vince knows you."

Archer shrugged. "Can't place him."

"You're better than I expected, Archer." Will leaned back against the door frame. "I'm impressed. I don't believe you, but I am impressed."

"I don't give a shit what you are. You don't have no business with me, so you can both leave. I didn't do nothing, I barely left this trailer since I got out of prison. I don't have no car, no job, nothing. I don't go nowhere." The look on his face was smug. "So you just go on out of here. I don't know no one named Vince, no one named Curtis whatever you said his name was. I don't know what they done, and I don't want to know, but it has nothing to do with me."

He pushed past Will to shove the door open.

"See you around, Archer." Miranda winked.

"Later." Will smiled and followed her out the door.

They did not speak until they were back in the car.

"He's better than I expected," Will said.

"We're better. Right now he thinks he's got the edge. Did you see that smug look?" She turned the key in the ignition, let the car idle. "So I think we'll just sit here for a few minutes and give him a little something to think about."

She fished her cell phone from her bag and rolled down the window, the phone in her left hand. "Let him think we're really on to something—which we will be, once we start to get to him."

She pretended to speak into the phone instead of to her companion.

"Okay." She made a show of dropping the phone into her bag. "Now he thinks we just reported to someone, so he's going to be a little more nervous about leaving home."

"You didn't buy that I-haven't-been-outside-these-four-walls-in-weeks routine, either, eh?"

"Are you kidding? He's twenty years old; he's been locked up for months. I noticed a bar about a quarter mile from the trailer park. I'll bet that's where he hangs out."

Miranda put the car in reverse and backed out of the small parking pad, then took off slowly down the wide black-topped road.

"Maybe we should stop back this evening and see."

"Maybe we should."

Will turned to look at the bar in question as they sped past.

"Looks like a biker bar I used to hang out in, once upon a time."

"A biker bar? Were you undercover?"

"No, this was before I came to the Bureau."

She frowned. Biker bar? Mr. Conservative from the Heartland of America Will Fletcher?

He smiled with satisfaction. "Thought you knew all there was to know, did you?"

Vowing not to ask, she bit her lip, and hit the gas.

Archer stood in the tiny bathroom and peered through the curtains, watching until the Spyder backed up and drove off.

What the hell was that all about?

Had Vince Giordano given him up? Had he?

No, no, that wouldn't happen. He and Vince and Curt, they had this pact. Vince would never . . .

But even if he had, so what? It was his word against mine. And he's a convicted killer. An admitted murderer. Sure, sure, Vince could have said something. Maybe he did. But who the hell can prove it? They got nothing to tie me to Vince. Nothing at all.

He thought about Vince's last victims. Two of the three had connections to Archer. And the last intended victim, Amanda Crosby, well, okay, Archer had served time for stalking her.

But what does that prove? Maybe Vince saw her

and maybe he sorta flipped for her, too. She's pretty hot, isn't she? Who wouldn't want her?

And Curtis, well, he's stone dead, isn't he? He ain't talking to no one.

It was then that Archer realized he'd started to sweat.

Hey, come on. No big deal. They got nothing on me, and I ain't killed no one.

"And guess what, Vince?" he said aloud as he went back into the kitchen for a beer. "I ain't going to kill no one."

He paused, contemplating the irony of having Miranda Cahill show up at his door. He'd thought he was hallucinating when he first read the name on the identification she'd held up. The old spider and fly thing crossed his mind, but he pushed right past that. For one thing, it didn't matter who she was, since he wasn't gonna do nothing to no one. For another, there was that big guy with her.

"But hey, Vince, you and Curt, you did your thing, I respect that. But I am out, and I am staying out. Ain't no one knows about the game, and as far as I'm concerned, this game is over. Curt is dead, and you are never going to see the light of day, old buddy. There ain't no reason for me to kill nobody. Ain't no one who cares whether I do or not. Except maybe you, Vince. And we both know where you are, don't we?"

He tipped his beer in the general direction of the county prison where Vince Giordano sat in his little cell, laughed, and took a sip. He thought about the three people who had made his life so miserable.

The three people who were responsible for his spending these past months behind bars. The three people Vince Giordano had agreed to take out for him.

Two of the three were now dead, thanks to good old Vince.

That the third was still out there, well, two out of three ain't bad. He could live with that. Archer's anger was gone now, his life was going to move ahead, and he was never, ever going to look back. Not on Amanda Crosby, not on Vince Giordano or Curtis Alan Channing. Not on the game he himself had proposed that cold February morning.

"Game over." He raised the bottle in a toast to his absent companions. "I win."

CHAPTER FOUR

"So, what do you think?" Will asked as he looked around the dimly lit bar where he and Miranda had just finished dinner.

"What do I think about what?" Miranda frowned. "The three pieces of greasy fried chicken I just ate? I think I'm going to be sick."

"I don't recall anyone force-feeding you. And I don't recall you ever turning your nose up at fried food in the past."

"Yeah, well, maybe I've gotten a little more discriminating."

He laughed, and she made a face at him.

"What time do you suppose he'll show up?" she asked. "If this is, in fact, his watering hole."

"This is it, all right." Will glanced around. "Close to home—critical when a guy has no wheels—and there's a fair share of single ladies. All regulars, judging from the conversations I overheard around the bar while I was waiting for our beer. This is the neighborhood hangout. This would be his place."

"So the next question would be, is this his night?"

"Every night is his night." Will looked over to the door as two laughing couples entered and went straight to the far end of the bar. "He has nothing else to do, nowhere else to go. You think he's sitting home with his mother every night? Nah. This is home base for him. Trust me."

"Been there, done that," she muttered.

He was about to respond when the door opened and Archer Lowell walked in. He peeled off his red-and-black-plaid jacket and tossed it in the direction of the coat hooks that lined one wall. He missed his mark and had to stoop to pick it up. Red-faced, he hung it on the hook. Passing the pool tables, he called something to a dark-haired girl who was just about to take a shot, but she turned her back on him as if she hadn't heard. Shaking off the rebuke, Lowell proceeded to the bar, where he took a seat next to two men who'd been there when Miranda and Will arrived.

"What'd I tell you?" Will took a long pull from his beer, watching Miranda's face.

"Do you ever get tired of being right?"

"Nah."

She glanced at the bar, then back at Will. "He just saw us."

"Want to take bets on how long it takes him to come over here?"

"Less than ten minutes," she said without hesitation. "He won't be able to stand it."

"I'm not so sure. On the one hand, he could act impulsively and rush right over. On the other, he might want to prove to us how cool he is. Show us that it doesn't matter to him that we're here."

Will appeared to weigh the matter.

"I'm going with more than ten. I'm going with twenty minutes, maybe even more."

"I think you're going to lose this one, Fletcher."

"I don't think so. Though I think if you were alone, he'd be right over. Oh, yeah, he'd be making a beeline for the table if you were sitting here all by your lonesome. That would sure show the other guys in here something. That he could sit down with this incredible babe and strike up a conversation and not have her toss him on his ear? That would definitely win him points around here."

"Babe?" Miranda repeated flatly.

"Looking at you strictly from a guy's point of view, Cahill, you are one incredible babe. You're the total package."

She cautioned him with one raised eyebrow.

"Okay, you get my drift. But Archer Lowell doesn't know just how complete that package is. He doesn't know how smart you are, or just how good a shot you are with that little Sig Sauer you carry around—you still strap that thing to your thigh?—or what a truly gifted investigator you are. Nor does he care about any of those things. He's a guy, and he looks at you and just sees a babe, because he doesn't know any better. He just doesn't understand that you're functional as well as decorative."

"Was there a compliment in there someplace? There might have been, but I'm not certain I'd recognize a compliment from you."

"Hey, I'm just telling you what a guy like Archer sees when he looks at you."

Movement from the direction of the bar caught Will's eye. "Looks like you might have won this round."

"Ha! My lucky day."

"Yeah, well, sooner or later, the odds had to change." Will stole a glance at his watch. "Less than five minutes."

"What do I win?" she asked, keeping her eyes on Will and deliberately avoiding looking at the figure approaching their table.

"A prize to be determined at a later date."

"My choice?"

"That's to be determined later, too."

Archer Lowell's shadow fell across the table.

"What are you guys doing here?" Lowell held a bottle of beer in one hand, a cigarette in the other.

"Having dinner. A few beers. Soaking up some local color," Will replied.

"Have you tried the fried chicken, Archer?" Miranda asked. "It's a little too greasy for my taste, but—"

"Come on. What are you doing here?"

"I just told you, Archer." Will's voice dropped an octave. "We just had dinner, and now are enjoying a few beers."

"You are full of shit. You're here because you thought I'd be here." Lowell looked nervously from one to the other.

"If that were so, that would mean we guessed right, wouldn't it?" Miranda said brightly. "We FBI special agents are really good at figuring things out, aren't we?"

Archer rolled his eyes.

"How smart do you have to be? I mean, it's the only bar within walking distance of my house."

"Did you see how fast he put that together, Will?"

"Yes, I did. And isn't that exactly what I said to you? That this is the only bar within walking distance of Archer's house, and—"

"Stop it. You're giving me a headache." Archer ran his hand through his wheat-colored hair. "I want you to go away. I haven't done anything that concerns you."

"Actually, Archer, it's what you're going to do that concerns us." Miranda tapped her fingers against the side of her glass.

"I'm not going to do anything." Archer leaned forward and lowered his voice. "I swear to you, I am not going to do a thing. I have served my time for what I done, and I do not want to ever go back inside that place again. Not ever."

"Well, I guess we'll just have to stick around a while and see."

"You can stick around for as long as you want, but there won't be nothing for you to see, 'cause I ain't doing nothing the law needs to know about." His face a grim and frustrated mask, Archer turned heel and stomped back to his place at the bar.

"What do you think?" Miranda's foot poked Will's ankle under the table. "You think he's going to renege on his part of the deal?"

"Sounds like it, doesn't it? I mean, without admitting that there might have been something he was expected to do, he's pretty adamant that he's not going to do it."

"You believe him?"

"Do you?"

"Now that he's out of prison, I don't see any advantage for him to go through with a deal he may have made with the deadly duo." Miranda drained her glass and set it on the table. "Like you said yesterday, Giordano will never see the light of day again, and Channing's dead. I'm having a hard time seeing this kid as a killer. I heard that when the police showed him photographs of Giordano's victims, he nearly passed out. Remember, these were people who had crossed Archer, people who were expected to testify against him. People he wanted dead."

"And . . . ?"

"According to Sean Mercer, the police chief down in Broeder who showed Archer those photos, the kid went totally green. Said he'd never seen a dead body before. He all but gagged."

"You don't think he was faking for effect?"

"I have yet to meet the person who can change the color of his skin just like *that*"—she snapped her fingers—"and Sean said that kid went green in the blink of an eye."

"So you think maybe now that he knows we're on to the game, and he knows he's being watched, he'll forget he ever met Channing and Giordano?" Will asked.

"I think the odds are good. Just look at him, Will." Miranda nodded toward the bar. "He's a mess. You think he's smart enough to plan, then carry out, three murders? You think he has the balls?"

"Actually, no, I don't. And that being the case, I suppose our work here is done." Will drank the last of his beer.

"First thing in the morning, I'm going to check in with the chief of police, let them know what's gone on, what we suspect. Ask them to keep an eye on Archer for a while, let us know if he leaves town, that sort of thing. And we should probably check in with his probation officer while we're at it."

"That's a good idea. Hanging around Fleming waiting to see what, if anything, Lowell might do is probably a waste of time. I left a serial killer and two pedophiles on my desk, so it's not as if there are no other cases either of us could be working on," Will said, nodding. "You ready? Since we've made our impression on Lowell, we might as well head back to the inn. I want to read through the rest of the files that Jared left for me before we drop this in the lap of the Fleming police and head back to Virginia tomorrow. I want to make sure we haven't missed something."

Miranda slipped her suede jacket on, then stood up, grabbed her purse, and followed Will to the door. She'd hoped to get back to the inn early enough to grab a good dessert and a cup of Barrie Lee Duffy's delicious coffee. Pleased at the prospect, she was oblivious to the eyes that watched as she tucked herself into the front seat of Will's Camry and the car left the lot to disappear into the darkness of Edgemont Road.

*   *   *

Barrie Lee Duffy smiled a greeting at the handsome couple who wandered into the foyer.

"Did you want a table?" she asked. "The kitchen's pretty much closed, but I'm sure we can find something for you if you're hungry."

"I'm heading up to my room," Will addressed both Barrie Lee and Miranda at the same time. "I have some reading to do. Guess I'll see you tomorrow. . . ." With a smile that was meant equally for both women, he climbed the steps.

"I'll take that table, Mrs. Duffy," Miranda told her as she slipped out of her jacket.

"Right this way." The innkeeper took the jacket from Miranda's hands and led her to a small table midway between a tall window and the fireplace.

Miranda smiled and took the chair offered to her. "Perfect."

"Did you want dinner, Ms. Cahill?"

"I want a cup of your wonderful coffee and a slice of that divine-looking chocolate something that I saw on the cake plate over there." Miranda grinned and nodded in the direction of a tea cart that held all manner of tempting confections.

"Excellent choice on the dessert. I'll be right back with your coffee."

Leaning back in the chair, Miranda studied her surroundings. The room was wide and airy and warmed by the glow of the fire. Over the mantel hung a painting that appeared to be a historic battle scene. She rose from her seat to take a closer look.

"That's a scene from the Battle of Gettysburg," Barrie Lee said as she placed Miranda's coffee on the table. "The man there on the black horse, that's Captain James Brady. Some ancestor of my late husband's."

"Your husband . . . ?"

"He died last year. Drunk driver ran him off the road." Barrie Lee turned her back and pretended to straighten the cloth on a nearby table.

"I'm so sorry."

"This inn has been in his family for over a hundred years. He really wanted to keep it going. It really meant a lot to him." She turned back to Miranda with a fixed smile.

"I'm sorry."

"Thank you. So am I. Your dessert will be right over."

Miranda returned to her table and sat down, feeling more depressed than she had in a while. She'd just started to stir her coffee when she looked up to see Will enter the room, a file under his arm.

"I had a few thoughts," Will said, as he joined her without waiting for an invitation, "including one about our friend Archer."

"And what might that be?"

"I think you may be right about him not planning on going along with whatever deal he'd made with the devil. Or in his case, devils."

"You couldn't have read that entire file in fifteen minutes."

"No. But I'm looking at the whole picture. His profile aside, as already established, he has no car. He has no job, so unless he was planning on stealing a car, which is also unlikely, since he knows he's being watched, he won't have any means of transportation. Chances are, any potential victims named by Channing would not be local, right? Since Channing was from Ohio, originally. His tracks are going to be hard to pick up between the time he left home after he graduated from high school, and the time you saw him six years ago and questioned him." He paused, then asked, "Do you think he remembered you, when your paths crossed last year?"

"We didn't come face-to-face last year. I met with Giordano a couple of times, but not Channing. I doubt he'd have remembered me, though. Rookie agent, fumbling through my first field interviews. I probably didn't make much of an impression on him."

"Well, there's really no way of knowing one way or another now, is there?" Will suspected that any man who'd come in contact with her over the years would have had some recollection of the meeting. She was one of those women who made a lasting impression.

Miranda smiled past him, and he looked over his shoulder in time to see Mrs. Duffy approaching with a china plate, upon which rested a chocolate concoction.

"Flourless chocolate cake with raspberries and just the tiniest bit of cinnamon whipped cream," Barrie Lee announced.

"Oh, my God, it looks perfect." Miranda beamed, admiring her choice.

Will made the mistake of picking up a spoon and tilting it in the direction of her plate.

"Don't even think about it," she whispered darkly.

"Just testing." He backed off.

"Shall I bring you one?"

"If you don't mind. I seem to be sitting in the no-share zone."

"Coffee?"

"Sure. Thanks."

Miranda took a spoonful of chocolate, closed her eyes, and licked the spoon.

"This is fabulous," she said dreamily.

"It's chocolate cake, Miranda. Get a grip."

"You call it chocolate cake. I call it a gift from the gods."

"Christ," he muttered under his breath.

Mrs. Duffy reappeared with the second plate, which she set in front of Will. "Your coffee will be right over. We're making a new pot. Enjoy."

"Hmmmm. It is pretty good," he agreed after sampling.

"Pretty good. Ha." She sighed happily. "So go on. You were saying . . ."

"I think I'd rather wait until I know for certain you're paying attention and not lost in some gustatory orgasmic experience."

"You're just jealous," she whispered, "because it's not as good for you as it is for me."

He laughed out loud.

"Back to what you were saying. Don't mind me."

"Miranda . . ."

"Your coffee, sir." A pretty young waitress poured for him and left the pot on the table.

"Go on, Will."

"We were talking about whether or not you'd made an impression on Channing."

"We're past that."

"Okay, then, we were talking about the fact that there is a long period of time when we don't know where Channing was or what he was doing."

"Well, I think maybe we've already established what he was doing."

"You mean the reports that came back from CODIS."

"Well, sure. We now know that all that time, he was merely honing his skills. He didn't wake up one morning and just decide to be a serial killer. That was working on him for a long time. By the time he met up with Giordano and Lowell, he'd become quite accomplished."

"You think they knew what he was? Giordano and Lowell?"

Miranda paused, considering the question. "Tough call. Giordano was a killer himself, maybe he recognized it in Channing. Lowell, on the other hand, is pretty much oblivious to most things, don't you think?"

"I'd say that's a fair assessment, judging by what I've read."

"Well, I'll bet if we look real hard, we'll find there are more unsolved murders that could be traced back to Channing, some that maybe aren't even showing up in the database."

"Because he didn't leave DNA behind."

"Right." She nodded. "Since he was still in the southern Ohio area when our paths crossed, maybe he'd stayed in that area for a while. Maybe there's more buried there—no pun intended—than has already shown up. If we could trace his footsteps by following where he'd been, maybe we can find some others who'd crossed his path back then."

"People who might have pissed off Channing enough for him to have remembered. Enough to have made a lasting impression. Enough to have put them on his hit list."

"Right." She nodded.

"I'll see if I can come up with a time line when I get back to Virginia. Maybe something will stand out when we put it all together."

"Think we'll find a pattern?" Miranda asked.

"I don't know. I don't really know enough about Channing to venture a guess. I'll have a better feel when I start looking over the data."

"We could still come up empty, though, as far as finding three potential victims is concerned."

"True. But suppose we do come up with a few names that could be on the hit list. What if we find these people? What do we do with them, once we have their names?"

"Don't you think we should warn them?" Miranda asked.

"Warn them about what? That there may or may not be someone coming around someday who might want to kill them? I don't know how responsible that is."

"You have a better idea?"

"Maybe it's moot. Didn't we just agree that Archer isn't likely to go after anyone?" Will reminded her.

"We agreed that he isn't likely to go after them now, when he has no job and no means of transportation."

"I checked with the DMV. Lowell doesn't even have a valid driver's license."

"Yes, but do we want to take the chance that his circumstances will never change, that he'll never have a change of heart?" Miranda sipped at her coffee. "As I see it, if we can identify a few likely targets and at least give them a heads-up, I think we are obligated to do that."

"You mean, show up at some poor sucker's door and say, 'Hi, I'm just here to let you know that your name may or may not be on a hit list because at some point in the past, you may have pissed off a guy named Curtis Alan Channing. . . .'"

"I think we could clean that up a bit, at least find out if there was some argument or bad feelings between that person and Channing. Will, keep in mind that anyone we could definitely finger as a potential victim, at this late date and with no clues from Channing, well, if it's that obvious to us, he or she just might be the right one."

"I guess it's worth the time to take a look, see if there is anyone out there who might be a target."

"You just put those legendary investigative skills to work. If anyone can dig out potential victims from a twenty-year-old slush pile, it would be you." She paused and looked at his plate, where a small amount of chocolate remained. "In the meantime, are you going to finish that?"

*   *   *

Genna Snow found her way through the darkened cabin, counting bed frames until she reached her own narrow bed at the end of the last row. She lowered herself quietly to the edge of the mattress and sat, leaning forward to untie her shoes. It was cool in the cabin, so her wool socks were still on her feet when she slid under the blanket and huddled herself to keep warm on the cold sheets. It was snowing again, and the leather shoes she'd worn when she entered the compound hadn't been made for snow. She wondered what she'd been thinking when she'd taken them out of her closet the day she'd left for Wyoming.

Of course, she reminded herself, it hadn't been snowing in Virginia when she left four weeks ago, and hadn't been snowing here, for that matter, but winter was moving across the mountains more quickly than had been forecast.

She lay in the dark, her hazel eyes staring at the ceiling. She missed her husband. Missed her bed. Missed the cat they'd gotten from the animal shelter last Christmas. She hadn't expected to be here, in the Valley of the Angels, for this long. It was now more than a month since she'd first shown up at the gates of Reverend Prescott's compound and asked to be admitted. She'd made nice with all the gentle folks she met those first few weeks, proved to one and all that she was gentle folk herself. That she'd come into this camp with no weapon, well, that had been an act of faith on her part, one that had made John absolutely crazy when she told him she couldn't take even a small handgun into the compound. If it was found on her, they'd know she wasn't who she was pretending to be.

And so Special Agent Genna Snow transformed herself into teacher Ruth Carey, and had sought a place in the compound. As Ruth, the résumé she'd brought with her had attracted the attention of Reverend Prescott himself, as she'd known it would. Ruth Carey had been terminated from her last teaching position for overzealously disciplining her charges.

"It's important, you see," Ruth had explained to the reverend, "that young girls—adolescent girls— understand that they must tame their emotions. Discipline, partnered with the proper reward, of course, is what children need if they're to understand their place in society, their function in this world."

"And that function is, Ms. Carey?" Reverend Prescott had asked.

"Why, to submit to the will of their elders. To understand that, as young women, they lack the judgment to know what is best for them. They must accept whatever lot is chosen for them, because they simply aren't capable of choosing for themselves."

"And who chose for you, Ms. Carey?" His eyes had narrowed.

"My father, of course." She had met his stare head-on. "He met you several years ago, at a lecture you gave in Pennsylvania. He was already ill at the time, but he never forgot your lessons. He bought all of your books, all of your tapes. He did live a very spiritual life, Reverend Prescott. He tried to live up to your example, and encouraged me to do so as well."

"You speak of him in the past? Has he . . . ?"

"I am sorry to say, I lost him last summer. After I was asked to . . . to leave my job, I was at a loss. Then, when my father passed away, it occurred to me that perhaps there might be a place for me here. I've heard about the wonderful work you do with runaways, Reverend. How you seek out those poor lost young souls and bring them here to help them discover their true spiritual nature. I've been wanting to offer my services to you, and to the young girls whom you've taken in, but while my father was alive, I believed that my place was there."

"And it was, of course it was." Reverend Prescott had leaned across his desk and taken her hands between his own. It was all she could do to not pull away in disgust. Not because he was coming on to her, but because she'd been touched by the hands of a pedophile before, and her skin had never forgotten what it felt like.

She forced a smile.

"Thank you for understanding, Reverend Prescott." She looked away modestly. "Do you think there could be a place for me here?"

"I think perhaps we could fit you into our staff."

"Even though I was . . . dismissed . . . from my last teaching position?"

"I've read the reports, Ms. Carey. How short-sighted those fools were to have let go a woman of your moral caliber and obvious spiritual nature." He shook his head slowly, side to side. "The world out there is awash in misguided theories and adrift on a sea of ignorance. Anyone can see that today's children need a well-marked course in life. They need guidance—and yes, discipline—to help them chart that course. To help them understand what is expected of them."

"Especially the young girls, Reverend." She'd looked up at him piously. "There are so many dangers to young girls in the world. It's a challenge to prepare them properly to take their place in the world."

"I can assure you, Ms. Carey, when a young girl leaves the Valley of the Angels, she is well prepared for her role."

He rose from his chair and extended a hand to her to assist her in rising.

"I look forward to seeing what you might contribute to our girls' education, Ms. Carey. You'll be addressed as Miss Ruth here." He walked her to the door and opened it. "Now, I'm going to hand you over to Miss Eleanor. She'll get you settled in as a cabin mother with some of the older girls, and on Monday, you'll start your new life as a teacher here in the Valley of the Angels."

"Reverend Prescott, I can't thank you enough for taking me in. For giving me a chance to be part of the wonderful work you do here."

"Well, I'm sure you'll become an integral part of that work, Miss Ruth."

A woman in her mid-fifties waited outside the door.

"Miss Eleanor, please take Miss Ruth to cabin twelve. She'll be the new cabin mother. Please help her get settled, introduce her to the girls . . ."

Miss Eleanor nodded and gestured to Genna to follow her. Genna wondered if perhaps her companion had taken a vow of silence until they reached the outer doors of the building and stepped outside.

"Do you have a suitcase? We're not supposed to have but two changes of clothing, so you'll have to go through your things and decide what it is you want to keep. The rest will go into the communal closet." Eleanor had continued to chat all the way to cabin twelve, explaining the rules and regulations set up by Reverend Prescott to simplify life at the compound.

Over the weekend, Genna—as Miss Ruth—had acclimated herself to life behind the compound walls and laid the groundwork for her true purpose in being there. In addition to gathering evidence that would shut down the child-prostitution ring that masqueraded as a shelter for the homeless and runaway girls whom Reverend Prescott lured to the Valley of the Angels with the promise of a home off the streets, she searched the face of every girl she met for Julianne Douglas. Late on Saturday afternoon, she found her. Genna was certain that the pretty young blonde girl known as Rebecca was Mara Douglas's daughter, who'd been kidnapped by Mara's ex-husband the day after their divorce had become final.

Before leaving for Wyoming, Genna had studied computer-enhanced photographs created using software that could age faces in photographs. It had been used with a photo of the five-year-old Julianne to show how she might look now, at age twelve. Rebecca was the very image of the sketch Genna had memorized, but even without it, she'd have recognized the girl who bore such a strong resemblance to her aunt. Looking at Rebecca was like looking into the past and seeing Anne Marie McCall at that age.

Over the next several weeks, Genna had had to earn the confidence not only of Rebecca, but also of Reverend Prescott as well. She was almost there, she knew. Almost at a place where she could leave the compound with Rebecca—Julianne—and disappear with her. Tomorrow would test whether or not her scheme would work.

Genna turned over, restless. If she failed in convincing Reverend Prescott to permit her to spend an afternoon in town with one of the girls as a reward for lessons well learned, she'd have to come up with an alternative plan, and fast. She was running out of time. Soon the worst of the winter snows would begin to hit, and she'd be stuck here until such time as spring decided to arrive. How many months might that be?

Too many. She shook her head in the dark. She'd already spent too many nights away from John. And in the time she was there, three girls had disappeared from the compound.

In her mind, she rehearsed what she'd say to Reverend Prescott in the morning.

"It's occurred to me that perhaps a bit of competition among the girls might inspire them to even better work," she would say.

When pressed, she'd explain, "I'd like to have the girls write weekly essays. On appropriate topics, of course. As a reward, I will accompany the writer of the best essay into Linden for an afternoon. We can ride in with whoever goes in for supplies. As part of her reward, the girl will pick out a small treat—a journal, perhaps, or some colored pencils for her artwork, whatever she fancies—then we'll have lunch there at the diner."

She practiced this over and over, thinking how she might reword this part or that, until she fell asleep.

And the next morning, it had gone just as she'd suspected it might.

"What on earth would be the purpose of that?" Reverend Prescott's eyes had darkened with suspicion.

"To promote healthy competition." She'd smiled. "As well as to gain some greater insights into what the girls are really thinking. Besides, discipline without occasional reward rarely works well over time. There has to be some positive incentive."

He'd stroked his chin and stared out the window for a long moment, then turned back to Genna.

"Have you already discussed this competition with the girls?"

"Of course not. Not without your approval. Though I do have a stack of essays I've read through."

"I'll let you try it this week; we'll see what the results are." He turned back to her. "But you understand that the girl is never to be out of your sight. That you are not to become involved in conversations with the people in town. And that you are not to call attention to yourself or to the girl in any way."

"Certainly not," Genna responded defensively.

"People in Linden are naturally curious about the Valley of the Angels." He softened slightly at her obvious offense. "And there are those who cannot accept that what we do here, what we do for these girls, we do from love, with only their best interests at heart. There are those who are suspicious of our motives, those who would take the girls away from here, but what would happen to them then? They'd simply run away again, just like they did from their own homes, their own families. The last thing I want is for any of these girls to be exploited by someone on the outside. A careless word—"

She held up her hand. "Please. I understand. And I assure you that the girls' best interests are my own. We'll be very discreet. We'll simply have our little treat, and we'll be back before the dinner bell rings."

"Then go ahead, Miss Ruth." He watched her gather her wrap around her. "Any idea about who might be the first lucky little girl?"

"I think perhaps Eileen." Genna smiled. "She wrote a very lovely paper on submission."

He nodded approvingly. "Excellent. I'd like to read it."

"I'll have it brought right over."

She'd left his office with her heart pounding, her stomach roiling. He was a disgusting excuse for a human being. He rescued girls off the streets only to clean them up—no one wanted a girl who looked like a junkie or a prostitute—to be sold into slavery, trading one form of hell for another.

And yet, how clever, preying on girls who don't want to be found, and dealing only with men who'd been investigated as carefully as modern technology would allow. Prescott's finances, so far, had withstood scrutiny, since his fund-raising efforts were so successful.

Who could refuse a man who showed the before-and-after photos of the young girls he'd rescued from the streets? Besides raking in money from the sale of the girls, he brought in thousands each week in donations.

But once the first hints of the girls' eventual fates had begun to leak out, the FBI had looked for a way to get inside and determine if the Valley of the Angels was in fact a front for trafficking children. Genna had demanded the assignment, and even her reluctant husband could not deny that she was the best qualified for the job. As a long-time friend of Anne Marie McCall, finding Julianne Douglas living within the compound walls had been a huge bonus for Genna personally.

No one had spoken of the girls who had disappeared in the night, except to say that they'd been chosen to do the reverend's work. That none of the other adults in the compound seemed to question this seemed absurd to Genna, but then, if they're all involved in this together, perhaps not. . . .

Well, it was her job to find out all she could about who was involved and where the girls were disappearing to. She still had to determine exactly what role Jules Douglas played here. She'd confirmed that he was there, had even seen him several times, though she'd not recognized him at first. These days, he sported a beard and slightly longer hair than he'd had in the old photographs Annie had produced, and he'd walked with a swagger she hadn't expected. He seemed more arrogant, more aggressive than she'd imagined, and physically, he was taller, stronger, a far more imposing figure than she thought he'd be.

Somehow, she'd expected a man who was quiet, reserved. The man she met at the compound was anything but. The Jules she met in the Valley of the Angels was nothing short of intimidating.

If she could prove that he was actively involved in laundering the money, and that he knew where that money was coming from, she could make yet another case for a long prison term for Mara's ex-husband. After all he'd put Mara and Annie through over the years, Genna was more than a little eager to see that he paid the price. The kidnapping charges could turn out to be the least of Jules Douglas's worries.

In the meantime, Genna had already confirmed the presence of Julianne Douglas within the compound, and she laid the groundwork for her escape. This week, knowing she'd be carefully watched, she'd take a girl other than Julianne into town. Next week, to avoid any lingering suspicions Reverend Prescott might have, she'd take a second girl. But the following week, she'd take Julianne.

Genna wished only that she could be there to see the expression on the face of Reverend Prescott—and Jules Douglas—when it was discovered that the conscientious Miss Ruth had left the Valley of the Angels for good, and had taken young "Rebecca" with her.

_____ CHAPTER _____
FIVE

MIRANDA STOOD ON THE TOP STEP OF THE INN'S FRONT
porch, one hand over her eyes to shield them from the
glare of the early-morning sun, searching from one
end of the street to the other for Will's familiar form.
He had to be out here somewhere. She'd knocked on
his door at seven—certainly loudly enough to awaken
a light sleeper, as she knew Will to be—but he hadn't
answered. Since then, she'd had breakfast and made
several phone calls, but he hadn't shown up.

Oh, well. Will's the proverbial bad penny, she reminded herself. He'll turn up sooner or later.

And sure enough, just as she was about to go back
inside, there he was, crossing the street, jogging
toward the inn.

"Waiting for me?" he called.

"You wish."

He was barely breathing hard. How annoying.

She crossed her arms over her chest. "I just came
out to see what the weather was like."

"Hey. Navy pinstripes today. I like it." Before she
could respond, he said, "Did you know that Fleming
had its own tea party of sorts back in the days of the
Revolution? Only they didn't throw the tea into the

harbor—because, hey, no harbor—but they dumped it into the gorge on the outskirts of town. Pretty neat, huh?"

"Ummm, neat."

"There's a statue down in the center of town commemorating the event. Right across the street from the tattoo parlor."

"Sounds like Fleming has a little something for everyone."

"Though you'd have thought the town fathers might have been a little more selective in what type of business moved into that part of town, but then again, when you have a lot of empty storefronts, I guess you have to take what you can get."

"I guess." She backed up as he approached, as if consciously or unconsciously keeping space between them. "Did you finish reading the file?"

"Yes. We'll talk about it over coffee, if that's all right with you. Let me take a quick shower, and I'll meet you in the dining room. Ten minutes. I have an idea."

He went into the inn before she could respond.

She muttered under her breath and followed him inside to the lobby, watching—despite her attempts not to—as he jogged up the steps to the second floor.

It doesn't hurt to look, she reminded herself, as long as she wasn't tempted to touch.

And I am not tempted. I am not, am not, am not. . . .

She helped herself to a cup of coffee from the breakfast buffet and sat down at a sunny table. It was a perfect autumn day, perfect for . . . what?

What would she do, if she had the day to herself? Walk in the woods, maybe, fallen leaves crunching underfoot, the smell of autumn in the air, geese honking overhead. Or maybe stroll along the shore, breathing in cool salt air and listening to the crash of waves upon the sand. Or visit one of those old churchyards she'd passed on the way into Fleming, and take some rubbings off the old battered grave markers . . .

Her mind wandered back through pictures in her mind, and she was startled when she realized she'd done all of those things, but not alone. She'd done them with Will.

Walking along the paths in Rock Creek Park, in D.C., on a crisp late November morning. Layers of leaves crackling as they moved, single file, through the early mist, following the trail of a killer on Miranda's second day in the field. They'd met in the parking lot at dawn, after they'd been called in to help search the woods for a man believed to have shot and killed several customers in a convenience-store robbery, and had taken a live hostage. The hostage was a woman who happened to work for the Bureau, and the team had been gathered in record time. Later Miranda admitted to herself—though she'd have died before she'd have admitted it to him—that she'd been a bit starstruck at working on a case with Will. He was well known around the Bureau for being intuitive, smart, and capable, and was respected by his fellow agents for his easygoing manner and keen humor. The men counted themselves lucky if they called him friend. Most of the women wanted to call him something else.

Miranda had been impressed with his handling of the case, with the respect he showed the body they found tossed behind some rocks and covered with leaves and brush. She'd been almost flustered— almost—when, hours later, after their work was completed, the evidence gathered, the body removed, he'd asked her to join him for a bite to eat.

He'd taken her to a Middle Eastern restaurant downtown, where they'd eaten and talked and laughed until midnight. They'd connected, right from the start, on several levels. Certainly the chemistry had been dynamic. Even now, her cheeks burned as she recalled that she'd taken him home, and he'd stayed the night. Something she'd never, ever done in her life—before or since. Mostly she hadn't even kissed on the first date. But there'd been something about him that had turned her inside out and had banished rational thought along with most of her inhibitions.

Of course, it had made for an awkward next morning, an awkward day in the office. She'd been spared having an awkward week or two, however, since Will had been sent to Florida to assist in a drug bust. By the time he returned, she was in North Carolina, investigating the kidnapping and assault of several young girls on the Outer Banks.

It had been several months before she'd seen him again.

Will appeared as if out of the air and plunked a file down on an empty chair. "I'll just grab a cup from the buffet, and I'll be right back."

Miranda moved the window curtain aside and

watched the neighborhood kids gather at the bus stop on the opposite side of the street.

"So what's your plan, Agent Fletcher?" she asked when Will returned.

He sipped slowly at his coffee, then set the cup back into the saucer. "We've already agreed that we need to identify people from Channing's past who may have irritated him sufficiently that he might have wanted a little revenge. Other than Albert Unger, of course."

"Right. And I suppose you've come up with a means of identifying them?"

"I've come up with a starting point."

"Which would be . . . ?"

"I think we need to start at the beginning, with Claire Channing."

"Curtis's foster mother." Miranda nodded. "Good choice. She might know of someone from his past who had done something that Channing might have wanted revenge for."

"And from there, we move on to Albert Unger. We can stop and see him while we're in Ohio. Maybe he'll know of someone Channing had a problem with."

"Unger, yes. I guess that's as good a place as any. I don't recall there being too many other people from his past mentioned in the file."

"There wasn't anyone else mentioned. Just these two."

"So when would you like to go?"

"You tell me. You're in charge of the case." He drained his cup and, without waiting for her reply, pushed his chair back and returned to the buffet for a refill.

"Is that bothering you?" she asked when he sat down again. "That John made me the lead on this case?"

"No, not at all. It makes perfect sense. You know the players. You have the history."

She stared at him.

"And you're a damned good investigator. You're a natural for this one, Cahill. I wouldn't have it any other way." He smiled. "So. You make the call. What next?"

"We go to Ohio. We chat with Mrs. Channing, Mr. Unger. I don't know that either of them will have much to contribute. Channing left home as soon as he graduated from high school, and I don't think he's seen Unger since the man was arrested for murdering his mother. But since we have nowhere else to start, I say, let's break out those frequent flyer miles and give it a shot." She finished her coffee. "I'll check in with John and let him know what we're doing. Meanwhile, I have a meeting with the chief of the Fleming Police Department."

Miranda slid her purse from the back of the chair where she'd hung it, then stood.

"So, while you're finishing your breakfast and getting ready to leave, I'm going to have a chat about Archer Lowell."

"You're going to ask him to keep an eye on Archer for us while we're gone?"

"Her." Miranda grinned. "I'm going to ask *her* to keep an eye on him for us."

"Sure you don't want me to come along?"

"What for? I think I can handle a conversation with the local chief all by myself. Good to know you're here, though, in case I need backup."

"Well, then, I guess I have time to sample the eggs Benedict, after all." He looked pleased at the prospect.

"Just as long as you're ready to roll when I get back."

"You know where to find me." He smiled and returned to the buffet.

The Fleming Police Department was housed in what must have been at one time an elegant private home. Of course, that time had been well over a hundred years ago. Fleming had an abundance of old buildings, and it appeared to Miranda that the borough had made an effort to repurpose as many of them as possible.

Chief of Police Veronica Carson was waiting, as promised, promptly at eight-fifteen.

"So, Special Agent Cahill," the chief said after Miranda had introduced herself, "what can the Fleming PD do for the FBI?"

Ignoring the tiny bite in the question, Miranda sat where she'd been directed to sit.

"Actually, I'm here to share information with you." Miranda crossed her legs and settled into the chair.

"Oh?"

"We've been following a case for several months,"

she explained. "It has, ultimately, led us to Fleming. We thought you should know."

"Go on." Chief Carson removed her glasses and laid them on her desk. Without breaking eye contact with Miranda, she buzzed the receptionist and asked that coffee for two be brought into her office.

Miranda explained the connection between Fleming and Archer Lowell, Vince Giordano, and Curtis Channing.

"I followed those cases." Chief Carson nodded. "I know Sean Mercer down in Broeder quite well. He's a great cop. And I've known Evan Crosby for years. He's at the National Academy right now, I heard, for some special training."

"He is. It was my good fortune to work with him on the Lyndon case. I worked with Chief Mercer on the Broeder case, as well. They're both top-notch." Miranda turned as the door opened and the woman she'd met minutes earlier at the front desk brought in two mugs of steaming coffee.

"Did you make this, or did Sergeant Foley make it?" the chief asked.

"I made it," the woman told her.

"Thanks. Foley's coffee could peel the paint off a cruiser." Veronica Carson smiled for the first time since Miranda had entered the room. She passed a mug to Miranda, who moved closer to the desk to take it from her hands.

"So, Agent Cahill," she continued. "I have to think this visit is more than merely giving me a heads-up."

"Yes, to be truthful, I was hoping to enlist your assistance in this case."

Chief Carson sipped at her coffee, burned her tongue, and set the mug back down. "Hot. How can we help you?"

"If you could keep an eye on Lowell . . . let us know if he does anything out of the ordinary. Call me if he leaves town . . ."

"You want the Fleming police to do your surveillance so that you can go do something more important, is that it?"

"No, that's not it." Miranda's back arched just slightly. "We're trying to identify and track down Lowell's potential victims."

"If in fact there are any potential victims."

"Yes. Ohio—where Channing grew up and made his early kills—appears to be the logical starting place. It's tough to be in two places at the same time."

"So we keep an eye on Lowell while you see what you can dredge up in Ohio."

"Yes. If you're willing."

"Agent Cahill, I have a very small force here. There's no way I can spare an officer to watch one person all the time. It just isn't possible." The chief leaned forward in her chair. "Especially since it really isn't clear if Lowell is going to do a damned thing. You said yourself it's unlikely he'll go through with whatever deal you think he made with these two killers."

"Believe me, I understand the situation you're in. Unfortunately, the Bureau is shorthanded now, too. We have more agents overseas than we've ever had, and it's hindered us in investigating cases like this."

"Okay, I will do this, because I'd hate like hell to

have something happen to someone if I could have prevented it. I'll instruct the officers to watch for him at night at the Well. That's the bar you spoke of. I can't think of a better way to monitor his comings and goings. If he fails to show up on any given night, chances are he's either ill or he's left town. There's really no place else to go around here, if you're that age. I can have someone stop in there at night. Several of our officers do, anyway."

"Thank you. We appreciate that." Miranda slid a business card across the desk. "The quickest way to reach me is on my cell. Call any time, day or night."

"I'll give this number out to the entire department, if that's all right with you." The chief stood to indicate that the meeting had concluded. "If anyone sees anything you should know about, we'll let you know."

"We can't ask for more than that. Thank you." Miranda took her cue, shook the chief's hand, and found her way out to the parking lot, relieved that someone would be keeping an eye on Lowell while she and Will searched Channing's past for likely victims. While Chief Carson had not agreed to surveillance, at least someone would be watching to see if he left town. Miranda really couldn't ask for much more than that from the small department.

She glanced at her watch. There was still plenty of time to stop in Lyndon on her way home and check in with Lowell's probation officer. Since she and Will arrived in separate cars, she'd just make a quick stop at the inn to pick up her bags, check out, and be on her way by noon.

* * *

"Archer? Archer Lowell?"

The voice on the phone was low, but forceful all the same.

"Who is this?" Archer rubbed his eyes and turned over to look at the clock. It was ten in the morning.

"A friend of a friend."

"What friend?" Archer sat up.

"A friend at High Meadow."

Archer's jaw moved, but no sound came from his mouth.

"You there, Archie?"

"I don't have no friends at High Meadow. And I don't like to be called Archie."

"Oh. Right." Even in agreement, there was menace in the tone.

"Who are you? Why are you calling me?"

"Your old buddy Vince asked me to."

"Vince who?"

"Don't even try to play me, Archie. It pisses me off no end when people try to play me. And you do not want to piss me off. Understand?"

"Yeah . . . yes." Archer wrapped the blanket around himself. All of a sudden, he felt very cold.

"Okay, then." A long drag off a cigarette, a long exhale. "I want to know what your plan is, Archie."

"My plan?"

"Your plan to carry out your part of the deal. The deal you made with Vince and that other friend of yours, the one who died. I want to know what you're going to do."

"I . . . ah . . ." Archer slammed down the receiver.

"Holy shit," he whispered. "Holy shit . . ."

He went into the tiny bathroom and relieved himself, then splashed cool water onto his face with hands shaking so badly they barely held water.

Calm down. You don't know who that was. Coulda been anyone.

Anyone who knew about the game . . .

Then it had to have been Vince. Yeah, that's it. It was Vince. Calling from High Meadow. Pretending to be someone else.

Why would Vince pretend to be someone else?

To scare me. Yeah, just to scare me into thinking it was someone on the outside.

Had the caller said he was on the outside? He couldn't remember.

But it had to be Vince. It had to be.

No one else knows, right?

Right?

Could even have been the FBI. Yeah, it coulda been them.

He tried to remember if he'd said anything that could incriminate him. He didn't think he had.

He pulled on the jeans he'd worn the day before and a flannel shirt from the pile of laundry in his room. Grabbing his jacket, he left the trailer, then paused out front. He avoided the road and walked along behind the other trailers until he reached the end of the mobile home village. He looked around and, seeing no cars, no strangers, he exhaled deeply.

Still, he felt jumpy. As if he were being watched.

He debated with himself, then set out across the field that lay between the trailers and the back of the Well. A short walk and he'd be at the bar, a cold beer in his hand. He'd taken that route on several occasions when he couldn't beg a ride home from anyone. It was dark and a little creepy late at night, but this was broad daylight.

It was with great relief that he rounded the corner of the building and pushed open the door. He went straight to the bar and ordered a shot and a beer, then another. His nerves mildly anesthetized, he finally relaxed, entered into some mindless chatter with the bartender, who was obviously bored. There was only one other person drinking at that hour of the morning, a regular from town who never spoke to anyone.

By noon, Archer was buzzed. By three in the afternoon, he was sleeping in a chair in the back room. Later that night, he was back at the bar with his friends. At midnight, the morning's fear forgotten, he left the bar by the back door, intending to return home the same way he'd arrived.

The door was barely closed before a large hand grabbed him by both lapels, dragged him around the corner, and shoved him back against the back wall of the bar.

"Who . . . ?"

"I hate it when someone hangs up on me before I've said what I had to say."

The figure was large, the face indistinct in the dark. Archer cringed and tried to melt through the wall.

"Now, I'm going to ask you one more time. What are your plans for carrying out your end of the deal?"

"I hadn't really thought about it. I just got out. . . ." Archer tried to calm himself. Tried to sound as if he wasn't ready to pass out from fright.

"Well, then, let's think about it now. You and me."
The man dragged Archer deeper into the shadows.

"Who are you?" Archer asked, hoping to buy himself time.

"You can call me Burt. And I'm the man who's going to make sure that you don't fuck up, little buddy." His breath was hot and sour in Archer's face. "I'm the man who is going to be watching every move you make until the job is done, understand?"

"No."

"Think of me sorta like your conscience." He chuckled, but to Archer it sounded more like a growl. "You know how your conscience tells you what to do? Keep your word, that sort of thing?"

Archer nodded slowly.

"Well, I'm gonna make sure you do what you said you'd do."

"I was gonna do it," Archer whispered. "Soon as I could, you know, get a plan together."

"This is your lucky day, Archer. Because I am here to help you with that plan." His grip on Archer never loosened. "Tell me the names. Convince me that you're still in the game, that you know what you have to do. . . ."

Archer whispered the names.

"Very good, Archie. Very good. At least you know that much."

"Hey, I know what I'm supposed to do, okay? Just haven't gotten around to doing it. First I need to get a job, I need some money to get around, you know what I mean?"

Archer felt himself lowered so that his feet once again touched the ground.

The stranger backed off slightly, then stuffed something into Archer's left jacket pocket.

"Now that's one excuse you don't have anymore. Tell me what your plan is, Archie. Walk me through it. . . ."

Jesus. Jesus.

Archer sat on the ground behind his mother's trailer and shook all over. He'd run all the way back from the bar in the dark, all the way across the field, stumbling, his neck craning this way and that. Terrified that the stranger was following him, that he'd let him get halfway across the field and then he'd pop up and just break his neck or slash him to ribbons. Like one of those bad scary movies. Jason. Michael. Freddie.

Burt was scarier.

Archer was crying softly by the time he arrived home. Not soft enough to risk going inside, though. He'd wake up his mom, sure enough, and there was no way he wanted her to see him like this. Geez, he was crying like a girl.

I can't help it. He was scary. Burt was the scariest person I've ever seen close-up.

Scarier still, knowing that he was going to be watching until this was over. Until he'd . . .

Archer started crying all over again.

I don't want to kill anyone. I never did; I never want to.

He thought of the photographs of Vince's victims,

the ones the chief of police from Broeder had shown him while he was still in prison, when they wanted him to talk about Vince. A man with a single hole in the back of his head, a larger one in the front. A woman with her throat slashed, her chest a mess of stab wounds, blood everywhere. Her eyes had been open.

Jesus.

He stopped shaking for a minute. Miranda Cahill—he cringed at the irony—had been here just the day before yesterday. He could have told her. He could still tell her. He could get the FBI to help him. Protect him.

Yeah, Miz Cahill, you were right. It was just supposed to be a game, that's all. Something to pass the time while we were in the courthouse waiting. I swear to you, it wasn't supposed to happen. I never thought it was going to happen. But then, see, Channing got out, and he did Vince's hits. Then Vince, he gets out, and he's thinking, hey, Channing did it, I have to do it, too. That's what I think happened, anyway. I think Vince didn't want to feel like Channing was, you know, a tougher man than he was. So then, Vince is out, and he picks up the game, and he does . . . he does these people that I had said pissed me off. I didn't really want them to die, you gotta understand that. I never thought anyone was really gonna die. . . .

He whimpered aloud.

And then I get out, and all I want to do is just live my life. Get a job. Find a girl. Live my life. I had no intention of playing out the game.

And then this guy came along and said I had to. . . .

And what was he going to say when they asked him who the stranger was?

"I don't know," he said aloud. "I don't know who he is. I never even seen his face. . . ."

Like anyone is going to believe *that*.

Archer hugged himself in the dark, and tried to think of a way out of the mess he'd gotten himself into, preferably one that would not require him to kill or, in the alternative, to be killed.

Right at that moment, he wasn't sure which would be worse.

———— CHAPTER ————
SIX

CLAIRE CHANNING WAS WATCHING FROM THE LIVING room window of her well-kept white clapboard ranch house as the man and woman crossed her lawn, headed for her front door. Even if they hadn't given her the courtesy of a phone call, she'd have known just by looking at them that they were law. She'd seen more than enough law enforcement types over the past six months. After the investigation into the circumstances surrounding the death of her foster son, Curtis, had concluded, she'd thought she'd seen the last of them.

Apparently not. Her face was etched with sadness as the doorbell rang. Would there never be an end to the questions?

"I appreciate you being on time," she said wearily as she opened the door.

"Mrs. Channing, I'm Special Agent Miranda Cahill. We spoke earlier on the phone." In the agent's left hand were her credentials.

Claire Channing had seen her share of those over the past months, as well.

"I'm Agent Fletcher, ma'am." The second agent introduced himself.

"Do come in, Agent Cahill, Agent Fletcher." Mrs. Channing stepped back, offering a weak smile as the two agents eased past her. "I'm afraid things are a bit disheveled right now. . . ."

"You're moving?" Agent Cahill asked.

"Yes. With everything that's happened over the past several months, I just need . . ." Mrs. Channing shook her head.

"A change of scenery." Agent Cahill completed the sentence for her. "Of course you do. I'm sure this whole matter has been terribly stressful for you, Mrs. Channing. It's very nice of you to give Agent Fletcher and me a few minutes of your time. We won't keep you any longer than necessary, I promise."

"Thank you. It has been an ordeal." Mrs. Channing sat on the arm of a club chair; several boxes had been stacked on its seat. "After Curtis . . . well, there was so much . . . commotion. Reporters and police, it just got to be too much. I spent some time in Florida with my sister, and that time away made me realize that there really wasn't anything to hold me here anymore. My husband has been gone these years, and Curtis . . . Curtis won't be coming back. So I listed the house for sale, and the agent found a buyer. We settle in two weeks. It's taking me longer than I expected to pack, though. It's not easy to pack up fifty-two years of your life in a month's time, you know."

"I'm sure it's very difficult for you, Mrs. Channing. We'll make this as easy for you as we can," Will assured her.

"Well, then. What exactly do you need to know

that no one else has asked me over the past six months?"

"Can you think of anyone Curtis might have had a grievance against? Someone he might have wanted to take revenge on?" Agent Cahill appeared to choose her words carefully.

"What kind of a question is that?" Claire Channing was taken aback. "Curtis is dead. What is this talk of revenge?"

"Mrs. Channing, we have reason to believe that before Curtis died, he and two other men made a pact . . . an agreement." More carefully chosen words from Miranda Cahill.

"A pact?" Mrs. Channing frowned. "What kind of a pact? What are you talking about?"

"They made an agreement to kill for one another, Mrs. Channing," Will Fletcher said. "The women whom Curtis killed earlier this year—all have ties to one of the other two men. Then, two months ago, two people having ties to another of the men was killed by the second. We believe a third man is about to kill three people having ties to Curtis."

"This is crazy. Just crazy." Mrs. Channing walked out of the room. The agents followed.

"Mrs. Channing—"

"This is crazy talk, Agent Cahill." Claire Channing sat at the table in the sun-filled kitchen, staring at her hands. "Curtis . . . killed those women. I know he did that. But it was because of what had happened to him so long ago, when he was just a little boy. It wasn't for revenge or for anything like what you're talking about."

She looked from one agent to the other, appealing for their understanding.

"Things happened to him. Things that made him . . . not right. Not that it's an excuse for what he did to all those women. I know nothing could excuse what he did. But if you understood what happened to him, you'd know that there was something inside him that just wasn't right. And God help him, it wasn't his fault. He didn't ask for those terrible things to be done to him."

"We know, Mrs. Channing. We've read the files," Will told her gently. "We know what happened to him . . . what his mother did to him."

"Then you know that he just . . . couldn't help but be what he was. How could any child be right when they've had to endure such abominations. And at the hands of their own mother." Tears started down her face, and she ignored them. "We tried, Marshall and I, to make it up to him. To give him a good home. Love. A family. Good times. Good memories. We tried to make up for all the bad. But it wasn't enough, you see. It could never be enough. . . ."

"You and your husband did your best, Mrs. Channing." Miranda knelt in front of the elderly woman and took her hands in her own. "If one thing was clear from reading the files, it's that you and Mr. Channing were the best thing that ever happened to Curtis. He cared a great deal for you. But there's no way that you could change what happened to him, and you weren't responsible for that."

"This . . . this revenge thing you're suggesting."

Mrs. Channing shivered. "This is different. It's colder, somehow."

"We're sorry to have upset you, Mrs. Channing, but we need to know if you can think of anyone from his past—from high school, even—whom Curtis would have wanted to . . . hurt." Miranda spoke softly.

"You were going to say kill."

"Yes."

"I can't think of a soul." The elderly woman shook her head slowly. "I'm sorry. I can't think of anyone Curtis ever had problems with."

Miranda handed her a business card.

"My phone numbers are on here, Mrs. Channing. If you think of someone . . . someone he didn't get along with, or someone who gave him a hard time . . ."

"I can't think of a one. He had a few friends in school, not many. He was a loner. But he got along with everyone. I never heard him say anything negative about anyone."

"If you remember anything . . . any incident, however small or insignificant it may seem . . ."

"Of course, Agent Cahill. I will call you."

"Thank you." Miranda stood. "I'm sorry we upset you."

Claire Channing merely nodded her head.

"We'll see ourselves out," Will told her. "Thank you for your time, Mrs. Channing."

Once outside, Miranda exhaled a long, slow breath.

"That was painful," she said as they walked to the car. "Poor, poor woman. After all she's gone through, all the pain of the past few months, she finally thinks it's all behind her, then we turn up, asking questions. Bringing it all back . . ."

"What's the likelihood she's forgotten?" Will asked as he unlocked the rental car.

"Oh, I'm sure it's on her mind at least once every day. She'll never get over it."

She slid into the passenger seat and strapped herself in.

"How do you get over something like that?" Will started the car and checked the rearview mirror before pulling out onto the road. "You think you're doing something wonderful, you take in this little boy who's had such a tragic life. You give him a loving home; you treat him as if he's your own flesh and blood, and in spite of it all, he grows up to be a serial killer."

"She seems like such a sweet woman."

"She is."

They drove in silence for several miles.

"So what now?" Miranda asked.

"On to Albert Unger."

"He should be easy enough to find. Assuming he's still working at the same place he was working when Aidan and Mara found him."

"I hope so. He's the closest thing we have to a potential victim," Miranda reminded him.

"So, what do we say when we find him?"

"I'm still working on that. I'm hoping that, by the time we reach Telford, I'll have that figured out. . . ."

There was silence for several miles, until Miranda broke it. "I've been meaning to ask you," she said, "did you specifically ask for this car, or was this all they had left at the rental-car place today?"

"Few things happen by accident, Cahill." He smiled. He was wondering when she'd say something about the truly ugly bottom-of-the-line sedan he'd leased.

"Really? You really called the rental agency and asked for the slowest, oldest, butt-ugliest car they had?"

"You know that budgetary restrictions determine what car we can get," he said loftily, his eyes straight ahead on the road before them.

"Most of us manage to do a little better than this. Think it will make it all the way to Telford?"

"Guess we'll find out, won't we?"

"Wake me up when we get there." She closed her eyes.

"You're supposed to be thinking of an opening line for our approach to Unger."

"I'm sleeping on it, Fletcher." Her eyes still closed, she reached her hand down next to the seat, searching for the controls. Finding it, she slid the seat back as far as it would go and stretched out her long legs. "I do some of my best work with my eyes closed."

Amen, he silently agreed. *Amen . . .*

Archer Lowell stumbled along the perimeter of the field, then headed for the woods well beyond the trailer camp.

"Don't like this," he muttered to himself. "Don't want to do this . . ."

The gun that he'd shoved into the waistband of his

jeans was cold and heavy and foreign. Today would mark the third day in a row he'd spent at the shooting range, practicing putting a single hole in the middle of the bull's-eye. Just like the stranger—Burt, he'd said his name was—had told him to do. Practice, practice, practice.

"Yeah, well, I practiced," he said aloud. "Today's the last day I'm doing this. I know how to shoot the damned gun. Don't know what he thinks I am, that I have to keep going back. I told him I done good enough with it the first day. But nooooo."

Archer kicked at a clump of dry earth in his path.

"Just all craziness, anyway," he mumbled as he walked along. "I hate him. *Hate* him. I should use this fucking gun on him, that's what I should do."

He kicked another clump.

"Making me do this thing I don't want to do. Kill some man I don't even know. Shit."

His hands started to shake just thinking about it. He was going to have to kill a man. Burt had given him until Friday to leave for Ohio, which was where this guy Unger lived. He already had his bus ticket. Burt had bought it for him and left it in his mailbox.

Shit. He wiped at his nose with his sleeve as he walked along. At the very least, Burt coulda driven him. Who takes a Greyhound to make a hit?

──── CHAPTER ────
SEVEN

AT TWENTY-FIVE MINUTES PAST MIDNIGHT, IN THE empty movie theater, the frail, stooped man slid his broom under the front row of seats. Methodically, he swept the debris into a central pile.

"Mr. Unger?" Will said. He and Miranda approached the old man slowly, so as not to alarm him.

"I'm Al Unger." The man stopped pushing the broom he held with both hands and leaned upon it, his expression guarded.

"My name is Will Fletcher. This is Miranda Cahill. We're with the FBI."

"Jesus, not again." Unger looked from one agent to the other. "Curt come back from the dead and kill someone else?"

"Not yet," Miranda told him. "But we're thinking he might do just that, in a manner of speaking."

"What the hell are you talking about? I know he's dead. I was one of the few people at his funeral who actually knew him."

"We're aware of that, Mr. Unger." Miranda hesitated. "Is there someplace we can talk?"

Unger gestured toward the empty movie theater.

"Got the whole theater to ourselves. Oughta be good enough."

"How about we sit down here in the front?" Will pointed to the row of seats.

"Long as it don't hold me up too long. I don't want to miss my bus," Unger told them as he sat. "Now, what the hell is this all about, talking about Curtis coming back from the dead? What kind of nonsense is that?"

Miranda and Will filled him in on the FBI's theory.

"You have got to be kidding. You think Curt asked someone else to kill me?" Unger's eyebrows shot up nearly to his sparse hairline. "Why in the name of God would he do that?"

"Before Curtis died, he'd been holding a woman captive. Her name was Anne Marie McCall. She's an FBI profiler," Miranda told him.

"I remember that. She was the sister of that girl Curt been trying to find."

Miranda nodded.

"Curt told Dr. McCall that he hated you for killing his mother."

Unger stared at Miranda blankly.

"Hated me for that? For killing her and stopping his suffering? Shit." Unger shook his head. "You'd think he'd a been thanking me. Why would he hate me for that?"

"Because he'd wanted to kill her himself."

Unger nodded slowly. "That, I can understand. I can understand why he would have wanted to been the one . . . but he was just a little boy then. Eight, nine, maybe. If she'd a kept on doing what she'd been doing to him, he wouldn't have lived long enough to grow up."

"That's probably true, Mr. Unger," Miranda agreed.

"But the problem we have now," Will told him, "is that someone else might be thinking about doing that job for him."

"Curt killed someone for him, you said, so you figure now this other person is going to kill me for Curt?"

"Close enough." Will nodded.

"Well, then, best I can do is watch my back." Albert Unger stood slowly. "Any idea what this guy looks like? The one who wants to kill me?"

"He's young, about twenty. Tall, lanky. Bad skin . . ." Miranda opened the leather bag that hung from her shoulder.

Unger started to laugh.

"Miss, that's a fair description of maybe half the young men who come into this theater."

"Maybe this will help." She handed him a photograph. "That's his mug shot. He looks a bit different these days. His hair's a bit longer; he's lost some weight, . . ."

"Still looks like half the kids I see on any given day. I can't be running every time some young kid comes through that door."

"We're not suggesting that. We just want you to be aware of people. A little more watchful, maybe. And here." She took a card out of her wallet. "If you even think someone is watching you, if anyone makes you feel uncomfortable, or uneasy, I want you to call me.

Stay right where you are until we can get someone to you, okay?"

He studied the card, then slipped it into his pocket.

"Sure. Thanks." He stood up, leaning on the broom handle to get out of his seat. "You know, someone was by a few weeks ago. Some writer. Said he used to get mail from Curtis. Said he wants to talk to me, maybe do a book about me and Curtis. That'd be something, wouldn't it?"

"It sure would," Miranda agreed.

"Well, I better get back to work here. I lock up, you know, after I'm done, and if I'm too late turning the lights off, the local cops come in to see what's going on, and the boss always hears about it. Thanks for letting me know what's what."

"You're welcome. Just be careful."

"Will do, Agent . . ."

"Fletcher," Will told him.

"Pleased to have met you." Albert Unger went back to pushing his broom under the seats, and brought a wide swath of popcorn and candy wrappers into the light.

"Mr. Unger," Miranda paused on her way up the aisle, "what was the name of the writer who contacted you?"

"Don't remember, offhand." Unger turned to her. "Got his card at home someplace, though."

"When you find it, or if he calls you again, will you let me know?"

"Sure, sure." The old man nodded. "Be glad to give you a call."

"Collect," she called over her shoulder. "Call collect . . ."

"Will do." He went back to sweeping the floor.

"Kind of a sad old guy, isn't he?" Miranda said as they left the theater.

"He's had a sad life." Will held the door for her, and together they stepped out into the night air. "Falls in love with a woman who has a young son and addictions to drugs and alcohol. Robs a store to keep her in what she needs, gets caught, and goes to prison. Meanwhile, she still needs."

"So she pimps out her little boy to feed her addictions," she said as they reached the car.

"And when Al gets out of prison and finds out what she's done, he kills her." Will unlocked the car doors. "Spends the next thirty years of his life behind bars."

"During which time the little boy grows into a man with very terrible needs of his own." Miranda summed it up as she slid into her seat. "End of story."

"Not quite." Will started the car. "There's still that little epilogue that Archer Lowell might be thinking about writing."

"That's our job, to keep him from doing just that."

"Think he took us seriously?" Will asked. "Unger?"

"I think so. I expect to hear from him, if anything odd is going on. He spent thirty years behind bars. He's just getting his life back again. I'd think he'd want to hang on to it for a while."

"Well, then, we're just going to have to be smart enough to make sure he does just that."

* * *

Two days later, Archer rested his head against the window of the bus and stared into the dark beyond. Several hours had passed since he'd boarded the Greyhound and taken a seat all the way in the back, where he could sit alone and think about what he should do.

He knew Burt had been watching him. Knew if he hadn't gotten on the bus there'd have been hell to pay. He bit a straggly fingernail and wondered how Burt would know whether he killed this old man in Ohio.

Of course, he'd know. He's *Burt*. He knows everything.

For a moment it crossed Archer's mind to wonder if perhaps Burt was really not of this world, like some of the movies he'd seen. Maybe he wasn't really a flesh-and-blood man; maybe he was from another dimension. Like in the comic books or video games. It could explain how Burt seemed to know so much about what Archer was thinking.

Like this morning, when the phone rang, even before Archer was out of bed.

"Are you packed?" the voice had asked. Archer knew, of course, whose voice it was.

"Um, yeah. Yeah, I'm packed." Archer sat up and ran a hand over his face. "I'm ready."

"You wouldn't be thinking about not making this trip, would you?"

"No, no. I told you I would . . . do it."

"You want to be on that bus when it leaves this afternoon, Archie. You don't want to know what will happen if you miss it."

The phone had gone dead before Archer could reply.

"Shit," he muttered aloud in the dim corner of the bus. "Shit."

He leaned back in the seat and wrapped his arms over his chest, pondering his options. And, of course, when Burt had called back later in the morning, he'd given him options. Archer could go ahead and kill this old man, this Unger guy, or Burt would take Archer's sister.

It had crossed his mind to ask where Burt would take her, since getting her out of his life, as far as Archer was concerned, would be no big loss. As miserable as she was, Archer had been sorely tempted, but it would kill his mother if anything happened to the bitch, so it really wasn't much of a choice. Besides, there'd been something in the way Burt had said his sister's name—*Angelina*—that had sent a chill right up his spine.

Of course, *most* of what Burt said sent a shiver up his spine.

Archer sighed. This was a real good example of what his grandmother would say was making your bed and lying in it. Well, he was lying in it, all right.

He patted his shirt pocket and felt the slip of paper upon which Burt had listed all the information Archer would need to do the deed: the victim's name, his home address, and the address of the theater where he worked.

Shit. He'd said *victim*. He ran a hand through his hair. This old guy was gonna be his victim. A murder victim. And that would make him, Archer, a murderer.

"Shit."

Restless, he surveyed the other passengers, wondering if Burt might have someone on the bus to watch him and report back. That was a possibility he hadn't considered before. That guy there in the black leather jacket, maybe. Or maybe that girl with all the curly brown hair up near the driver. Could be Burt's girl. Sure, Burt would have a dishy-looking girl, wouldn't he?

The bus pulled to the side of the road and the driver announced the stop. Archer removed the folded paper from his pocket and strained to read in the dark. This was Oak Avenue. Two more stops and they'd be at Ridge, which was where he was supposed to get off. He rubbed his sweaty palms on his pants and stood up. If someone was watching him, someone here in the bus, he'd better get off at the right stop. Once off the bus, he'd figure out where to go from there.

Two stops later, Archer walked the length of the bus, his eyes darting from side to side to see if anyone seemed interested in his leaving. No one appeared to be, but then again, anyone working with Burt would be too smart to let themselves be caught watching, wouldn't they?

He hopped down the steps, his heart in his mouth. There, right there, not two doors down, stood the movie theater. Archer took a deep breath and walked toward the ticket booth, trying to appear as nonchalant as possible under the circumstances. He bought his ticket for the nine-forty-five show and went in through the heavy glass doors.

The Telford Theater was one of those old-fashioned movie theaters you didn't see many of these days. A single-screen theater. There were few patrons for the last screening of the sappy comedy that was playing. Archer sat in the back row, huddling in the dark in the far-left corner and taking stock of the others in the audience. A random couple or two, but mostly single people here and there throughout the theater. He wondered if any of them had been sent by Burt to make sure Archer stayed behind after the movie ended, like he'd been instructed to do.

"Before the movie ends, you crouch down there on the floor. When everyone else has gone, you creep down to the front on your hands and knees. When you hear the old man start to sweep, you get as close as you can, plug him, and leave."

"What if someone else is there, what if everyone doesn't leave?"

"Then I guess you follow the old man home and plug him on the way. Best to do it in the theater, though. He's usually the last one there."

"But what if someone hears the gun?"

"It's a small caliber, won't make all that much noise if you get real close up. And besides, like I told you, the old man closes up after the last show. Won't be no one around to hear nothing. Just take care of your business, walk down to the bus stop, and wait for the next bus."

"But . . ."

"Archie. No buts." Burt had started to sound a little testy at this point, so Archer had shut up.

"Okay." Archer had sighed.

"Don't let Vince down, Archie." Burt had hung up while Archer was still trying to figure out what bus he was supposed to get on after he shot the old man.

The movie theme song began to play louder, and the credits began to roll. Reluctantly, Archer slid off his seat and onto the floor, landing in a pool of something sticky. He moved quietly toward the end of the row, wiping his hands on the carpet in disgust. Discarded bits of popcorn exploded under his knees and clung to the legs of his pants. He cursed under his breath as he slunk forward toward the front of the theater. At one point he paused and ventured a peek across the room. The theater was empty. There was no one left to see him, but still he crawled along the floor. He did not want to see the face of the man he was supposed to kill. If he stayed down here, he could wait for the man to come into the theater, creep up on him from behind, and shoot him in the back of the head. That way, he wouldn't have to look the man in the eyes. He wasn't sure he could pull the trigger if he knew what the man looked like. Right now, Al Unger was sort of a blank man. Like pictures you see in the newspaper or in magazines, where they show the shape of a head but no facial features. That's how he wanted to think of Al Unger. A face without features.

A shuffling sound from the front of the room stopped Archer in his tracks. Cautiously, he peered over the rows of seats. A frail little man with a broom under his arm was dragging a large shop vacuum cleaner into the pit area in front of the first row of seats.

Archer made his way to the far end of the front row, still on his hands and knees, and watched the old man clean under the seats with the broom. When he'd accumulated a hefty pile of debris, he turned on the large shop vac and began to suck up the trash.

This was it. This was the moment.

As soon as Unger turned his back, Archer forced himself to his feet. Still crouching, as if he'd be struck dead if he stood up, Archer rounded the corner and approached Unger from behind. He took the small handgun from his pocket and, with it in his right hand, walked up behind Unger. Raising the gun and aiming straight at the back of the man's head, Archer fired one bullet.

The vacuum handle fell from Unger's hand and hit the ground. Slowly, the body crumpled, falling where it had stood. Archer opened his eyes and saw Al Unger's head hit the floor, facedown. Backing away, Archer stuck the gun back into his jacket pocket. Refusing to think about what he had just done, he walked halfway up the side aisle and through the closest exit into the deserted parking lot.

His breathing coming harder, faster, he went around the building and, pausing to get his bearings, leaned flat against the hard brick wall. Tears streamed down his face.

"I'm sorry," he whispered to the night. "I'm sorry . . ."

*　　*　　*

A rustle from the dark, a soft scurry among the discarded chip bags and candy wrappers had Archer scurrying off as well. He wiped his face on his sleeve, swatted the popcorn off his pant legs, then walked to the end of the alley and crossed the street to the bus stop. Grabbing onto the sign, he held on for dear life and prayed his legs would not give out on him.

He'd just killed a man. God, he'd really done it.

He stood at the corner—staring straight ahead and trying to keep from crying—until the next bus arrived. He hopped aboard, took a seat near the back, and shook like a man who'd just come in from the cold. Once the bus reached the terminal in Cincinnati, he sat quietly while he waited for morning and the bus that would take him on to his designated stop, the refrain running over and over through his brain:

I killed a man. I put a bullet in the back of his head, and he fell down and died. I didn't even know him, and I killed him.

He'd boarded the bus he'd been told to take, once again huddled in the back, his head in his hands, the sound of his heart pounding loud in his ears. Crying silent tears, he begged forgiveness from a God he'd never really believed in, and from the old man whose life he'd taken that night.

And he knew that if he didn't come up with something fast, he'd be forced to do it again. And again . . .

CHAPTER EIGHT

WILL FLETCHER TOSSED THE NEWSPAPER ONTO THE recycling pile in the corner of his kitchen, noting that the pile had grown considerably over the past few days. He made a mental note to bundle up the papers and get them outside in time for the next scheduled end-of-the-week pickup. He'd missed the past few weeks, once because he'd gone into the office early to check up on something regarding a case, and once because he'd simply forgotten until it was too late. This week he'd make the pickup. He found a ball of string to wrap the papers in and set it on the counter. The doorbell rang before he could begin his hunt for the scissors.

Miranda stood on his front porch, her color pale and her eyes vague and distant.

"Hey, Cahill. This is a pleasant—"

"We fucked up."

"What are you talking about?"

"He did it. The son of a bitch did it."

"Who . . . ? You don't mean Lowell . . . ?"

"Yes. I do mean Lowell. Unger is dead. So much for the combined smarts of that all-star FBI panel that convened last week."

"What happened?"

"I got a call this morning from the Telford police." She shoved her hands in the pockets of her jacket and recited the facts. "A passing patrol car noticed the lights in the theater were still on at two-thirty this morning, so they stopped in. They found Al face-down on the floor, a bullet through the back of his head."

"Damn," Will muttered. "*Damn* it. I thought they were going to keep an eye on him."

"Apparently their idea of surveillance is limited to twice-nightly drive-bys." Her shoulders dropped. "May I come in?"

"Of course. Sorry." Will stepped back to allow her to enter, then closed the door.

"I feel like an idiot. We were all so sure Lowell was such a pussy he'd never do something bold like kill a man. God, we are so stupid."

"Whoa, take it easy, Miranda. Even Annie, who is usually right on the money when it comes to figuring people out, thought Archer would be a no-show when it came to finishing up the game."

"Well, it just goes to show you, like Annie always says, profiling is not an exact science."

"Do we know for a fact that it was Lowell? Or are we assuming?"

"Well, wouldn't it just be the biggest coincidence in the world if someone other than Lowell pulled the trigger?"

"Good point." Will took her arm and led her through the house to the kitchen. "Come on. You look like you could use a cup of coffee."

"Bastard had us all fooled," Miranda said. "No one figured him for a cold-blooded killer."

"Here, sit down." He pulled a chair out from the table, and offered it to her. "What exactly did the police say when they called?"

She sat, turning the chair slightly to the left when he sat down next to her.

"A cruiser passing by the theater early this morning noticed the lobby lights were still on, which is not normal for that hour. So the cops stopped to investigate, found the door unlocked, went into the lobby, heard the vacuum cleaner running. They entered the theater, saw the vacuum but not Al. When they walked down to the front, they found the body. There was no one else around, and a canvass of the neighborhood has turned up nothing. No one saw anything; no one heard anything." She blew out a long, exasperated breath. "And the Telford police are telling me they have no suspects."

"What do you mean, they have no suspects?" Will frowned. "We told them who to watch for, even gave them a picture of Lowell."

"Yeah, well, they're saying there's no evidence to tie Lowell to the murder. We can't even prove Lowell was in Telford last night."

"They think this whole thing is one big coincidence? Who else could it have been?"

"Do you think there's a chance there could have been a fourth person in on this game?" Miranda asked.

"I don't see how. The only time we can place Lowell, Giordano, and Channing together was in the police van one morning back in February, and even then, according to the guards and the driver, they did not speak to one another. There was one other inmate in the van that morning, but he's spending the rest of his life behind bars." Will paused, then added, "As a matter of fact, on the morning in question, this other prisoner had escaped into the courthouse and held up things for hours. Put the entire courthouse on lockdown for a good part of the day until they found him."

"I don't recall hearing about that." Miranda frowned.

"It was in an amended report that Evan Crosby filed. It's in the packet of material Jared put together for us."

"What were the other three doing while the courthouse was on lockdown?"

"I don't know. Good question, though. Maybe we should give Evan a call and see if he knows."

"If he doesn't, I'll bet he can find out."

"I have his card in my desk. I'll be right back. In the meantime, think you could throw together a pot of coffee? The coffee maker is there on the counter. Coffee and filters are the same place they were the last time you were here."

By the time Will returned to the kitchen, the coffee was just beginning to drip and Miranda was leaning into the open refrigerator, searching for a carton of milk.

"I had to leave a voice mail for Crosby."

"He'll call you back. He's real good about returning calls. He'd make a great agent. Bet it wouldn't take much to convince him, either. I think he's really got a thing for Anne Marie."

"Has anyone notified the Fleming police?"

"I called them on my way here. God knows I had plenty of time. Honestly, could you have found a house farther out than this?"

"There was a time when you liked my little bungalow in the woods." He turned his attention to pouring coffee into two mugs that had SOUVENIR OF NAGS HEAD, N.C. in faded blue paint on the front and a pair of equally faded pelicans on the back.

"It has a lot of promise, I'll give you that. But I'll bet those narrow roads up the side of those hills are hell in the winter."

"Guess I'll find out over the next few months," he said, handing her a mug.

"Guess you will." She opened a cupboard and surveyed the contents. "No artificial sweeteners?"

"Sorry. Only the real thing. Sugar's in the bowl on the counter."

She opted for milk only, stirring it as she spoke. "Anyway, Fleming sent a patrol car to the Lowell trailer. If he's there, we're going to have to consider the possibility that it wasn't him. I should be hearing from them soon."

"It's not impossible to drive from Telford, Ohio, to Fleming, Pennsylvania, between midnight and eight or nine in the morning." He dumped a teaspoon of sugar into his mug and stirred it thoughtfully. "But would you really expect to find him there? You think he'd be dumb enough to go right back home?"

"Do I think he's dumb enough to shoot someone

we expected him to shoot, and then go right back home where we can find him? Two words, Fletcher. *Archer Lowell.*"

"So you think he's home."

"It's a starting place. Where else would he go?"

"On to victim number two?" Will asked.

"I suppose that is a possibility," she conceded. "It would sure help if we knew who that was going to be."

"It would help, too, to know how Archer's getting around. We know he doesn't have a car, he can't rent without a license, and I don't think he's smart enough to steal a car. So he's either gotten a friend to drive him—unlikely, that would require some explanation—or he took public transportation." Will paused, mentally picking through the possibilities. "My guess would be a bus. A train would be faster, but it's also more expensive, and as far as we know, Archer has no source of income."

"You might be on to something." She set her coffee down on the counter and rummaged in her bag for her phone. "I'm going to call Veronica Carson back and ask her to check the nearest train and bus terminals in and around Fleming. But that's a little crazy, isn't it? I mean, isn't that like taking a bus to your prom?"

She punched in the numbers, and, while she waited, Will opened the back door and stepped outside onto the small porch he'd rebuilt over the summer. It had rained overnight, and the birdbath the previous owner had left in the yard overflowed water onto the slate patio, the construction of which had followed the porch. There were two chairs and a small table. The patio was too narrow to accommodate anything else.

The air was thick with autumn, the sky dark with leftover storm clouds. Crows screamed at one another in the trees at the back of Will's property. Will stood on the bottom step and felt a little like screaming himself.

Having Miranda in his house, sitting at the kitchen table in the morning once again, had unsettled him. He thought he'd done a damn fine job of hiding it, but now, out of her presence, he was having a tough time holding the memories at bay. He'd meant it when he'd told her she was the total package. Her physical beauty was only part of it. When he was with her, it was easy to forget he'd ever been with another woman. And God knew it had been a while since he had. Miranda just had that effect on him. She'd taken his breath away the first time he'd seen her standing in the door of John Mancini's office on the day she'd reported for work. She still took his breath away. He thought he'd become accustomed to it—to that punch he felt in his gut when he looked at her, when he remembered their time together.

Apparently he was wrong.

The scent of wet earth took him back to a day almost two years ago, when they'd worked a case together in a small western Pennsylvania town where they'd gone to help track a serial killer who left his victims propped up against headstones in the local cemeteries. It had been the first time they'd worked together in months, the first time they'd seen each other in weeks, and Will recalled with total clarity the way he'd felt when he'd seen her get out of her car and walk among the graves that lay between the road and the place where he stood.

He hadn't been able to take his eyes off her. Her hair blew around her head in dark ribbons, and the wind plastered her jacket to her body. By then, he'd become intimately familiar with every curve and hollow, and that familiarity burned deep inside him as he watched her approach. She'd acknowledged him with a slight gesture, a small wave of the fingers of her right hand, and he'd had to force himself to concentrate on the business he'd been sent to do.

The first body they'd found that day had been left sitting against a headstone. The victim's hands had been folded demurely in her lap, and her chin rested on her chest. She'd been a pretty girl before she'd been snatched from her pretty life and stabbed to death. They'd found three more bodies that day, and later, much later, when they returned to the motel where they'd been booked, he'd caught up with Miranda in the bar. They'd gone back to his room, and sought to forget the ugliness they'd seen that day by losing themselves in each other. Later, in the wee hours of the morning, Will had found Miranda out on the balcony, wrapped in a blanket, staring up at the sky.

"When I was younger, my sister and I used to do rubbings in cemeteries," she'd said without turning around. "You know, wax rubbings of headstones. We used to look for old cemeteries, the ones with the really neat stones. Where people have been resting for years. For centuries, sometimes. Some of the stones were so pretty, some of the inscriptions so poignant. We'd walk along and read the names and the dates. We'd find graves of men who fought in the Civil War, and babies who'd only lived a day."

"Like the cemetery we were in today," Will had said, and she'd nodded.

"I don't think I'll ever be able to do that again. Not after seeing what he did to those women . . ."

He'd coaxed her back inside, and they'd made love until the sun came up. Later that day, he took her to another cemetery, this one outside of town, and they walked along the quiet graves, reading the inscriptions to each other. Two hours later, he was on his way to Maine, she to Phoenix. . . .

"Carson is sending someone to the bus terminal with Archer's mug shot, and they're also going to get in touch with his probation officer, see if we can get a warrant issued for Lowell," Miranda announced from the doorway, oblivious to his disquiet. "She's already had someone out to talk to Archer's mother. Mrs. Lowell said—surprise, surprise—she hasn't seen Archer since she left for work on Friday morning. He wasn't there when she got home yesterday, and he didn't come home last night. She's very worried about him."

"I'd be worried, too, if he were my son. But I thought someone was supposed to be keeping an eye on him."

"I think the Fleming police might have attended the same surveillance workshop as their brothers in Telford. In any event, the police are going down to the Well to talk to the bartender and some of Archer's drinking buddies, see if he mentioned to any one of them that he'd be leaving town." She opened the screen door and stepped outside. "You've done a lot of work on the house since the last time I was here. It's really nice, Will."

"Thanks."

She descended the steps and stepped onto the patio. "This is really pretty. I bet it's nice to sit back here and drink your coffee in the morning, read the paper. Or have a drink at the end of the day."

"It is. I'd invite you to have a seat, but as you can see, everything's wet from the rain."

"Too bad. It's so cozy." She looked around the yard. "You put the fence in yourself?"

"Yes."

"Planted all those trees?"

"Yes."

"You do all that over the summer?"

"Yes."

"You were busy."

"I had some time on my hands."

"You take any time off at all?"

"Only to dig another hole," he told her.

"I noticed the inside of the house was all newly painted, too. And there's real furniture in the living room."

"I did that back in June."

"You fixing the house up to sell it?"

"No." He shook his head. "I like it here. I want to stay here."

"It's a great house, Will. You've done wonders with

it. Hard to believe it's that same ramshackle old heap of shingles you bought back when."

"Thanks."

The phone in Miranda's pocket began to ring.

"Cahill . . . yes. Thanks. Give me a minute to find something to write that down." She disappeared into the house, then returned a few minutes later. "I appreciate the information. Thanks so much . . ."

"Telford PD," she explained as she tucked the phone back into her jacket pocket. "I'd asked them to check Unger's room for a business card from anyone who might be a writer. They found one with the name Joshua Landry on it. Sound familiar?"

"Of course. True-crime writer. Picks up on cold cases and tries to solve them. Does all the talk shows, the morning shows. Made a big splash a year or so ago when he solved an old murder in Wisconsin, then another in Michigan. I have a bunch of his books."

"Me, too. He's really good."

"Agreed. So, he was the writer who came to see Al Unger a few weeks back. Not too tough to figure out what he was interested in. Wonder what his angle was going to be."

"I think we should ask him."

"I think you're right."

"Should we call, or pay a visit?"

"I think we should speak with him in person."

"I agree," Miranda told him. "I'll call him first just to make sure he's home today."

"Where does he live?"

From her pocket Miranda pulled the slip of paper

on which she'd written the information given to her by the Telford police.

"New Jersey. Near Princeton."

"Maybe we can catch an afternoon flight."

"Last minute on a Saturday? Doubtful. It will take less time to drive." She dialed Landry's number and smiled up at Will. "Especially if I drive . . ."

The ride to Joshua Landry's home wound through several miles of flat farmland outside the Princeton borough limits. Following the directions Landry had given them over the phone, they found his two-hundred-year-old farmhouse at the end of a long lane, guarded by trees splendid in autumn golds and reds and overlooking a small, peaceful pond. Mature woods along the back of the property added yet more color, and a large well-kept barn completed the picture of pastoral serenity. All was as perfectly composed as a painting, and impeccably maintained.

"Who says crime doesn't pay?" Miranda said dryly as she parked next to a Jeep near the barn.

"He's sure found a way." Will got out of the car and stretched the kinks from his long legs. He wished Miranda had fallen in love with a car that had a little more legroom.

"Wow. He's got, what, twenty, thirty acres here. Pool and pool house out back. Tennis courts over near the barn. Looks like a little guesthouse out there as well. Nice." Miranda nodded as they walked to the front porch. "Very, very nice."

Will leaned past her and rang the doorbell.

A moment later, the door opened, and a woman in her mid-thirties greeted them. She wore faded jeans and a cornflower-blue sweater that matched her eyes. A haze of blonde hair framed her pretty face.

"Agent Cahill?" the woman asked.

"Yes. This is Agent William Fletcher," Miranda replied.

"I'm Regan Landry. Please come in. My father is waiting for you in his study." She smiled and stepped aside to permit her guests to enter, then closed the door behind them. "This way . . ."

They followed her down the hall, over highly polished oak floors upon which lay a well-worn carpet of reds and creams and golds. American primitive artwork flanked the walls on either side, and a huge bouquet of fresh flowers sat on an antique table. The overall impression was one of comfort and quiet wealth.

"Dad, your visitors are here," Regan announced as she showed the two agents into a large square room, three walls of which were lined with bookshelves. The fourth wall was mostly glass and looked out over the pond.

"Well, come in, come in." Joshua Landry rose from his leather chair near the window and greeted them with enthusiasm. He was a tall, well-built man in his late sixties, with broad shoulders and a shock of white hair and piercing eyes that were the same intense shade of blue as his daughter's. "Please, sit. Here, Agent . . ."

"Cahill. Miranda Cahill." Miranda shook the hand he offered.

"Will Fletcher," Will introduced himself.

"Welcome, both of you. Here, let's sit over here." He ushered them toward the sofa. "You've met my daughter. . . ."

"Yes." Miranda smiled as she took a seat.

"What can we offer you? Tea? Coffee?" Landry seemed to hover.

"You don't need to—"

"Of course, we do. It isn't every day that we get a visit from the FBI."

"Tea would be fine," Miranda said, "if it isn't too much trouble."

"I was just making a pot." Regan smiled hospitably. "My mother was English, and she and Dad lived outside of London for years. They always had tea together around this time every day, so we still do. Old habits die hard." She turned to Will. "Agent Fletcher?"

"Actually, water would be fine."

"I'll just be a minute, then." She glanced over at her father before leaving the room. "Need anything, Dad?"

"Just tea. Thanks, sweetheart." After she left, Landry turned to Miranda and Will and said, "I had a bit of a go-round with my cardiologist this week, and everyone's acting like they expect me to keel over at any minute. Which I can guarantee you is not going to happen."

"Oh. Are you sure you want to—" Miranda began.

He waved away her concern.

"It's nothing. Doctors always make a big deal out of the least little thing, don't you think? I wish I hadn't even mentioned it to Regan. Since her mother died, she thinks she has to watch over me, you know? Only child and all that."

"Well, I'm sure she's concerned . . ." Miranda said, and once again he waved her off.

"I keep telling her, Get on with your life. But she keeps taking these guest lectures within a stone's throw of my front door. This semester she's at Penn, so she's just an hour away in Philly."

"Does she live here, then?" Miranda asked.

"No. She's staying with a friend from college in the city until she finishes up there, then she'll go back to her own place. She bought herself a nifty little place on the Eastern Shore, spends most of her time there. These days she just drops in often enough to get on my nerves." He laughed. "I know she means well. And I appreciate her, I do. I just don't want her to worry so much about me. Now," he moved past the subject of his health, "you mentioned on the phone that you were looking into the death of Albert Unger. Why would the FBI be interested in the death of an old man whose claim to fame was the murder of a junkie prostitute some thirty years ago?"

"We wanted to ask you the same question about your interest, Mr. Landry," Will said. "Unger told us you paid a visit to him, not so long ago."

Landry sat back in his leather chair and crossed his legs. "It certainly shouldn't surprise you that I'd be interested in speaking with him. After all, he is the man who killed the mother of Curtis Alan Channing, a man whose . . . career . . . is most interesting to me. And to the public. He's become quite notorious in a very brief time. With his death earlier this year, and the coming to light of his crimes, well, naturally, I'm going to gather all the information I can."

"Unger mentioned that you and Channing had corresponded at one time," Miranda said.

"I was about to get to that, yes. Actually, it was a bit one-sided at first." He paused as Regan came into the room with a tray. "Do you need help with that?"

"No, thanks." She set the tray on the table that stood between the chair in which he sat and the sofa. She proceeded to pour tea and pass out cups.

"Yes, I received my first letter from Channing about six or seven years ago. Right after the publication of *The Killer Next Door*."

"I remember that book," Will told him as Regan handed him an ice-filled glass and a bottle of spring water. He thanked her and continued. "It followed the careers of several serial killers who had committed most of their murders right under the noses of their unsuspecting neighbors."

"Yes." Landry nodded. "People always seem to have this idea that serial murderers are evil-looking men whose very appearance gives them away. The truth is, there is no type; there is no look. It can be— and often is—the boy next door."

"In every case—at least, in every case you wrote about in that book—when the arrests were made, the neighbors all said, 'But he was such a nice young man. . . .' "

"Exactly the point of the book," Landry told him.

"Why did Channing write to you?" Miranda asked.

"Because he'd read the book. He said that at first he'd picked it up because he thought perhaps there was some connection, some psychic nonsense—my middle name happens to be Channing—that our having the same name was a sign that he should read the book. Later I realized he probably meant, his being a serial killer, and my studying, writing about them."

"He told you he was a killer?" Miranda's eyebrows rose.

"No, no. It wasn't difficult to figure out over time, though. Of course, by the time I figured it out, he'd disappeared." Landry stirred his tea absently. "The first letter, he took me to task, telling me where I'd gotten it all wrong."

"Where you'd gotten what all wrong?"

"I delved quite deeply into the backgrounds of the four men I'd written about, which, of course, one would have to do if one was looking to explain such violent, aberrant behavior. All of these men were from terribly abusive homes, and had all either run away from home or had been shoved out of the nests by the time they were in their early teens. I stressed environment as the determining factor in making them what they had become."

"And Channing disagreed?" Will asked.

"Channing believed you were born bad and stayed bad. That environment played no part," Landry explained.

"He must have been in denial." Miranda set her cup on the saucer. "You'd think that coming from his background—where his own mother had traded him, as a very young child, for drugs—he'd know damned well what part environment played."

"Ah, but he never mentioned any of that to me. He spoke of his parents as exemplary folks, loving, kind. Perfect parents," Landry said.

"Those would have been his foster parents," Miranda told him. "They knew of his background and made every effort to help him overcome it. They were, by all accounts, wonderful people. But by the time he'd gotten to them, he'd been irreparably broken."

"Of course, I didn't know that at the time." Landry nodded. "It certainly explains a lot. He was very adamant that I did not know what I was talking about and insisted that I should write another book and admit I was wrong."

"How many times did he write to you?" Will asked.

"Several times, but he stopped writing when I started asking him questions about how he knew so much about the criminal mind. I invited him here to chat, offered to give him an opportunity to explain his point of view, but I never heard from him again. After a time, I just chalked him up as a crazy and forgot about him," Landry said. "Then, a few months ago, I read about his long life of crime, and I looked up the letters—"

"You still have the letters?" Miranda appeared surprised.

"Yes. I don't know why I kept them, frankly. Must have subconsciously suspected I'd hear of him again."

"May we see them?" Will asked.

"Certainly. They're in my office." He started to get up, and Regan stopped him.

"I'll get them, Dad. I know exactly where they are." She turned to Miranda and Will and said, "I've reviewed them several times over the past few weeks, ironically, in preparation for a new book."

"R. J. Landry," Will said. "You've cowritten several books with your father."

"Yes." Regan nodded and appeared to be pleased by the recognition. "I'll be right back with the letters."

"She's the real brains." Landry tilted his head in his daughter's direction. "Much better writer, much cleaner insights. Sharper instincts . . ."

Regan rolled her eyes and laughed as she left the room.

"Now, tell me, what exactly are you looking for in Channing's letters?" Josh Landry ran a hand through his thick white hair. "I mean, the man is dead, and I can assure you he never mentioned a thing about having killed anyone. I would, of course, have gone straight to the police had he done so."

"We're sure you would have, Mr. Landry, but the truth is, we're not investigating an old murder. We're trying to prevent a future one," Miranda told him. "Let me explain . . ."

She proceeded to tell him about the unholy trio who had put into play a game that required each man to kill three people who had, in some way, been a thorn in the side of one of the others.

"Hmmmm." Landry stroked his chin, his eyes

bright as he contemplated the scenario. "So you think this last fellow, this Lowell, is going to kill three people named by Channing. Interesting."

Regan came back into the room carrying a red file, which she handed over to Miranda.

"Most of the letters are here," Regan told her. "There are several others we're still looking for. I think a few might have been misplaced when Dad hired a new secretary. She moved some files around, and there are some things still missing. But these will give you a start."

"Thank you." Miranda opened the folder.

"This Lowell . . . you say he's not the killer type?" Landry directed the question to Will.

"We certainly didn't think so. At least, not until Al Unger was murdered," Will replied. "Even our profiler believed that Lowell wouldn't play it out."

"Wait a minute. What did I miss?" Regan asked. "Who is Lowell?"

"Archer Lowell," Miranda said, and repeated the connection of Lowell to Channing.

"Three killers?" Regan's eyebrows raised, and she glanced at her father. "There's a story for you."

"Indeed. I admit to being intrigued by what Agent Cahill has shared with us. Now, back to this Lowell fellow. You were saying that your profiler thought he wasn't the killer type. Most people are repelled by the notion of killing, you know. Most normal people, anyway."

"According to the reports I've heard, Lowell was definitely repelled by the photographs of Giordano's victims," Miranda told him as she skimmed the contents of the file.

"Then I suppose it needs to be determined what could have coerced this young man to kill," Landry noted. "If in fact he did kill Albert Unger. You're certain there was no fourth player?"

"As far as we know, there are only the three involved."

"Hmmm. Certainly a lot to think about. A real puzzle to be solved." Landry looked pleased at the prospect.

"Mr. Landry—" Miranda looked up from the letter she was reading "—Channing says in this letter, 'You need to tell it the way it is. You set it straight, or someday I will set you straight. I hate people like you who think you know, when you don't know. You talk about these things like they are truth, but you do not know the truth. You are getting rich telling lies. My mother always said that liars are found out. Maybe someone should find you out and show you the truth. Maybe someday I will. . . .' "

Miranda held the letter up. "Does that sound like a threat to you?"

"Not really." Landry shrugged. "Besides, Channing is dead and . . ." He paused for a moment, then said, "Oh. I see. You're wondering if maybe mine was one of the three names?"

"The thought is crossing my mind."

"What an intriguing idea. Me, a victim."

Regan looked up sharply.

"Dad, I don't think you should be so cavalier. If

this man was part of this killing club, and there's reason to believe that you might have been singled out—"

Landry waved a hand as if to dismiss her. "Those letters were written six or seven years ago. I'd be surprised if Channing even remembered writing them," Landry told her. "And I'd be surprised if this was all that important to him even when he wrote them."

"It's been thirty years since Unger killed Channing's mother," Regan reminded him. "And Unger's now dead."

"True, but that's entirely different. According to the news reports I read, Channing watched from a closet as Unger murdered his mother. He was eight years old at the time. Of course he would harbor a long-term resentment."

"Not for the reason you might think," Will said. "He told our profiler he hated Unger for killing his mother because he, Channing, had wanted to kill her himself."

"Oh." Landry mulled over this information. "That might put just a slightly different spin on things."

"Mr. Landry, we're trying to locate people who we think might have angered Channing at some point in his life. It sounds from those letters that your books set him off."

"Well, then, supposing you're right, Agent Fletcher. What do you suggest we do about it?" Landry's daughter's eyes clouded with worry.

"I think the first thing we need to do is get your local police involved," Miranda said. "And we need to assess your security here."

"I assure you my security system is top of the line.

I have all faith in it." Landry smiled and added, "As for the local police, well, let's just say I have more faith in my alarm system, and we'll leave it at that."

"There's always private security, Dad. You can always hire someone."

Landry made a face. "I think you're getting a bit carried away, honey."

"And I think you're being a little too cocky about the possibility of your name being on a hit list. It isn't a game, Dad."

"Oh, but apparently that's exactly what it is." Landry appeared unfazed.

"Any other red flags in those letters?" Will asked Miranda.

"No. It's interesting, though, that he wrote at least one of them right around the time I interviewed him about the Ohio murders." Miranda passed the file on to Will.

"The Ohio murders?" Landry turned his attention from his daughter to Miranda.

"About six years ago, there was a series of murders in southern Ohio. Several suspects were picked up. Channing was one of them. I interviewed him, couldn't get a thing from him, so we had to let him go. But at the time, he just gave me the feeling that . . ." Her voice trailed off.

"That he was involved?" Landry completed the thought for her.

"Yes. But it was my first case, and I didn't know at the time if I just had unusually good instincts, or if I was seeing things that weren't there because I wanted to crack the case. I just hadn't learned to trust myself then."

"These are the cases that were recently linked to Channing through DNA, the ones I read about in the paper?" Landry asked.

"Yes," Miranda said.

"So your instincts were right on, after all." Landry leaned over and patted her arm.

"Fat lot of good it did us." Miranda shook her head. "After he was interviewed, he disappeared."

"So you scared him off," Landry noted. "You could possibly have saved the lives of several unsuspecting women."

"Only to put others in jeopardy," Miranda replied. "We now know that later that same year he killed four women in Kentucky, and several other women in other locales. There are probably more. We're still piecing his movements together."

"Well, then, it appears you may have stymied him at a critical time. Stopped his forward motion, so to speak. I doubt he'd have been too happy with you at the time." Joshua Landry leaned forward, his arms resting on his thighs. "As a matter of fact, I imagine it would have made him quite angry. Aren't you just a bit worried, Agent Cahill?"

"Worried about what?" Miranda frowned.

"Worried that perhaps your name is on that list as well."

_____ CHAPTER _____
NINE

"So what did you think of him?" Will asked as he settled into the front seat of Miranda's car.

"Landry? I liked him," she replied. "I liked him a lot. The daughter, too. She seems pretty sharp, don't you think?"

"Sharper than the old man, in some respects. But I liked him. I hope we're wrong." He hesitated for a moment. "I hope he's wrong."

"About what?"

"About Channing being pissed at you."

"I doubt Channing ever gave me another thought once he'd left that interview room. I can't think of one good reason why he would."

"Well, as Landry pointed out, you did stop his forward motion."

"You think it made a difference to him? He just moved on and started over." She turned on the ignition and backed the car out of its spot near the barn. "Now, Joshua Landry, he's a different story. You read those letters. Landry really had old Curtis pissed off."

"You think he's taking this seriously?"

"Not as seriously as Regan is."

"That was my impression, too."

"He did seem almost amused by the prospect of a killer coming after him, didn't he?" She shook her head. "Writers. Every one I've ever met has been just a little off, you know what I mean?"

"Yeah. But I feel better knowing that the local police will be keeping an eye on things."

"Ah, may I remind you that we just went through this in Telford?"

"Well, with any luck, these guys will do a better job than the Telford police did with Al Unger."

"Though the officers who came out to Landry's in response to his call seemed genuinely fond of him," Miranda noted. "Guess he's somewhat of a local celebrity. I think they'll keep tabs on him. Plus, he has that mega security system. Hopefully, he should be all right until we find Lowell."

"Well, I'll feel better if Regan is successful in getting her father to agree to hiring someone to watch his back. She seemed concerned about leaving him when she goes back to Philly tomorrow. She doesn't look like she'd be much of a bodyguard."

"I don't know about that. I read an article about her last year. She's pretty accomplished. She's supposed to be quite the marksman. She's a black belt in tae kwon do and competes in triathlons."

"Maybe so, but I don't think watching out for Landry is a job for his daughter."

"I think I'd have more faith in her than in the local police."

"Speaking of whom, you didn't hear back from Fleming yet, did you?"

"No," she said, shaking her head. "Maybe I should pull over and make a call."

"Why don't we stop for dinner at one of those restaurants out there on Route One? I noticed there were quite a few when we came in."

"Good idea. I'll never make it back to Virginia on an empty stomach."

"Me either."

They rode in silence for a mile or two, down the winding country road.

"This is Grovers Mill," Will noted as the car rounded a curve that wrapped around a large lake. "See the sign back there?"

"Is that supposed to mean something to me?"

"Sure. Orson Welles. *War of the Worlds.*"

"You're talking about the novel?"

"I'm talking about the radio show, back in the late thirties. The night before Halloween, 1938. The novel was adapted as a radio play and rewritten as a live news broadcast. Actors described the landing of a force of invaders from Mars. It was supposed to have happened on a farm right back there in Grovers Mill."

"I think I might have heard about that but don't recall the details."

"It was really famous. As a matter of fact, you can buy the entire broadcast on tape. I'll see if I can find it for you; you can listen to it yourself. People tuned in, not realizing it was a play, and there was all kinds of panic. People hid in cellars, locked themselves in their houses, boarded up the windows, and loaded up their shotguns, ready to take on the Martians. The broadcast was so convincing, people really believed the United States was being invaded by a force from outer space."

"Didn't they tell the public it wasn't real?" She frowned. "That's not very responsible."

"They did make it very clear at the beginning, and occasionally reminded the listeners that it was just a play. But you know how it is, if you turn on the radio or the TV in the middle of something, you often have no idea what's going on. If it looks like a real broadcast, sounds like real news coverage, you think it's real."

"So if you tuned in at the wrong time, you thought we were under attack?"

"Apparently, a lot of people really believed it."

"And they broadcast from back there?"

"No, they just said they were there."

"Why'd they pick that place? It's in the middle of nowhere."

"That's probably why they picked it. I guess if they'd said they were broadcasting from someplace like Times Square, everyone would know it wasn't real."

She stopped at a stop sign, tried to get her bearings and remember which way they had come.

"Take a right here," Will said.

"You sure?" she asked, then, rather than wait for an answer, said, "Oh, of course, you're sure. You're always sure of yourself, aren't you, William James Fletcher, special agent for the FBI?" She slanted him a look from the corner of her eye and hit the gas.

"Right now the only thing I'm sure of is that I'm

likely to die in this car with you behind the wheel," he muttered, and she laughed.

Minutes later the Spyder was pulling into a parking spot in front of a busy diner, and Miranda was digging into her purse for her cell phone. Will got out of the car while she made the call to Fleming, and wondered if there was any real possibility that Miranda's could be the third name on the list. He didn't have a good feeling about it. The thought of it caused his insides to twist.

"I had to leave a message for Carson to call me back," she said as she stepped out of the car and locked it. "Ready?"

Will nodded and they walked up the steps of the diner.

"You're awfully quiet," Miranda said after they'd been seated.

Before he could reply, a waitress in a black dress appeared with menus in one hand and flatware in the other.

"Specials are inside," she told them as she set their places for them. "I'll be back with your water in a sec."

"Efficient, isn't she?" Will noted as he opened the menu.

Miranda looked at him over the top of hers. She knew the look on his face, the set of his jaw. Something was working below the surface, and she was going to find out what it was.

"I think I'll have the turkey sandwich," Miranda told him. "How about you?"

"I'm going to have the pork chops," he said.

The waitress returned with their water, and they placed their orders.

"So," Miranda said when the waitress disappeared. "Are you going to tell me what's bothering you?"

"You have to ask?"

"You're wondering how we let Lowell get to Unger and how we can make sure Landry is protected."

"Bring it a little closer to home."

"You're thinking about Landry's suggestion that I'm the third?" She frowned.

"I think we need to discuss it with John. I don't think we can take this lightly."

"I'm not taking it lightly," she said softly. She hadn't. But she'd pushed it aside to think about later.

"Tell me about the interview you had with Channing six years ago. Tell me everything you remember. What he said, how he said it. How he looked when he said it. Let's go over it, bit by bit."

"I don't recall all the details." She played with her spoon, spinning it around slowly on the table. "But if we could find the file, there is a tape."

"A tape of the interview?" he asked. "He let you tape the interview?"

"Yes. Actually, he seemed amused by the prospect."

"It has to be in the file, though I don't remember seeing a tape when I looked for your reports a few months back. I'll check again as soon as we get back to the office. I think we need to listen to the tape and see exactly what he had to say to you back then."

"I remember his tone—he was pretty cocky with

me, I remember that. As if he knew exactly what I wanted to know, but he wasn't going to give me a thing."

"Was he aggressive? Combative?"

"No, no. More like he was toying with me. The impression that I had was that he seemed more amused than angry. At least in the beginning, he did." She continued to play with the spoon. "I think if he was angry at all, it might have been toward the end of the interview. I seem to recall there'd been a shift in his demeanor, somehow."

"What kind of a shift?"

"Oh, it was subtle. Might have been nothing at all. And I might have been imagining it."

"Try to remember. Was there anything in particular he might have said?"

"Will, I just don't remember." She shook her head. "It was six years ago. And even though he'd made me uneasy at the time, I doubt I could have told you even then what it had been that made me more suspicious of him than I was of any of the others I'd interviewed that day. Maybe if I listen to the tape, something might strike a chord."

"Then we'll put finding the tape at the top of the to-do list." He leaned back to permit the waitress to serve their food. "We'll see if anything jogs your memory."

"Funny, but I don't remember any of the other suspects I spoke with that entire week, but I never forgot him."

"Tell me what you do remember. Maybe if you talk

about it, something might come to you. Who picked him up and brought him in, and why?"

"He worked at the restaurant with the vic. We spoke with all of her coworkers."

"Was he resistant to speaking with you?"

"Not at all. When we first starting talking, he was very relaxed, very matter-of-fact. Said he was washing dishes at the time of the murder, and wasn't it just terrible, poor Jenny. He said he had seen her off and on during that night, but that she'd worked her shift and left by the back door at closing time." Miranda leaned her head back against the seat. "However, when we went over our notes, we realized that several other employees mentioned that Jenny had left through a side door. And when pressed, none of them could remember actually seeing Channing just before closing."

"And, of course, when you wanted to question him again, he was gone."

"Right. Disappeared into thin air."

"And there was no physical evidence to tie him to the crime scene?"

"None. There'd been no fingerprints to match—he must have worn gloves—and he had no record, no DNA to match."

"I'm assuming his apartment was searched."

"He'd been living in a rented room. Week to week. By the time we got there, he'd cleared out."

"Seems as if he'd have been a likely suspect at that time. I'm surprised they gave up on him as easily as they did."

"Keep in mind that the local cops had another

suspect—a neighbor of the victim's—who looked pretty good to them for a while. By the time he was cleared and we decided to take another look at Channing, he'd taken off."

They'd finished their meals and the waitress returned to ask if they wanted dessert. When Miranda shook her head, Will reached across the table to place a hand upon her forehead.

"Hmmm, you don't appear to be feverish." He frowned. "Was there something wrong with your dinner?"

"No. I'm just not in the mood for dessert." She took a sip of water from her glass. "I'm tired. As a matter of fact, I was just thinking about asking you to drive home."

"This is a first, Cahill. Are you sure you're not sick?"

"No. Just tired. You ready to leave?"

"Yes. I'll just grab the check from the waitress, and we can go."

"I'm going to go on outside and see if I can get Veronica Carson again. I really want to know what's going on out there in Fleming." Miranda slid out of the booth and swung her bag over her shoulder. "I'll meet you out by the car."

By the time Will got outside, Miranda was in the passenger seat in the recline position, the key was in the ignition, and the engine was turned on.

"All warmed up and ready to go," she told him as he got into the car.

"Great." He adjusted the driver's seat and the mirrors, and put the car in reverse. "Were you able to get through to Carson?"

"No. I had to leave another message." She closed her eyes. "I hope she's not avoiding me. I can't think of any reason why she would."

"Do you want the heat on?" he asked.

"No, thanks."

"Want to put my jacket over you?"

She thought about that for a minute, then shook her head no.

"You all right?"

"I'm just tired, Will. I haven't been sleeping well. And I barely slept at all last night."

"Thinking about Unger?"

"Thinking about how we screwed up."

"That's the second time you said that. How do you figure we screwed up?" He put on the right turn signal and followed the signs for I95 south.

"We should have been more aggressive with the Telford police, should have been stronger in our approach to them."

"As I recall, we made it pretty clear that there was a good chance Unger might be the target of a killer. Then again, there was a good chance that he might not be."

"We should have—"

"Stop it. We gave the police all of the information we had. It was their responsibility to follow through. You can't be everywhere and do everyone else's job, Miranda. I feel every bit as badly as you do that Unger is dead, but I can't think of one thing I could have done to have prevented it." He paused, then added, "Other than watch him myself."

"Maybe we should have had someone watching him. Maybe we should have someone watching Landry."

Maybe someone should be watching you, Will thought.

"Let's toss it all around with Mancini when we get in to the office tomorrow. See what he has to say." When she didn't respond, Will glanced over and found her head dipped to the side and her mouth parted just ever so slightly. He turned down the radio and turned up the heat just a little.

She slept all the way to Maryland, waking only when Will pulled into a gas station and got out.

"Want anything while we're here?" he asked softly. "They have a little market there."

"No, thanks."

He paid for the gas and climbed back into the car. "You sure you don't want anything? Last chance . . ."

She shook her head no.

"You're awfully quiet," he said as he headed back onto the highway.

"I'm just worn out." Her eyes were closed again, and he couldn't help but wonder if she was really sleeping, or if she was feigning to avoid getting into a conversation with him that might lead to places neither of them wanted to go.

He decided if avoidance was what she wanted, avoidance was what she would get. If she changed her mind and wanted to chat, she was welcome to open her mouth. Otherwise, he'd just let it go for now.

After all, what was there, really, to talk about—

other than work? What was there that he could put into words?

He drove along through the darkness, fighting off the thought that Archer Lowell might come after her.

"Over my dead body," he whispered aloud, then glanced over to where she slept, wondering if she'd heard. If she had, she gave no sign. Her dark lashes still lay against her cheek, and her mouth was still just open the tiniest bit. Her hair fell down around her face like a dark veil, and her chin rested on her chest.

The thought worried him all the way home.

When he arrived at his house, he drove slowly, so as not to shake her awake as the car traveled over the rough stones. He turned off the ignition and turned to look at her as she stretched awake. The effort not to reach over and smooth that black hair from her face all but killed him.

"Where are we?" She yawned, breaking the silence.

"We're back at my place."

"Can I come in and use your bathroom before I head home?" She sat up.

"Sure, but don't you think you should stay? It's late and—"

"No, I don't think I should stay." Unexpectedly, she opened the passenger door and got out. "That's done, Fletcher. Over."

"Miranda, I wasn't suggesting that you and I—"

"Oh, right, the thought never crossed your mind."

He got out of the car. "Well, of course, it's a little hard not to think about—"

"Just give me the keys and I'll stop at that little bar just before the highway." She held out her hand.

"Don't be an idiot."

"I don't want to sleep under your roof tonight or any other night. We're not going back down that road again, Will."

"I swear, I was not suggesting that we do. I only meant, it's late—after midnight already—and you have at least an hour drive."

"I'm well rested."

"At least come inside and use the bathroom and get something to drink." They stood in the darkness and stared at each other. "Look, we've been pretty successful these past few days at moving past what . . . what was. If you can accept that we've moved on, I'll accept it, too."

She continued to stare at him.

"Friends?" he asked.

"Sure. Okay." She nodded slowly. "Friends . . ."

"Then you shouldn't have a problem staying in the guest room tonight and driving home in the morning." Before she could protest, he said, "The roads are dark; they're windy and dangerous if you're not familiar with them. It just doesn't make sense for you to leave now, unless of course you're only doing it to be stubborn."

She laughed and threw up her hands.

"Okay. I give in. You really have a guest room?"

"It's more like a spare room with a bed in it. But it's a nice bed. I brought it up here from my grandmother's house over the summer. She moved into an assisted-living place and couldn't take most of her furniture with her, so she divided it up between the grandkids."

"And there's a lock on the spare-room door?"

"I'm wounded that you'd think such a thing of me." He took her by the elbow and led her up the dark path to his front porch. "However, feel free to put a chair in front of the door if it makes you feel better. I think there's a chair in there—"

"No, no. You're right," she said as he unlocked the front door. "We're both adults, and right now, we have to work together. We'll have to work together again, I'm sure, in the future. We should both be big enough to put all . . . put the past behind us and move on with our lives, right?"

"Right."

Once inside, she stopped in the hallway, framed by the light from the front porch, and looked up at him.

"I can do it if you can do it."

He gritted his teeth, not sure, after all, that he could.

"Sure." It was easier to just agree at this point. "Great."

"Great." She smiled and snapped on the overhead light. "Which way is the guest room?"

Archer sat on the edge of the bed in the cheap motel room he'd rented for the night, just like Burt had told him to do, and waited for the cell phone to ring. He wished he could call home, let his mother know he was all right and not to worry, but Burt told him when he gave him the phone that it was only to be used to communicate with him. Still, Archer was tempted. How would Burt know, anyway, if he called home?

Forget it, he told himself. Burt seemed to know everything.

He wished he knew who Burt was. Maybe if he had a last name, he wouldn't be so scary.

Nah, Archer decided. Knowing his last name wouldn't make much difference. Burt would always be scary. He was just a scary kind of guy.

His hands over his eyes, Archer tried to make sense of his life. It had all gotten too crazy, too fast. One minute he's at the Well trying to score with Lisa Shelton; the next minute he's putting a bullet in the back of some old man's head.

God, I didn't mean to . . . I never meant to . . .

The cell phone rang rudely, and he looked at it for a long moment. What if he didn't answer it? What if he took the money Burt had given him and just disappeared forever?

What if this all turned out to be nothing more than a bad, bad dream? That the past twenty-four hours had never happened? He'd wake up in his old bed. And, back in Telford, that old man would still be alive. . . .

The phone continued to ring. Finally, he answered it.

"Where were you?" the voice demanded.

"I was, ah, in the bathroom."

"Next time take the phone with you."

"Okay."

"Now, where are you?"

"I'm still in the motel, like you said. You told me to stay here till I heard from you."

"Well, I think it'll be okay if you leave now. Take the next bus to the place I told you about. You'll be okay. No one knows it was you; there's nothing to connect you to the old man."

"They know. That woman . . . Cahill . . . she's gonna know. . . ."

"What?" Burt's voice went cold. "What did you say?"

"She's gonna know it was me. They already knew about the game, her and that other guy. The big FBI guy. They came to my house. They told me they knew what—"

"When were you planning on telling me this, asshole?" Burt's anger rumbled like an avalanche through the phone.

"I . . . I . . ." Archer began to stutter.

"You . . . you . . . what?" Burt snapped. "The FBI was at your house, and you didn't bother to mention it? *She* was at your house and you didn't think that was important enough to tell me?"

"I didn't get a chance," Archer began to whine. "You didn't let me tell you anything. You never give me a chance to say anything."

"What exactly did they say? What did they want?"

"They . . . they said they knew about the game. About Curtis and Vince and me."

"You tell me this now, *after* you do Unger?" Burt swore under his breath.

"I tried to tell you before but you—"

"You didn't try hard enough, did you?" Burt's breathing came a little faster now, and the sound of it through the phone made Archer's heart beat almost out of his chest. "How did they know?"

"I don't know. Maybe . . . maybe Curtis told them before he died. Maybe they just figured it out."

"All right, this is what you do. You stay there, keep your head down. You got enough money left for another day, right?"

"Yes. I think so."

"Well, you're just going to have to." He paused again, as if thinking. "If you're right, maybe they'll be watching for you. Shit. I guess I'll have to drive out for you myself."

Archer's insides twisted.

"Then, we'll go over what you need to do next. Get it over with fast and be done with it before they can track you down. You been thinking about who you're going to do next?"

"Yes." Archer closed his eyes. *NO.* "But if they know who—"

"Did they say they know?"

"Well, no, but—"

"Then they don't know. You got two choices, Archer. You decide who goes next—and how you plan to pull it off—or I'll decide for you."

The phone went dead, and Archer turned it off.

Shit. Burt was coming for him. He was going to want to know who was next on the list and how he was going to do it.

Shit.

Well, not much choice involved in the how. He only had the one weapon. The gun Burt had given him, the one he'd used to kill Unger, was in his backpack.

As for who, well, how was he supposed to do that? Maybe he should let Burt decide.

He shook off the idea. Maybe Burt would just see that as a weakness on Archer's part, and he'd probably shoot Archer instead. From his pocket, he took a quarter and tossed it back and forth, one hand to the other. He'd have to flip for the name.

Mentally, he assigned heads to one name, tails to the other, then he tossed the coin on the floor and watched it roll across the worn carpet.

Tails.

Shit.

_____ CHAPTER _____
TEN

THE ALARM SHRILLED AWAY DANGEROUSLY CLOSE TO Will's head at half-past six. He'd set it for an early hour so that he could get a shower and slip downstairs before Miranda woke in order to make coffee and maybe even start breakfast. She wanted friends, he'd give her friends. He'd be the best friend she ever had. And then, maybe she'd see that beneath the cloak of friendship, there was so much more.

At least, that was the plan he'd come up with a few hours earlier, after having lain awake most of the night trying to think things through. He and Miranda had such a jumbled past. They'd never worked a job together that hadn't ended up with the two of them in bed.

Not that that was a bad thing.

But lately, it had occurred to Will that he wanted more from her. Over the past several years, the routine had been pretty much the same. Work together, sleep together. Go their own way. Work together, sleep together. Go their own way. And that had been fine, for a while.

Will could point with certainty to the exact moment when he realized that was no longer fine.

Miranda had been working a job—alone—in New Jersey's Pine Barrens, playing guard dog to Kendra Smith, the Bureau's favorite sketch artist. Kendra's house had been broken into by the serial killer who had more than a passing interest in her, and in trying to protect Kendra, Miranda had been coldcocked. In the resultant fall down the steps, she'd cracked her head open on the newel post, and spent the next twelve hours unconscious. Will had been sent to join in the hunt for the killer, which had served the dual purpose of allowing him to be involved in the investigation as well as to be at Miranda's bedside when she awoke.

"Oh, God," she'd groaned when she opened her eyes and focused on his face. "I knew it! I've died and gone to hell. . . ."

He'd laughed then, and he chuckled now, remembering how her smile had beaten back the fear that had spread through him when he'd first seen her in the hospital, her face black and blue, stitches running into her hairline. But remembering that forced him to recall the rest of that day, when a massive blunder on his part had almost cost Kendra her life. Assigned to keeping Kendra under wraps until her official FBI escort had arrived, in his eagerness to return to the hospital and Miranda, Will had handed Kendra directly into the hands of a madman.

It had taken him months to live down what could have been a fatal mistake, months before he could look at himself without loathing, cursing himself for his stupidity and knowing that only Kendra's own quick thinking and resolve had saved her life. Will had retreated to his house in the woods and had ventured back into the office no sooner than he'd had to. He had three weeks' vacation coming to him, and opted to take all three right then.

"Will, we all suffer from poor judgment at times," John had told him when he'd finally reported back in.

"Kendra could have been killed. She almost *was* killed," Will reminded his boss.

"Thank God it didn't turn out that way."

"How can you gloss over this?"

"Oh, make no mistake, Fletcher—" John had frowned "—there's no glossing over here. What you did was stupid. You handed a woman over to a serial killer and walked away without a second thought."

"So why aren't you firing me?"

"Because in spite of your carelessness in this one instance, you're a fine agent. You've done outstanding work in the past, and I've no doubt you'll do outstanding work in the future. You're an integral part of my team, and I need you." John's chair swiveled back and forth slowly, and he faced Will straight on. "And I have to admit, looking back over my career, there have been times when I've done incredibly stupid things. Yes, even handed a witness or a potential victim over to another law enforcement agent without thoroughly checking their identification. In your case, there were several dozen cops, other agents, and state troopers on the scene. I can see why you would have assumed that the man who identified himself as the agent expected to take Kendra Smith off your hands was exactly who he said he was. Who expected to find a serial killer right there in the midst of all those lawmen?"

"I've relived that minute over and over—"

"Don't." John stopped the chair's back-and-forth motion. "It's done. Move on. Learn from it, and move on."

"John, when I think about what that guy could have done to her—"

"I understand, and I'd have serious reservations about you if you'd shrugged it off without a second thought. But at this point, you need to move past it. If you can't, you will become a serious liability to the unit, Will. You'll spend too much time second-guessing your every move. Sooner or later, that kind of hesitation is going to get someone hurt. So I repeat. Learn from the mistake, and move on to your next assignment." John reached across his desk for a file. "Which I happen to have right here . . ."

Will had taken the file and left the office, determined to regain his standing within the team. He'd moved on to that case, and then to the next, and then to the one after that, keeping as low a profile as possible within the unit, spending as little time in the office as he could get away with. He'd pretty much avoided everyone, for a while. For as long as John allowed him to lick his wounds, anyway. Moving back among the ranks of his unit hadn't been quite as bad as he'd feared, though the first time he'd had to face fellow agent Adam Stark had been a bit tense. Adam, who'd been quietly in love with Kendra for several years, had been the last person Will had wanted to see. But Adam had been reasonably civil, if not cordial, and even Kendra had not been accusatory when they'd run into each other briefly in the hall several weeks later.

It had taken him a while, but he soon reestablished himself as one of Mancini's top dogs.

But not the alpha dog, he reminded himself as he strolled to the shower. Not today, anyway, but that was okay. Today he was going to be Mr. Nice Guy. Mr. Best Friend. At least until he could figure out just what was really between Miranda and him.

He showered and dressed in record time. He hummed softly on his way past the room where Miranda slept, pausing to listen outside the door. There was no sound from within.

She must really be zonked, he thought as he quietly ran down the stairs and went into the kitchen.

He surveyed the breakfast possibilities. He had bread and eggs. Maybe he'd surprise her with French toast. Cahill's sweet tooth was known to act up in the morning from time to time. He was filling the coffeepot with water when he glanced out the window.

The little white Spyder was MIA. Hadn't he left it right at the end of the drive?

Damn, he muttered on his way down the hall. When he got to the front door, he realized it was already unlocked. Stepping out onto the porch in his bare feet, he saw that the Spyder was indeed gone.

He sat on the top step, his arms resting on his knees, and watched a few big yellow leaves float down from the maple at the end of the drive. Another minute passed before he took the cell phone from his pocket and speed-dialed her number.

"I guess you're not on the way back from the

neighborhood store with groceries," he said when she picked up.

"Hey, you're awake."

"Where are you?" He forced a light tone, not wanting to sound as peevish as he felt.

"I'm just pulling into my driveway."

"Why?"

"Well, since I slept most of the way between New Jersey and Virginia, I was awake most of the night. Still awake at five, so I figured I might as well get up and get some work done. Unfortunately, I had nothing to work on there, and since I didn't know how long you'd be sleeping, I just figured I'd come home. Besides, the whole idea of me sleeping there last night was to keep me from driving home in the middle of a very dark night, so I figured driving at dawn would be fine."

"Oh, sure. It is fine. I was just wondering what happened to you, that's all."

"Well, that's all that happened. I came home because I was wide awake." She paused, then asked, "So what are you doing up so early?"

"I got up to make breakfast."

"You're kidding."

"Nope."

"What are you making?"

"French toast."

"Yum. My favorite."

"I know. I was making it for you."

"Oh." She fell silent, and so did he.

Finally, he said, "No big deal. Twice as much for me."

"Next time, Fletcher."

"Sure." He wondered if there'd be a next time.

"Oh, before I forget, did you ever hear back from Evan?" she said, deftly changing the subject.

"Don't know." He got up and went inside. "I'll have to check the messages on the answering machine."

The phone sat on the edge of the old worn desk that had once stood in his grandfather's study. It pleased Will to have it in his home now. He'd had to trade with his cousin Jen, who'd arrived at their gran's house before he did on the day Gran was giving away her furniture, but it was worth giving up two or three other prized objects for the desk. It was the one piece he'd really coveted.

He hit the message button.

"Hey. It's Carole. We just wanted to let you know that Junie had her baby last week. Baby boy, cute as can be. They named him Nathaniel. Give us a call when you get a chance. You have the number. . . ."

"That was my cousin," Will explained as he hit the delete button.

"Cute name, Nathaniel."

"Yeah." He made a mental note to send something to cousin Junie for the baby.

"Will. Evan Crosby. Got your message late, I'm just back from the training program at Quantico, trying to catch up here. To answer your question, I did ask my old partner from the Lyndon PD to find out if there's any record at the courthouse of the three amigos spending time together, but I haven't heard from him. I will be back at my county job on Monday, so

I'll ask around and get back to you. By the way, I heard about Unger getting it. I can't believe we were all so wrong about Lowell. Annie's taking it hard, that she so misread him. Anyway, I'll be talking to you." There was a brief pause, then, "Oh. Were you and Miranda able to come up with any other likely victims? Just curious . . ."

"You heard all that?" Will asked.

"Yes," Miranda said. "Poor Annie. I'm sure she does feel badly. I think I'll give her a call. . . ."

"You going into the office?"

"Today? It's Sunday," she reminded him.

"That's never stopped you before."

"True enough. Yeah, I'll probably take a run in."

"Well, maybe I'll see you there."

"Okay. See you. And thanks. For the bed in the middle of the night. For thinking to make breakfast for me."

"Anytime," he said, and disconnected.

Will sat on the edge of the desk and tried to decide if Miranda had really left because she was wide awake, or if she just didn't want the intimacy of facing him over breakfast this morning. It was a tough call. Given their history, *just friends* might be harder to pull off than he'd expected.

On the other hand, maybe friendship is overrated.

He tapped restless fingers on the desk, then went into the kitchen, where he tried to analyze the situation while he finished making breakfast for himself. Midway through the first stack of French toast he decided a phone call was in order. Between bites, he dialed Anne Marie McCall's cell and left a message.

By the time he finished eating, she'd returned the call and agreed to meet him at the office at one.

Back to work, he told himself as he drained his coffee cup and deposited it, along with his plate, in the dishwasher. *Keep it focused. Don't let the bad guys win.*

Watch Miranda's back . . .

Genna peered out the window and watched the snow pile higher around the fence that outlined the compound. She'd been hoping that the storm would pass by this time, but she'd had no such luck. For the second day in a row, the snow continued to drift. If it didn't stop soon, there'd be no way she'd be able to leave the compound that afternoon with Caroline, the girl whose essay on self-discipline had been chosen as the best of the week.

Last week's trip into Linden had been uneventful, but of course, that was the point.

She and Eileen had ridden with Daniel, a large, dour man who rarely strayed far from the reverend's side. When he parked next to the local market, Genna and her charge had jumped out. Knowing Daniel watched every step she took, Genna had put a hand on Eileen's arm to hold her back. Together she and the girl had walked—slowly—to the chain drugstore in the center of town. Once inside, the normally shy Eileen perked up a bit. After having been behind the gates of the compound for several months, she was dazzled by the array of products, as if she'd forgotten what it was like to shop. Then again, hadn't Genna heard that Eileen had lived in shelters and on the streets for the past three years? Even a modest shop might have been beyond her means.

With Genna by her side, the girl wandered from aisle to aisle, touching hair clips in one, nail polish in another, a long-handled bath brush in yet another.

"Do you see anything you'd like to have?" Genna asked.

"I don't know." Eileen had studied a box of fake nails. "Everything looks so . . . fun."

"Why not look for something you can enjoy for a long time?" Genna suggested. "I noticed that you like to write poetry. Perhaps you'd like a special notebook and a pen to write your poems with."

It had taken almost forty-five minutes, but Eileen had finally selected a fat spiral notebook with a cover the color of blue denim, and a pale yellow pen that wrote with blue ink.

"Thank you, Miss Ruth." Eileen had beamed when they left the store. "Thank you so much."

"You earned it. It's your reward for having done well with your essay."

They stood at the corner where the two main streets of Linden intersected. Across the street and down two blocks, the Linden Diner marked the boundary of the small town.

"We'll have lunch at the diner there," Genna had told her. "But we'll have to watch the time. We don't want to be late meeting up with Daniel."

Eileen had taken forever to order from the menu, giving them precious little time to eat. Spurred on by Jayne the waitress, Eileen had finally settled on a hamburger and fries, and an old-fashioned milk shake. Not having any particular interest in food, Genna ordered the same, then wondered if she'd be able to safely manage a phone call. She knew from her visit here on the day she first entered the compound that the phone was back behind the door leading to the restrooms. However, should Daniel come into the diner looking for them, he'd see Eileen sitting alone. If he found Genna on the phone, all the more problematic for her. On the other hand, she'd had no contact with John for several weeks, and surely by now he'd be worried, both professionally and personally. Of course, she knew there were other agents in the area. She just didn't know who or where they were, or what information was getting back to the Bureau. It simply had been too dangerous to risk bringing any communication device into the compound.

She'd decided she'd risk making a call, and was just rising from her seat when the door opened. Daniel had walked in, headed right for their table, and Genna's heart sank even as she plastered a smile onto her face.

"We were just finishing up," she'd told him.

"It's time to get back," he'd replied. All the way back to the compound, she'd wondered how the report to Reverend Prescott would go.

If Daniel had had negative thoughts, he must have kept them to himself, because aside from asking Genna if she'd enjoyed her outing, Prescott had had little to say. She assumed that she and Caroline would be permitted to leave with Daniel again today. Assuming, of course, that the snow stopped.

By noon, it had. At one, Genna grabbed her coat

and met the excited young girl at the front door of the block building that held the small classrooms.

"You should borrow boots, Miss Ruth," Caroline told her.

"I wish I knew someone who was willing to trade for a while," Genna said, looking ruefully at her leather shoes.

"Miss Joan is in the infirmary. Maybe she will let you borrow her boots for a while."

"Stay here, and wait for Daniel." Genna took off for the wooden structure next to the classrooms. "Tell him I will be right back. . . ."

Genna found Miss Joan way too ill with the flu to care who was wearing her boots just then. Leaving her own shoes under the bed in the makeshift hospital room, Genna pulled on the boots. They were a half size too big, but even so, they were warmer and provided more traction on the snowy ground.

"I'll bring them back later this afternoon," Genna had promised.

"No hurry," Joan replied without opening her eyes. "I'm not planning on going anywhere for a while. . . ."

Unlike Eileen the week before, Caroline knew exactly what she wanted. A sketchbook and some colored pencils, a pack of gum, and she was ready to go. A plate full of chicken fingers and French fries, a hot fudge sundae, and a Coke, and Caroline's day was complete.

"This is such a nice thing you do for us," she'd told Genna as she got out of the Jeep once they'd returned home. "You're the nicest person here. I can't wait to use my new sketchpad."

"Maybe you'll let me see some of your sketches," Genna replied.

"Maybe." Caroline nodded as she ran to her cabin to show off her new possessions. "Maybe . . ." she called over her shoulder.

Daniel had said little, but Genna knew he'd been watching her like a hawk. She and Caroline had barely been in the diner for ten minutes when Daniel had arrived. While he hadn't rushed them, he'd sat at the counter, ignoring the attempts of the friendly waitress to make conversation, and had watched through the mirror as Genna and Caroline ate. As soon as they finished their meal, Daniel rose and came to the table, silently indicating that it was time for them to go. Genna was certain that the reverend had grilled Daniel last week and would grill him again today. Well, she'd expected as much from Prescott, and she'd been careful not to do anything that might cause him to suspect her motives.

Genna stopped in at the infirmary to see how Joan was doing, and she found her no better than when she'd left earlier that day.

"Keep the boots." Joan waved her away. "I won't be out of this bed for another few days."

The storm had kicked in with a vengeance shortly after they'd returned from Linden, so Genna gratefully accepted the offer. The biting cold sent everyone shivering to their cabins for the rest of the afternoon. It was then that Genna noticed that Bethany, one of the older girls from her group, had not returned.

"Has anyone seen Beth?" she asked.

"No."

"Not since before lunch."

"She wasn't in class. . . ."

"Maybe she's in the infirmary," someone suggested.

Genna, having just come from there, knew that only one bed in the infirmary had been occupied.

"Maybe she's been cleansed," someone else said softly. "Maybe the reverend chose her for a mission. . . ."

The room grew silent, as everyone wondered just what kind of mission young Bethany had been sent on.

Do they suspect? Genna studied the solemn faces of the girls who gathered around Bethany's bed. *Do some of them know what fate awaited Beth? What fate awaits them all?*

A sense of urgency spread through her. How could she possibly wait another week before riding through the front gates with Julianne Douglas?

How long would it take her to file the reports that would bring the Reverend Prescott to his knees? To put his shameful network out of business forever? How would they locate the girls who had already been "cleansed" and sent on their way? And once rescued, how badly damaged would those tortured girls be?

_____ CHAPTER _____
ELEVEN

BURTON CONNOLLY TUCKED THE BROWN BAG STUFFED with snacks under his arm and pushed open the double doors that led from the food court of the turnpike rest stop to the parking lot, vowing that when this was over, he'd never eat fast food again. The selections here had been limited to burgers or chicken, and today he'd fancied neither. What he really wanted was a big steak, but that would require him to get off the turnpike and search for a restaurant in the Harrisburg area, and he just didn't have that kind of time today. He figured it would be at least another hour before he arrived at the motel where Archer Lowell was holed up, waiting for him.

Burt climbed into the cab of his new Ford pickup and dropped the bag onto the seat next to him. Before leaving the parking lot, he reached into the bag and pulled out a Snickers bar, unwrapping it as he drove onto the roadway. Traffic was light at this time on a Sunday morning, so he expected to make pretty good time. He took a bite of the candy and turned on the radio.

He sighed deeply, wondering just what to do about Archer Lowell.

Burt had been on his way out of High Meadow to his first taste of freedom in sixteen years when he'd run into his old buddy, Vince Giordano, who was on his way back in for a lifetime stay. They'd had a casual reunion of sorts, and Burt had been ready to leave when Vince called him back and asked him for a favor.

Since the favor would, in the end, benefit Burt far more than it would benefit Vince, Burt had said sure. Of course, at first, Burt had no intention of making good on his promise. After all, Vince, facing several murder charges, would never see the outside of the prison walls in this lifetime, and he would have no way of knowing whether Burt had kept his word or not. Now Burt was driving this fine new pickup, and living in a classy condo, and he had Vince to thank for it all.

All Burt had to do, Vince had explained, was to make sure that Lowell carried out a promise of his own.

"There's someone who has a job to do for me out there," Vince had whispered. "I just want you to make sure he does it."

"That's all I have to do? Make sure someone does a job for you?" Burt, too, had lowered his voice.

"That's all," Vince had said with a nod.

In return, Vince had told Burt where he'd find a metal box filled with cash.

"It's all for you, Burt-man. No one else knows it's out there. You just gotta keep this guy honest. Make sure he does what he's supposed to do . . ."

And Vince had proceeded to fill Burt in on the pact he'd made with Channing and Lowell.

Before Burt had left the intake room, Vince had whispered, "And if you come back with proof that the job's been done, I'll tell you where to find the other half of the money."

Of course, Burt had agreed. And of course, the first thing Burt had done when he left High Meadow was to track down that secret stash of Vince's, and damn if it wasn't there, just like he'd said it would be. It was more money than he'd ever seen in his life, and it was all for him. He'd bought himself the pickup right off, then some new clothes. Then he found himself a nice place to live. Found, too, that the ladies liked a man who dressed well, who had nice wheels and a ready wad of cash to spend. Life had never been sweeter for Burt Connolly, and he had Vince Giordano to thank for his good fortune. It hadn't occurred to him to keep his part of the bargain, of course, until he realized that if he was living well on half the money, how much better life would be if he had it all.

And all he had to do in return was to keep this kid Lowell focused on doing what he was supposed to do.

Nothing old Burt-man couldn't handle, though Lowell was turning out to be a real pain in the ass. Stupid, too.

Old Vince had sure read him right. It was obvious to Burt that Lowell was in no hurry to follow through with his part of the bargain. Burt figured Lowell planned on being a no-show as far as his promise was concerned.

Think again, little man, Burt muttered under his

breath as he wrestled the Ho Hos out of the bag and bit the plastic wrapper to open it. No way was Burt going to let Lowell weasel out of his obligation to Giordano. More important, no way was Lowell going to cheat him, Burt Connolly, out of the rest of the money.

He gunned the big engine of the pickup and passed an SUV that was going just over the speed limit.

Lowell was such a wimp; he could be scared into doing just about anything. Look at what he'd already done, shot that old man in Ohio. Burt shook his head in disgust, recalling how Lowell's voice had shaken, how terrified he'd been once the deed was done. Burt's plan had been perfect; there was no one who could have connected Lowell to the killing.

Except that the FBI already knew that the old man would be a target.

How stupid of Lowell not to have told Burt about their visit to the trailer. Would have served him right if the cops picked him up. It was almost enough to make Burt call off the hit on that writer guy, but there was no way anyone could know about that, right? He figured Unger wasn't such a stretch that the FBI agents couldn't have figured that out on their own, but who the hell would connect the writer to a hard-assed serial killer like Curtis Channing?

And if Lowell got caught, so what? He had no way of identifying Burt. He'd just have to make sure that he didn't leave his fingerprints on anything that Lowell could give up later.

Of course, if Lowell got caught, that would end the

game prematurely. There'd still be that one last hit. After that, well, he'd have to wait and see.

Burt had gotten a glimpse of target number three, and he'd sure liked what he'd seen. Maybe it wouldn't be so bad if Lowell was taken out of the game. Burt might have to jump in and pinch-hit, so to speak.

Wouldn't that be a shame? Burt grinned as he recalled watching Miranda Cahill fold those long legs of hers into that little car one night outside the Well. The sudden image of those long legs wrapped around his waist caused his heart to flip over in his chest. Wouldn't that be a pretty sight?

Well, first things first. Lowell had a job to do, and Burt was going to make certain the job got done and got done right. There was plenty of time to think about what was to be done about Agent Cahill.

"Hey." Will stuck his head into Miranda's cubicle.

"Hey, yourself." She smiled at him from her place behind the desk. "I was just going to call you."

"What's up?" He stepped through the doorway and leaned over the back of the visitor's chair that stood before her desk.

"I just got off the phone with Veronica Carson up in Fleming. No sign of our boy in town since Friday."

"I'm assuming the police have interviewed his friends. His bar buddies."

"According to Carson, they've spoken to just about everyone in town. No one has seen or heard from Archer since he left the Well on Thursday night. His mother says he couldn't have gone far because he had absolutely no money. He never mentioned to anyone that he was planning on leaving town."

"They checked the train and bus stations?"

"Carson said they showed his photo around. One of the clerks said he could have been in one day last week, then again, maybe not. There were no credit card sales in his name. Not so surprising since it's unlikely that Archer has a credit card."

"So if he bought a ticket, he paid cash for it." Will digested this. "And since we figure he was in Ohio three days ago, it looks like he may have gone to ground somewhere. He has to be staying someplace, he has to be eating. Where's the money coming from?"

"Good question."

"Before I forget, I just pulled the old file on the Jenny Green case. The taped interview with Curtis Channing is MIA. As so often happens around here."

"Damn. It could be anyplace. Could have fallen out in the file drawer, could have been left on someone's desk, could have gone out in the trash accidently in a pizza box with the remains of someone's lunch, for all we know." Miranda bit the inside of her lip. "Well, so much for going to the source, though frankly, I don't know that it would have helped us all that much in the long run. It was a good idea, but I don't know that there was anything on it that would have broken the case."

"Am I interrupting anything?" Anne Marie stuck her head through the cubicle's opening.

"No, not at all." Miranda waved her in. "Come in and join us."

"Well, actually, I'm a little short of time this afternoon. I have a lecture to prepare for tomorrow. " Annie touched Will's arm. "So. Ready for lunch?"

"I was just waiting for you." He straightened up and nodded to Miranda. "I guess I'll see you later."

"Sure." Her eyes flickered from one to the other. "See you later. Bye, Annie."

"Bye," Annie called from the hall.

Well. Miranda twirled a pen around slowly. *What was all that about?*

She continued to twirl the pen between her first two fingers for several moments. Then she stood up, went to the window, and looked out at the parking lot. Annie and Will were almost to his car. They walked close together, close enough that their shoulders touched every few steps. A small cold spot in her chest began to spread little by little.

I thought that Annie and Evan . . .

But Annie and Will? She sat back down and swiveled her chair from side to side slowly, wondering when *that* had happened.

Maybe all those times I thought he was playing it cool . . . maybe he just wasn't interested.

That gave her pause. Well, he did say he wanted to be friends, didn't he? When a man really cares about a woman, he doesn't go all buddy-buddy on her, does he?

She sat so still, she could almost hear the beating of her own heart.

You're jealous, a tiny voice inside accused, and she turned the thought over and over in her mind.

The admission surprised her.

Why, yes, I suppose I am. Shit . . .

Unexpectedly, John Mancini's voice shot through the intercom, jarring her out of her reverie.

"Miranda, you still in there?" he asked.

"Yes."

"Stop in my office when you get a minute, if you would."

"Sure. I'll just be a minute."

"Take your time."

Miranda stood and gathered the notes she wanted to take home with her, as well as copies of the letters she'd brought back from Landry's. She'd been looking forward to discussing the Unger and Landry cases with John, so she was pleased to have an opportunity to do so. She'd have preferred to have had Will along, but as he was otherwise engaged, she'd go it alone. On her way to John's office, she made copies of the letters.

Ten minutes later she was sitting in John's office, her chair pulled up close to his desk, her elbow leaning on the right corner. John sat back in his well-worn leather chair, one eye on his computer screen, his printer spitting out a stack of documents, the phone up to his ear.

"Okay. Thanks. Keep trying." He hung up, his expression unreadable. To Miranda's eye, his coloring appeared a shade or two paler than normal.

"So. What's the latest with your three amigos?" he asked.

"Lowell is missing. We're thinking he's on the run after having killed Unger in Ohio." Miranda cut to the chase. "His mother was the last to see him. That was Friday morning before she left for work. Fleming

PD reports that none of his friends have seen or heard from him since the night before."

John's brows knit together. "Any luck in identifying a possible second—or third—victim?"

"This is a tough call, because we still know so little about Channing other than his ever-growing number of kills. We don't know who he came in contact with on a daily basis, who he worked with, who he lived with, who over the years really pissed him off. So we're going into this blind," she reminded him. "That being said, however, we think Joshua Landry looks like a good candidate."

"Josh Landry, the crime writer?"

"Yes. Apparently Channing read one of his early books and took exception to some of Landry's theories. Channing wrote to him several times. I made copies of the letters for you. Landry's daughter made a set for Will and for me."

John nodded. "I'd like to see them."

"I thought you might." She took an envelope out of the folder on her lap and passed it to him.

"You've advised Landry that he could be a target?" he said as he slid the envelope to one side of his desk.

"Yes. He says his house is protected by state-of-the-art security. He also called in the local police while we were there, so we had an opportunity to alert them, discuss the situation. I think they have a pretty good understanding of what we're dealing with here. We left a photo of Lowell with the police and with Landry so they know who they're looking for. But I'm not certain that Landry really understands how serious the situation is. I think we need someone of our own on the scene."

"We'll send in Art Phillips. He's already in the area. New Brunswick, I think. Close enough."

"Actually, I was thinking about going myself—"

"I can't afford to have you sitting on Landry. For one thing, assuming that Landry is in fact going to be the second victim, we'll need to figure out who might be the third."

"Actually," she shifted uncomfortably in her chair, "there's a theory about that."

"I'm all ears."

"Landry thinks I might be the third target."

"You?"

"He thinks that when I interviewed Channing six years ago—in Ohio, that first field assignment I had?" John nodded.

"Well, Landry thinks that my focusing on Channing spoiled a nice little run he was having in southern Ohio, forced him to move on before he wanted to." Miranda looked across the desk at John. "He thinks that maybe Channing was angry that his fun was ruined. Landry referred to it as my 'stopping his forward motion.'"

"He was in his comfort zone, and you pushed him out of it."

"That's Landry's theory."

"Maybe you should back off the case, then." John frowned.

"No, no. First of all, I think I know Lowell better than anyone at this point. Second, we don't know if

Channing even remembered my name. And third, the plan is to stop him before he gets to Landry."

"You're working with Fletcher," he noted. "Who else do you need?"

"I don't think we need anyone else right now. With Phillips keeping an eye on Landry, and the local police involved, I think we'll be able to get our hands on Lowell." She grimaced. "Christ, if the FBI can't outwit a loser like Archer Lowell, we're in big trouble."

"So far, he's one up on the Bureau," John reminded her.

"I'm well aware." She nodded glumly.

"Frankly, I lay that one at the feet of the locals. You laid the whole thing out for them. Apparently they didn't take you very seriously."

"Let's hope the Plainsville police have more on the ball than their brethren in Ohio. In the meantime, over the next few days, Will and I will be going over the reports of all Channing's known kills. We need to look at the whole picture. Where he'd been, how long he stayed, see if we can identify anyone who had contact with him."

"You're going to try to re-create the last six years of his life through police records?"

"That's the plan. There has to be a pattern there someplace. We need to find it."

The phone rang, and he glanced at it with weary eyes before picking it up. He listened for a few moments, then snapped, "Find her," before hanging up.

"Someone lost?" she asked.

It was a long moment before he responded. Then,

finally, he said, "We seem to be having a problem with Genna's signal."

"Genna's still in Wyoming?"

"Yes. Before she left, we inserted a device in the heel of one of her shoes so we could keep track of her while she was in Reverend Prescott's compound."

"And the signal is lost?"

"The signal hasn't moved in three days."

"Maybe she took her shoes off. . . ."

"They're having record snowfalls out there right now. It's unlikely my wife is walking around barefoot."

The phone rang again.

"Anything else?" he asked, his hand on the phone.

"No." She stood to leave. "Listen, John, if there's anything I can do . . . I could go back to Wyoming, I could see what I can—"

He shook his head, waved her off, turned his back, and took his call.

"Thanks, Annie, for coming in to meet me today," Will said as he parked his car near the edge of the park.

"I'm sorry I don't have more time," she apologized, "but you sounded so worried on the phone."

He passed her the bag of sandwiches they'd picked up at the local drive-through. She opened it and searched for her selection.

"I guess I should just get to the point." He ran one hand through his hair. "Miranda and I paid a visit to Joshua Landry the other day."

He explained why they believed Landry could be a

focus of Channing's anger, then handed her copies of several of Channing's letters. She read through the first few while she unwrapped her chicken sandwich and nibbled on it.

"Well, I'd say that Landry certainly did push Channing's buttons," she said when she was finished reading.

"So you think he could be a target?"

"Oh, yes. Channing was clearly angry with him. There's no mistaking that. Channing even asked him to retract several statements Landry made in the book, and when he refused, he all but threatened him." Annie paused to take another bite, chewed slowly, then said, "But you figured that out for yourself."

"Miranda and I did, yes."

"So what is it that you really wanted to ask me?"

"There's one more letter you need to see." From the inside of his jacket pocket, he withdrew an envelope, which he passed to her. "Read this."

She did, then looked up when she was finished, and said, "Channing was really angry with this woman—this woman police officer—when he wrote this, wasn't he?"

"I don't think it was a police officer," he told her. "I think it was a woman FBI agent."

Annie raised a questioning brow. "Anyone we know?"

"Miranda interviewed him right about the time he's referencing in that letter. She apparently rattled him enough that he moved on, disappeared. She'd tried to bring him back in for more questioning, but he couldn't be located."

"So you think that maybe Miranda might be the woman he's referring to here? And could therefore be Channing's number three?"

"I'm asking you what you think. You're the one who has made a career of understanding these personalities. And you met Channing. You're the only person I know who spent time with him, talked to him."

She tapped the folded letter on her crossed knee.

"What you want to know is, do I think Channing gave Miranda's name to Lowell?"

"Yes."

"Well, let's look at what we learned about him from the Mary Douglas case. You've read the reports yourself, Will. Channing was a very organized killer. Took all his gear with him. Had his victims staked out ahead of time, knew where they lived, when they left in the morning, when they arrived home at night. He left very little to chance."

"Except he failed to properly identify his first victim."

"Yes, a failure that resulted in his killing three women more than he'd planned. Not that I think he regretted that." She shook her head. "Actually, I think it may have amused him, in an 'oh, silly me' sort of way."

"Do you think he would have remembered Miranda?"

Annie smiled. "Will, you're a man. You tell me.

How often does a man meet a woman like Miranda? How likely is he to forget?"

"That's pretty much what I was thinking."

"So the answer would have to be yes, I think he remembered her."

"We know he held a grudge against Unger for thirty years, but that was pretty personal. I mean, Unger was a part of his daily life; they lived together. They shared a defining moment in Channing's life." Will rubbed his chin thoughtfully. "But would his feeling toward Miranda have been that strong? Would he have held on to those feelings for six years? Would he have wanted to destroy her as he did Unger, as he might want to do to Landry?"

"Depends on how cozy he felt where he was, when she brought an end to it. Have you reviewed all of the identified cases?"

"Most of them, not all."

"I'm familiar with the ones Miranda had been investigating in Rockledge. All young women in their late teens, early twenties. All from roughly the same area in southern Ohio. All raped, strangled in their homes. All were left with one of their own scarves over their faces."

"Same as the ones we're looking at now, the murders he committed after he left Rockledge."

"But they didn't start up for two, three months after he left Rockledge," Will pointed out.

"Two or three months when he would have been stewing, wanting to kill but afraid of being caught." Annie thought it over, then nodded. "As Landry said, Miranda stopped his forward motion for a time. A time he probably spent quite frustrated. Angry, no doubt, because of it."

"Then you think there's a chance Miranda might be the third victim?"

"I think you should keep an open mind, keep scanning those files. See if you can identify a more likely candidate. But until you do, I'd say proceed as if Miranda's name is the third on that list."

"I guess I need to talk to John."

"The sooner, the better," Annie agreed. "Right now your focus is on Landry. Can we take the chance that Lowell's focus isn't on Miranda?"

CHAPTER TWELVE

BURT LOWERED HIMSELF SLOWLY INTO THE LONE chair in his motel room and rubbed his temples, trying to ease away the pain caused by forty minutes in the company of Archer Lowell, whom Burt had found to be one big fat pain in the ass. If Vince Giordano had simply asked him to do all this as a favor, Burt wouldn't have given it a second thought. But Giordano had thrown a whole shitload of money his way—more money than he'd ever seen in one place before—so what else could he do but take this all the way to the end?

He only wished he didn't have to take Lowell along in order to see it through.

Archer Lowell was a dangerous man, in Burt's opinion. Dangerous because he was so stupid. Burt had been really careful not to let Lowell see anything with his full name on it. He wore a hat and dark glasses that covered much of his face when he was in Lowell's company, and he made sure he wore gloves when he was in Lowell's room. He wanted to leave nothing behind that could tie him to Lowell once the shit hit the fan. He'd even muddied up some of his license plate so that Lowell couldn't give it up, should it ever occur to the twerp to turn on him.

He rubbed the back of his neck with his big, beefy right hand. That was something that had to be considered. What were the chances Lowell would just do what he had to do, then go quietly about his business? Would there come a time when, overcome with remorse, Lowell might go to the cops and spill the whole thing? The fact that, up to this point, he had gone along with the deal was no real guarantee that he might not someday regret what he'd done.

Burt was going to have to think long and hard about this. How to keep Lowell on track so that he could see this through and collect the rest of the money, and keep his head out of a noose at the same time.

It had been no surprise that he'd arrived at the motel to find Lowell had absolutely no plan for going after his next victim. The guy was totally clueless.

"I don't know," Lowell had whined when Burt had asked him what his next move was going to be.

"You got your vic picked out?" Burt had asked, trying to keep a rein on his temper, lest he belt Lowell in the head.

"Yes."

"So you know where you're going? How you're getting there? How you're gonna get the job done?"

"Not exactly."

"What exactly do you know, Lowell?" Burt's eyes had darkened. Lowell had visibly cringed at the menacing.

"I just know who. I don't know where he is. New

Jersey, I think. A farm or something. But that's all Channing told me."

"So you go on the Internet and you find him. You know how to do that?"

"Sorta."

"There's no sorta, asshole. You either know how to locate someone or you don't."

"I don't."

"How can a kid as young as you not know about computers?"

"I don't know." Lowell shrugged. "I just never learned computer stuff."

"This town must have a library. I'll go in the morning and look him up on the computer for you." His eyes lit. "I'll bet I can even get driving directions. . . ."

And he had gotten directions, practically to Landry's front door. Next he had to lay it out for Lowell.

"What you gotta do is study the place. See what's what. So's you know when to go in, when you can nail him."

"How do I do that? How do I get there? How do I . . ." Lowell had started to pace in the small motel room, and Burt had thought he'd explode. Or break a chair over Lowell's head.

"All right. I'll tell you what. I'm going to drive you there. You can figure out what to do from there, can't you?"

"I don't know," Lowell began to whine again.

Burt grabbed him by the throat and lifted him clear off his feet.

"Now you listen, and you listen good," Burt

growled into the younger man's face. "You are going to do this for Vince if it kills you. Frankly, I don't care if it does. You ain't nothing to me, you hear? I could just as easily plug you myself right here and now because you are pissing me off big-time."

Tightening his fingers on Lowell's neck, he repeated, "You ain't nothing to me, you understand that, punk?"

Gasping, his eyes bulging nearly out of his head, Lowell nodded.

Burt dropped him to the floor.

"I got that address for you, and I'll take you there. Then you're on your own. And you better not fuck up."

Burt had left the room, slamming the door behind him, and retreated to his own room down the hall. He turned on the television, surfed until he found ESPN, then leaned back to watch some college football.

Another couple of days, and this would all be over. Vince would tell him where the rest of the money had been hidden, and once Burt had the full amount in his pocket, he'd be on his way to Florida. He'd find himself some nice little town and buy himself a condo. Set himself up in some kind of legitimate business. He'd done a little Internet research himself and found that he could buy a water ice franchise for a couple of hundred thou—which, thanks to Vince, he'd have—and in a few more years, he'd be living the life.

He wondered what Sharon, his ex-wife, would say when he showed up at her door, a respected businessman, and demanded to see his kids. That'd be something, wouldn't it?

He had to remind himself that his kids were almost out of high school by now. Well, if they wanted to go to college, he'd step in and take care of that. Sure. They were his kids, weren't they? Not their fault that their mother had taken them away while he was in prison. Yeah. He'd offer to pay their tuition, that's what. Show them what kind of a guy he really was. And fuck Sharon if she didn't like it.

Of course, when she saw that new pickup, saw him dressed so fine in his new threads, her eyes were just about going to bug out of her head. Maybe she'd even try to put some moves on him, try to get herself back into his life.

Like that was going to happen.

He was going to find himself a new woman, that's what. Prettier than Sharon, younger, too. Someone who could appreciate him, who'd be proud of him and the business he was going to start. Maybe even have another family. One he'd be there for, not like last time.

Well, that was his old life. Water under the bridge. He didn't have to be pulling any petty-ass jobs anymore. He had his own stash, and he was going to have a hell of a lot more.

Thinking about the cash he had hidden in the well of his spare tire made him think about Giordano. Thinking about Giordano made him think about Lowell all over again.

He groaned and rubbed his temples.

Tomorrow was going to be a very long day. He got

up and grabbed his keys from the top of the dresser where he'd tossed them, then went out into the night. There had to be a liquor store around here someplace. He hadn't had a drink since this whole mess had started, but tonight, faced with the prospect of spending the next day or so with Archer Lowell, he figured he needed a little something to help him get through it without killing the assassin.

He thought about how it had felt to have his hands around Lowell's throat. It would have taken precious little additional pressure to have strangled him. The kid was so annoying, Burt almost wished he had. In that second, there was no doubt in his mind that he could very easily have taken Lowell's life and not thought twice about it.

Good to know.

CHAPTER THIRTEEN

MIRANDA'S DOORBELL BEGAN TO CHIME JUST AS SHE hung up the phone. She peeked through one of the living room windows to see who was there and, for some reason, was not surprised to see Will leaning against one of the faux colonial pillars that graced what passed for a front porch in Miranda's town-house development.

"Well, well," she said as she opened the door. "Let me guess. You were just in the neighborhood and thought you'd stop by." She glanced at her watch. "Could the fact that it's almost dinnertime and you have another hour to drive before you get home have anything to do with this impromptu visit?"

"No, but now that you mention it, did I catch you in the middle of whipping up some gourmet goodies?"

She held the door open and gestured for him to enter.

"Please." She rolled her eyes. "Remember where you are."

"Sorry. I lost my head."

She walked into the living room, knowing he'd follow, and sat on the edge of a large square plush otto-man the color of cocoa.

"How's your sister? Have you heard from her?" He took a seat on the sofa.

"She's fine. I just got off the phone with her. She's still in some undisclosed location in the Middle East; that's all I know." Miranda frowned. "I hate that she's over there. It's just too dicey to be undercover in an unfriendly region."

"Did she say she's in any particular danger?"

"No, of course not. This is Portia the Fearless we're talking about here. Even if she was scared to death, she'd never admit it."

"Even to you?"

"Especially to me."

"I thought identical twins were supposed to be like two peas in a pod."

"Yeah, well, we're mirror-image twins, so I guess that accounts for it."

"You're right-handed, she's left- . . ."

Miranda made a face. "That's the short version. I also think there's some left-brain, right-brain thing at work there, too. She would walk into the gates of hell unarmed with a smile on her face, like she's walking into a theme park and with about as much caution."

"You make her sound careless, and we both know that's not true."

"No, she's not careless. But she is fearless. Compared to her, I'm the family wimp."

"Don't be so hard on yourself. I can't remember the last time I saw you back down from a job."

"It's easy to look brave when you don't put yourself in dire situations." Miranda shook her head. "I've never done half of the stuff she's done. And I don't want to."

"And you think that makes you a wimp?"

"Compared to her, yes."

"Why do you have to compare yourself to her?"

"Because she's there." Miranda shrugged. "Besides, everyone's always compared us to each other."

"That hardly seems fair."

"It happens to twins all the time." She made a face again. "If it wasn't 'Miranda walked earlier, but Portia talked first,' it was 'Portia could read by the time she was three, but Miranda didn't read until nursery school.' That sort of thing. You grow to expect it after a while."

"I guess that can be tough, growing up."

"I suppose it could be, if one is way ahead of the other developmentally. Portia and I sort of seesawed back and forth, one did one thing first, then the other did something else. So, enough about me. What's going on?"

"What makes you think something's going on?"

"You never just stop in, Fletcher." She paused, then added, "At least, it's been a while since you just showed up at my door. Makes me think there's a reason."

"There is a reason." He nodded. "I had lunch with Annie today."

"So?" She knew that. She crossed one leg over the other and swung it slightly, trying to look as nonchalant as possible.

"We talked about this whole situation with Lowell

and who his victims are likely to be. She thinks Landry is definitely on the list. She also agrees with him, that you're likely to be on there, too."

"Swell."

"She further agrees that we need to see if we can find someone else from Channing's past who might fit the bill, but as it looks now . . ." He held both hands out in front of him, palms up. "Well, she thinks you just look too good. I'd be real happy if we were able to identify a more likely victim. But until we find someone else, we need to decide how best to watch your back, Cahill."

"I can watch my back." She frowned.

"Oh, and now you have eyes in the back of your head, do you?"

"You think Archer Lowell can get the best of me?" Her face hardened. "That is insulting."

"He's going to have an advantage over you." She started to protest, and he held up one hand. "He will know where, and he will know when. Two very crucial bits of information. You will have to be totally vigilant every minute of every day until we get him."

"It isn't as if I walk around in a fog all the time, Will." She was growing visibly angry.

"It's different when someone is after you. You can never let your guard down. And regardless of what you think, you cannot watch your own back, Cahill. No one can."

She glared at him. "So what are you suggesting?"

"That we have someone watching your house. Someone with you all the time."

She crossed her arms over her chest. "Tell me that you have not volunteered for that duty."

"I haven't, but I will." He watched her face but could not read her expression. "I haven't had this discussion with John yet, but I intend to, first thing in the morning."

"I already mentioned it to John. Sort of."

"That was before we had the opinion of our behavior specialist."

"Annie really thinks Channing remembered me?"

"She thinks there's a good chance, yes." He continued to watch her face. "Let's take this seriously, okay, Cahill? Let's pretend that there's no maybe. Let's pretend that it's a definite, and act accordingly."

"If we're wrong, I'll feel like the world's biggest ass."

"But you'll be alive."

She got up and moved around the room, for no apparent reason other than to work off a little of her restlessness.

"Portia will be home in a few weeks. She'll be here with me."

"And what do we do in the meantime, hope that Lowell can't figure out how to look up your name in the phone book?"

"How would he even know what book to look in?"

"You gave him your business card when we were at his trailer that first day. It had your office and cell phone numbers on it, along with the address of the office. Even he is probably smart enough to figure out that you most likely live somewhere relatively close to where you work."

"Is that why you moved out into the boonies? So that no one would be able to figure out where you live?"

"I moved to the boonies because I like it, and don't change the subject."

She sat back down on the ottoman and rubbed her temples, closing her eyes as if in pain.

"Christ, my sister is off fighting terrorists in the Middle East, and here I am, in Virginia, talking about having an armed guard outside my safe little townhouse. What is wrong with this picture?" She shook her head. "Portia's going to think I've really lost it."

"Portia's going to be thrilled that you're still alive."

"Okay. Do it. Just . . . do it." She stood up. "Was that it? That's what you stopped for?"

"Well, as you pointed out, it is dinnertime. I noticed a new restaurant out on Route 43."

"I'll get my coat."

She left the room, and Will stood up, stretching his legs. He walked to the front window and looked out across the parking lot. Fortunately, there were only two ways in and out of Miranda's townhouse. He made a mental note to check the locks on the back door, but he seemed to recall there was a dead bolt there. Not foolproof, certainly. And maybe he'd suggest that she get her security system upgraded.

He wandered around the room absently, thinking about how they might go about keeping Miranda safe without destroying her ego. He wandered into the hallway and paused at the small sideboard that sat near the front door. An envelope lay open, its contents spread across the top of the table. He leaned closer to take a look.

"What are you doing?" she asked from midway down the steps.

"Just looking at these photos," he said. "I hope you don't mind, they were laying here on the table and—"

"I do mind."

Surprised at her tone, he looked up at her.

"They're just baby pictures. You don't want me to see how cute you and Portia were as babies? These are pictures of you and Portia, aren't they?"

She nodded.

"You were beautiful babies. And your mother still looks a lot like she did back then, you know?" He peered closer at the top photo. "But who's the guy carrying you on his shoulders? In this picture here . . ." He held it up.

Without glancing at it, she said, "That's our father."

"Really? I don't remember him being that tall." Will frowned. "I met him that time you were in the hospital, after you got knocked out at Kendra Smith's house. I thought he was kind of short."

"That was my stepfather."

"Oh." He looked up at her, saw how guarded her face had become. His eyes went back to the photograph, which he studied more carefully. "You know, if I didn't know better, I'd think that this was—"

"Jack Marlow." She named the man in the photo

before Will could, her voice touched with frost. "Yes. He's my father. Can we go now?"

"Jack Marlow? Mad Marlow, the legendary English rocker and guitar god, is your *father*?"

"I understand these days he's not quite as mad as he used to be, and perhaps somewhat less of a god, but yes," she said with strained patience. "He's my father."

Will looked incredulous. "How could I have not known that?"

"It isn't something I generally discuss. Are we going to have dinner now or not?"

Will dropped the photo back on the pile.

"Learn something new every day," he muttered, and preceded her through the front door. "And set the alarm, damn it."

"Maybe we should get takeout instead." She activated the system. "Then we can come back and start going through those computer files, at least identify the cases we're going to pull tomorrow morning."

"I already did that."

"Well, then, we can make a list of all the reports we want to review from each of the files."

"Did that, too." He grinned. "And before you ask, yes, I printed out copies of all the case logs, all the reports, and all the police records from each. I thought we'd divvy them up between us and see if any one person stands out."

"You did all that this afternoon?"

He nodded.

"Damn, you really are good." She started down the

sidewalk and passed him, shaking her head. "Annoying, but good."

"So," he said as he caught up with her, "want to tell me how Jack Marlow, the guitar-smashing, drum-bashing rock idol, happens to be your father?"

"He slept with my mother."

She fished her car keys out of the bag that hung from her shoulder. Putting a lock on the subject once and for all, she asked, "Italian or Chinese?"

CHAPTER FOURTEEN

BURT PULLED THE PICKUP OFF THE ROAD AND ONTO the wide shoulder and put the engine in neutral.

"Tell me again what you are going to do."

"I'm going to walk down the side of the road here," Lowell pointed behind them, "until I get to the woods. I'm going to walk straight into the woods, and when I get to the fields on the other side of the trees, I'm going to walk that way," he pointed to his right, "until I see the house. The big yellow farmhouse."

"And then?" Burt said, with the same tone of voice he'd use for conversing with a five-year-old.

"Then I'm going to find a tree that would give me a good view of the farmhouse, and I'm going to climb it and sit and just watch."

"What are you watching for?" He handed Lowell a pair of binoculars, and Lowell slipped the strap over his head.

"I need to know who is up there. How many people are at the house. And see if I can figure out what he—Mr. Landry—does all day. If he comes out at any special time each day."

"And you think you're going to remember this because . . . ?"

"I can remember. Sure." Lowell's head bobbed up and down. "No problem."

Burt handed him a small notebook and a blue pen.

"Excuse me for seeing a problem, but I don't want you getting things mixed up. You're going to be watching this guy for the next couple of days. I don't think there's a chance in hell you're going to remember what time the mailman comes, what time Landry takes a walk *if* he takes a walk. Write it all down, then you won't have to worry about remembering anything. You're looking for patterns here."

Lowell scowled but tucked the notebook and pen in his jacket pocket.

"Now get out," Burt directed, and Lowell opened the passenger-side door.

"But you promise you're coming back for me, right?" Lowell whined.

Burt reached over and slammed the door.

"Walk," he commanded.

Lowell sighed heavily and walked past the back of the truck toward the woods. He jammed his hands into the pockets of his jacket and wished he was wearing that nice down jacket his mother had bought him. It was so much warmer than this wool thing he was wearing. Buffalo checks, his mother had called the red-and-black plaid, though Archer couldn't figure out why. He'd been meaning to ask. Now he wondered if he'd ever get the chance. If he'd ever see his mother again . . .

Shit. Don't go thinking like that, he berated himself. *Just gonna get upset.*

Like he wasn't already upset. Here he was, going to spy on some man so he'd know when would be the best time of day to go back and kill him. He'd already killed one man, and every night since he'd had nightmares of that old body facedown on the floor of the movie theater, shaking and jerking around, the blood pooling on the floor beside that gray head like syrup from a bottle. It had been just awful.

And now he was going to have to do it again.

He hunched inside his jacket and kept walking straight ahead on the shoulder of the two-lane country road. The woods were nearer now, and in minutes he'd be walking right through them. He wondered how long it would take him to get through them and out the other side to the fields. Of course, he wouldn't walk in the fields. Especially in this red jacket. Someone might see him and call the police.

And would that be the worst thing that could happen to him, he wondered.

What would be the worst that could happen to him?

He didn't even want to think about that. Burt scared the shit out of him. He still didn't know what the man's full name was, though he had tried to get a peek at the registration for the truck when they stopped for gas, thinking that Burt would get out and pump. But the attendant had pumped the gas—not like back in Pennsylvania, where you could pump your own—and he'd lost the opportunity to take a quick look through the glove box.

He stopped at the edge of the woods and looked past the trees. It was dark in there, spooky, even.

It's almost Halloween, he reminded himself, and hoped there were no unfriendly spirits about in the woods.

Shut up. Would ya just listen to yourself?

He shook his head in disgust and walked a little slower as a car passed. When the car was out of sight over a rise in the road, he slipped into the woods. Off to his right something crunched softly, and he stopped in his tracks, then slid behind the trunk of a maple tree, his heart pounding. After a few minutes, he peered out from behind the tree. Seeing nothing, he resumed his walk.

A sign they'd passed down the road claimed that the woods and fields surrounding the town had seen bloodshed during the Revolutionary War, when a lost platoon of redcoats had been ambushed by a handful of farmers. Archer looked over his shoulder from time to time as he walked along, half expecting to see the ghosts of British soldiers creeping up on him. Just the thought of it sent a chill up his spine. Before he could panic, he came to the end of the woods, where he gratefully stepped out into the sunlight and looked around.

The yellow farmhouse was off to his right. Archer slunk back into the shelter of the woods and, staying behind the trees, walked until he was directly behind the house, which was about three hundred feet beyond the woods. Archer stood and watched the house for a few minutes, but saw no one. He began to look for a tree to climb. There were lots of trees, but none were good for climbing, so he sat down on the stump of a tree and took the lens caps off the binoculars Burt had given him.

Holding the lenses up to his eyes, he adjusted the focus and scanned the property belonging to Joshua Landry.

The yellow farmhouse looked neat, like something from a magazine, with the pond and the pool and the tennis court. The barn was painted red, and it reminded Archer of the old toy barn he'd had when he was a kid. It had little plastic animals—a pig, a couple of sheep, a cow, some chickens—and a silo. The roof came off and you could see inside the barn, which had a loft on one side. He and his sister used to fill up the loft with dried grass and pretend it was hay. Archer studied Landry's barn and wondered if it had a loft. Lofts were good places to hide.

The back door opened, and a woman came out. Archer readjusted the lenses again, trying to see her face. She looked like she'd be pretty, with lots of blonde hair that sort of floated around her face. She was wearing jeans and a bulky sweater and got into a small white car. She drove the car in a circle, and, just as she passed the back door, it opened; a man walked out and waved to the woman in the car. She stopped and he leaned into the window.

Archer held his breath and studied the man as best he could. White hair. A little over six feet tall. Blue cardigan sweater. Khaki pants. Under one arm was a folded newspaper. He looked just like the picture Burt had ripped from the magazine he'd found in the library on Monday.

Archer stared through the binoculars.

The man laughed at something the young woman said, then stood up and tapped the hood with the newspaper as the car pulled away.

This was him, then. Joshua Landry.

His intended victim.

A shiver ran up Archer's spine at the thought of this man being a victim. God, but he hated that word. *Victim.*

He shook his head. *I'm not going to think about that right now.*

Landry walked in the direction of the pond. A small flock of Canada geese scattered at his approach, giving him a wide berth as he drew closer to the water. He stopped at the edge, then stood, hands on his hips, and stared out at the pond. Suddenly he turned and looked toward the woods. Archer's heart leapt into his throat, and he hunkered down behind a fallen tree where he slipped out of the red-and-black jacket. Landry turned again and took a few steps before stooping to pick up some object from the ground. He turned it over in his hand several times, then slipped it into his pocket. He glanced back at the woods for a moment, then headed back toward the house. Movement near the back door caught Archer's eye, and he trained the binoculars on the small porch. A second, younger man came down the steps and set out hurriedly toward Landry. When he caught up with him, he gestured in the direction of the house. Landry shook his head and went into the barn while the second man scanned the field behind the house. After a minute or so, Landry emerged with a rake in his hands. He walked toward the area behind the house and began raking leaves.

Archer watched through the binoculars as the young man studied the field from one end to the other before turning back to the house. Once on the back porch, he sat, all the while staring across the field right up to the woods, and beyond. Archer flattened himself as much as he could into the cold, damp grass, and prayed that the man didn't see him. All of a sudden he was afraid. He didn't know who the man was, but he sensed a threat, and it scared him.

After a while, twenty or thirty minutes, Landry returned the rake to the barn. Then he and the other man went back into the house.

Taking out the little notebook Burt had given him, Archer opened it and wrote on the first page.

Pretty lady left the house in a little white car.

Mr. Landry walked to the pond.

Another man came outside and talked to Mr. Landry.

Mr. Landry went into the barn and came out with a rake and raked some leaves under the tree.

The other man sat on the back steps and watched Mr. Landry and kept looking around.

Archer couldn't think of anything else to write, so he lay on the ground and looked up into the sky. A flock of birds flew overhead, so many he couldn't even begin to count them all. They landed in the trees above him, and he lay perfectly still so as to not scare them away. After a while he grew cold, and he decided he'd had enough for one day. When he stood, the birds directly overhead took off, followed by the others; for a minute, the sky was black with them. He grabbed his jacket and walked farther into the woods before putting it on, just in case that other man was looking into the woods with binoculars of his own. The thought spooked him, and he hurried along, hoping that Burt would come along soon to pick him up.

Daylight had already started to fade, and suddenly thoughts of ghostly redcoats taunted him. He walked faster and faster, his breath coming in ragged bursts, as he headed toward the road. He breathed a sigh of relief once he reached the tree line, then paused to lean against a red oak, trying to catch his breath. He patted his pocket for the notebook, and his heart took a dive when he realized it wasn't there. He searched the jacket and the back pockets of his pants, even though he knew he didn't have the notebook.

He knew where it was. Right there on the ground where he'd dropped it while he was watching the birds.

Oh, shit. Now what . . . ?

Burt was going to have a fit, that's what.

Archer looked behind him. The woods appeared even more foreboding than they had just minutes earlier.

He looked back toward the road. Burt would be along any time now to pick him up.

Burt was not going to be happy. The thought of Burt sent fear into Archer's very bones.

He turned back to the trees.

Ghosts or Burt?

He thought about the way Burt's eyes narrowed

and seemed to glow like the devil's when he got really mad about something.

Archer buttoned his jacket against the chill and hurried back into the woods. He'd take his chances with the redcoats.

CHAPTER FIFTEEN

WILL LEANED OVER THE DESK, THE PHONE UP against his right ear, while he took notes on the back of an envelope.

"That would be great, yeah. That's what we'll need. Thanks. I owe you one. . . ."

He hung up the phone and opened a desk drawer, hoping to find a piece of paper to transfer his notes to, when he noticed Miranda in the doorway.

"That was Evan," he told her as he opened the center drawer, rooted around, and found a pad of Post-its.

"Has he been able to identify the deputies who were on duty the day that Channing, Giordano, and Lowell were in the courthouse together?" She came into the office and draped herself over the back of the communal visitor's chair, which somehow had found its way into Will's cubicle today. A few days ago it had been in Miranda's cubicle, and before that she remembered seeing it in Livvy Bach's cubicle down the hall.

"He has the names, but he's only been able to speak with three of them. They were all assigned to the front of the building when the courthouse went on lockdown that day. He still has several others to track down. One retired in August and moved to Phoenix; another is on vacation; and another one just entered the police academy. But Evan will keep on it."

"If we can prove they were together, that they had opportunity to hatch this plan, we can go after Giordano on conspiracy charges." She gazed into space, thinking out loud. "If nothing else, the threat alone might make Giordano open up."

"And if we can catch up with Archer Lowell in the meantime, we can avert two more murders."

"All good, all around." She nodded.

"So what have you got?" Will asked. "You have that look in your eye."

"I may have found someone who could have pissed off Channing in a big way."

"Who's that?"

"A guy named Ronald Johnson. He was Channing's boss in a little restaurant in Wynnefield." She leaned back in the chair and looked just a little smug. "Wynnefield, Ohio, where three bodies were found within two weeks time. DNA was just recently matched to Channing."

"What's that got to do with Johnson?"

"Johnson fired Channing. Shortly after he lost his job, the killings stopped. Picked up about three weeks later in Union."

"Why'd he fire Channing?"

"It doesn't say."

"Maybe we should speak with Mr. Johnson."

"I've already made a call to the Wynnefield police." She smiled. "We're booked on a three o'clock flight to

Cincinnati. We'll pick up a car and drive on down to Wynnefield."

"Great." He glanced at his watch. They had another two hours before they'd have to leave for the airport. "Who put you on to Johnson?"

"The owner of one of the restaurants Channing worked for. I got the names of his prior employers by running the social security number he was using back then. I matched up the restaurants with the towns where we had confirmed kills that matched back to Channing. Seems he drifted from town to town for several years, restaurant to restaurant."

"Kill to kill," Will murmured.

"So it would seem."

"The owner didn't have a number for Johnson?"

"No. He said Johnson left his employ about three years ago, left no forwarding information. The Wynnefield police are doing a search for me. I'm expecting to hear from them." She glanced at her watch. "I hope they call back soon. I'd love to know what caused Johnson to fire Channing and how Channing reacted."

"Well, I say for now, we put Johnson's name on our list of maybe victims."

"I already did. You find anything interesting in your stack of files?"

"Only that there's a stretch of time when Channing seems to have disappeared from the area for a while." Will frowned. "For almost a year, there were no kills in the Ohio, Kentucky, Indiana, or Pennsylvania areas that we can attribute to him."

"You sent his DNA through CODIS; if he'd been active elsewhere, it would have shown up."

"*If* he left DNA behind. If he'd smartened up by then, who knows? He could have been just about anywhere."

"Did you imput his kills for similar MOs?"

"I just started doing that when Evan called."

"Want me to help?"

"No, thanks, that's okay. It's giving me an opportunity to take another look at his patterns."

"Let me know if you change your mind." She stood up and stretched. "By the way, I spoke with Regan Landry this morning. Apparently all's quiet on the Plainsville front. She isn't happy about having to be in Philadelphia right now—she feels she should be with her dad until this is over—and her father isn't particularly happy about having Art Phillips in his hair, as she put it."

"Her father would be even less happy to have Archer Lowell in his face."

"Regan agrees. But she said Landry and Phillips keep rubbing each other the wrong way. Landry goes outside without telling Phillips, Phillips gets pissed off. Landry gets pissed off."

"Sounds like one big pissing contest in the fields of New Jersey."

"That pretty much sums it up. Regan told her father he'd just have to live with it. She's trying to keep him in line, but you know, as she explained it, he thinks he's the authority on the criminal mind."

"Thinks he can outsmart Lowell, does he?"

"Well, so did we, if you remember."

"Ouch."

"Anyway, Regan's riding herd on her father to just ignore Phillips and just let him do his job."

"Let's hope he listens to her."

"Yeah, well, in the meantime, Livvy's ordering lunch. You want anything?"

"Where's she going?"

"Luigi's. They deliver. No one really feels like going out into this storm." She nodded toward the window. "Or hadn't you noticed it's raining like crazy out there?"

"I noticed," he said, nodding. "But I heard it's supposed to stop early this afternoon."

"Hopefully before our plane takes off. I don't relish going up in this. So. Are you ordering lunch?"

"Ham and cheese on whole wheat. Lettuce and tomato." He reached for his wallet.

"I've got it," she told him as she started for the door. "It's the least I can do, since you insist on picking me up in the morning and driving me home at night."

"Gotta keep you among the living, Cahill."

"There's a man in a van who is watching my house twenty-four hours each day now. I doubt I need an escort back and forth to the office."

"Tell it to the boss." He tilted his head in the direction of John Mancini's office. "Besides, it gives us a chance to go over what we're finding in the files."

"Ha. All we went over on the ride in this morning was Pink Floyd's *Dark Side of the Moon*."

"A classic, in the best sense of the word."

"Yesterday, it was *The Wall*. Tuesday, it was . . . what was that, anyway?"

"*The Piper at the Gates of Dawn*. Very sixties, very psychedelic."

"Yeah, well, it was a little too sixties for me. I've heard enough psychedelic rock to last a lifetime, thank you very much."

"What can I say? I just got the CD player in the car fixed. I haven't been able to play Floyd in . . ." He glanced to see the look on her face. "Oh. It's the Mad Marlow thing, isn't it?"

"There are some people who never left the sixties, Fletcher. My mother is one of them."

"Stuck in a time warp?"

"World's oldest living hippie."

"She looked pretty straight when I met her. So did your stepfather."

"Roger is an insurance salesman." She laughed and shook her head. "My mother waited twenty-five years for my father to come back and marry her, then turned around and married an insurance salesman."

"Hey, easy on the insurance salesmen. My favorite uncle sells insurance."

"Not that there's anything wrong with it. It's just that, well, look at Jack." Miranda shook her head. "He's a crazy man. I saw an interview with him on television a few years back. He has seven children by five different women in different parts of the world, one of whom, by the way, is reported to be a princess in some small, obscure European country."

"Hey, you're related to royalty." He tried to make light of it.

"No. I have Portia. I have my mother. Roger. That's it."

"Aren't you even curious about—"

"No." Her blue eyes darkened to cobalt. "Not about any of it. Not about Jack or his life, not about his kids or his music. He's never been involved in our lives, and he doesn't exist in mine."

"Those photos I saw the other day, he looked like he was pretty involved then."

"I think we were a novelty to him back then. After all," she said dryly, "we were his first offspring. He did support us financially when we were growing up, but he's never been a father to us. And we could have used one, since our mother wasn't much of a mother. I find his attempts to get in touch with us now little more than an annoyance."

"How did the two of you grow up to be what you are?" he wondered aloud.

"How could we have been any different? When you grow up fending for yourself, you get strong because you have to be. Your instincts about people grow sharp because they have to be. And you trust the law because you never learned to trust anything else."

"You're really something else, Cahill."

His phone rang, and she pointed to it. "Answer it," she said, and left his cubicle.

"So, have you thought about what you might want for your reward?" Genna slowed her stride as she and Julianne approached the drugstore. Her heart was beating like crazy. She'd been in more dangerous situations, surely, but she could count on the fingers of one hand the number that had held such personally high stakes. She'd gotten Julianne out of the Valley of the Angels. Could she get her out of Linden?

"I don't know." The girl shook her blonde head.

"Well, Eileen got a sketchpad, and Caroline picked out a journal. Maybe something along those lines?" Genna opened the door to the store and held it until the girl stepped inside.

"I'm afraid I'm not much of an artist."

"A journal is nice to write your thoughts in."

"My father . . ." she began, then stopped.

"Your father what?" Genna asked casually.

"He doesn't like me to be secretive. He always tells me to talk everything over with him." She smiled faintly.

"But every girl has her secrets," Genna whispered conspiratorially.

"I don't." The admission seemed almost apologetic.

"You tell your father everything?"

"He likes to know what I'm thinking about." Julianne stopped to look over a package of faux tortoise-shell hair clips. "I guess it's because I don't have a mom. That's why he makes me stay with him and Pamela, in their apartment, instead of in the cabins with the other girls. He wants me to know her."

Genna had seen Jules with his new young wife. She was pretty and blonde and, well, young. Barely of legal age, Genna guessed, though she suspected that Jules Douglas was just too smart to take an underage bride.

"You stay with them, not in a cabin, like the other

girls?" Genna asked, though she knew. It appeared Jules used his position as one of the reverend's financial advisers to keep his daughter from harm's way. For that, Genna grudgingly gave him credit.

"My dad says a family should stay together."

"Well, the cabins are a bit crowded. And I'm sure your father likes to have you close to him," Genna said. *And your father would probably like to keep you from forming any attachments that might cause you to ask too many questions when girls you become close to disappear.*

As she'd anticipated, Genna had had a hard time getting Jules to agree to permit Julianne to leave the compound today. Only the fact that Reverend Prescott approved of Genna's mission and would be sending Daniel to accompany them persuaded Jules to let his daughter leave the Valley of the Angels. Genna was grateful for Prescott's backing. There was something about Jules Douglas that she found menacing. The sooner she could get Julianne away from him and back in her mother's arms, the happier Genna would be.

"I think I like this little dish." Julianne stopped in front of a display of small ceramic items. "See, it has a little lid."

She carefully lifted the box to show Genna. "It has a tiny pink flower painted inside."

"Pretty, yes." Genna peered inside. "But what will you put in it?"

"Tiny stones, maybe." Julianne smiled. "Or other pretty little things I find."

"Sounds like a winner. Let's take it." Genna gestured for Julianne to follow her to the front of the

store and the cash register, where she paid the un-
smiling clerk for their purchase.

The middle-aged woman hadn't been the only person in Linden to show a lack of friendliness to Genna
and her charges over the past few weeks. It was an
odd position for Genna to be in. She'd made a solid
place for herself in the Bureau by being one who always fit in, wherever she was. Here in Linden, she
was the odd man out, identified as a member of Reverend Prescott's followers by the white scarf she wore
around her neck. Apparently the good people of Linden had their reservations about strangers, especially
those who dwelled in the Valley of the Angels.

As well they should have, Genna thought as she accepted her change and pocketed it. *What will they
think, once the reverend's little empire is exposed for
what it is?*

She could almost hear the interviews on CNN and
the morning news shows. "We always knew there
was something going on out there. . . ."

Soon enough, Genna told herself as she took Julianne by the arm and leaned into the wind that snaked
around them and blew the snow in whirls of icy mist.

Soon enough, of course, assuming that those who
were responsible for their escape from here on out
had everything in place. Genna simply had to trust.

The Jeep was still where Daniel had parked it outside the grocery store, but Daniel was nowhere to be
seen. They were just crossing the street when Julianne
tugged at her sleeve and said, "Look, there's Daniel."

They stopped in the middle of the street.

"Who are those men he's talking to?" she asked, and pointed to the three men in black who surrounded Daniel at the entrance to the store.

"Maybe someone from the compound." Genna hurried the girl toward the sidewalk on the opposite side of the street.

"They're not. At least, I don't think they are." Julianne had paused to study them. "I've never seen any of those men before."

"Well, I'm sure Daniel knows them, or he wouldn't be talking to them. Come on, Julianne. The diner is another block up the street. It's freezing, and I'm starving. Have you thought about what you might like?"

Minutes later, Genna and Julianne were seated in the diner, shaking off the cold. Every few minutes, Julianne looked out the window, as if watching for someone.

"Is something wrong?" Genna finally asked.

"I was just wondering if Daniel . . . if he was in some kind of trouble." Julianne looked up and down the street.

"I'm sure if he'd been in trouble he'd have said something while we were crossing the street."

"Can I bring you a nice hot cup of hot chocolate, honey?" The tall blonde waitress appeared with their menus. "It's pretty nippy out there today."

"Thank you." Julianne smiled. "I love hot chocolate."

"You, miss?" the waitress asked Genna.

"Coffee would be fine. Thanks."

They were ready with their sandwich orders when the waitress returned with their hot drinks.

"It's been so long since I've been in a restaurant," Julianne told Genna. "Thank you for bringing me here."

"You don't travel with your father when he leaves the compound?"

"No. He doesn't like me to leave. He didn't want me to come today," Julianne said sheepishly.

"What does he think will happen to you?"

"I think he thinks I'm going to be kidnapped or something." Julianne shrugged.

"Why would he think that?" Genna asked.

"I don't know." She shrugged again. "Maybe he doesn't really."

"You mentioned your mother earlier. . . ."

"She died when I was little." Julianne tore a tiny hole in the corner of her paper napkin.

"How little?" Genna asked.

"I was five."

"That's old enough to remember her," Genna said. "I hope you have some good memories of her."

"I don't know. Sometimes I think I do, remember things, that is. But when I ask my father, he says I should just put it all out of my mind. That it was a long time ago and none of that matters now."

"I lost my mother when I was nine or ten," Genna confided. "And it still matters."

"Did she die, too?"

"Eventually." Even now, Genna found it hard to talk about her past, about the parents who abandoned her, about the life she'd led up until the time

the state had placed her in the foster care of Patsy
Wheeler. Genna recalled that time as one of fear and
uncertainty, until she realized that with Patsy, she'd
found her home. Her heart ached for Julianne, for all
she would go through during the coming weeks and
months. Before the next forty-eight hours had passed,
Julianne would lose one parent and find another. She
prayed that the shock wouldn't devastate the child.

"You were old enough to remember your mother,
too," Julianne was saying.

"Yes. I remember her." Not always fondly, Genna
thought of the weak woman who had permitted a
tyrannical husband to rule their lives with an iron fist
and who had made fire and brimstone a part of their
everyday lives.

"I guess your dad raised you, too," Julianne continued.

"No. No, he died, too." Why go into that now?
Genna mentally shrugged it off. She was grateful
when the waitress appeared with their sandwiches.

"I love potato chips." Julianne grinned as she
munched a chip. "We almost never have them at the
compound. Mrs. Miller says they're fatty and greasy
and unwholesome. That's her favorite word. Unwholesome."

Genna bit into a pickle and wondered if Mrs.
Miller, the cook, knew of her boss's penchant for
young girls. Now *that* was unwholesome.

"Can I get you some more hot chocolate?" asked
Jayne, the waitress.

Julianne nodded. "Thank you." She turned and

looked out the window. "Oh-oh. Look at the snow. . . ."

"It is starting to come down, isn't it?" Genna bit the inside of her lower lip, wondering if the snow would help or hinder their escape.

"I wonder where Daniel is." Julianne stared out the window.

"Maybe he got held up someplace."

"I hope he comes for us before it starts snowing too hard."

"Don't worry. We'll be out of here in no time." Genna glanced up at Jayne as the waitress served Julianne's hot chocolate.

"You worried about getting a ride someplace?" Jayne asked.

"I'm sure our friend will show up soon," Genna replied.

"Well, hey, I'm off in about fifteen minutes. I'd be happy to drop you someplace."

"That's very nice of you, but I'm sure our ride will be along," Genna assured her.

"The offer stands," Jayne said. "Just say the word . . ."

"That's nice of her," Julianne noted after Jayne had cleared the table and disappeared into the kitchen.

"Very," Genna agreed.

"But I know Daniel will be along soon." Julianne yawned.

"Tired, sweetie?" Genna asked softly.

"I don't know why I am." Julianne covered her mouth as she yawned again. "I just feel so sleepy. . . ."

Genna looked across the diner and met Jayne's

eyes. Jayne nodded and returned to the kitchen. Moments later she came back out, her coat over her arm.

"Well, I'm leaving now. Are you sure you don't want me to drop you off?" she called to Genna.

"Well, maybe you could drive us a few blocks down, and we'll see if our ride is ready," Genna called back. "How 'bout that, Julianne? If the waitress drives us back to where Daniel left the car?"

"Not supposed to get into anyone's car except Daniel's."

"I know, sweetie, but this one time will be fine."

To Jayne, Genna whispered, "Was it necessary to sedate her?"

"Sorry, but yes. We need to get her out, and get her out fast. She'll be fine, Genna. Won't even have a headache when she wakes up. But I couldn't run the risk that she'd be kicking and screaming all the way across the parking lot. We just don't have time for that. There really wasn't any option."

Genna slipped into her coat, then helped the sleepy Julianne ease her arms into the sleeves of her jacket. With a nod to Jayne, the two women and the girl left the diner.

"This is my car," Jayne said, pointing to a black Jeep with tinted windows.

"It looks just like the reverend's car," Julianne said as the two women helped her into the backseat and fastened her seat belt.

"You strap in, too, Genna," Jayne told her as she hopped into the driver's side and slammed the door. "We really have to fly now."

"Why are we flying?" a sleepy voice asked from the back.

"Because we have to get you home, little girl." Genna turned around to see Julianne's chin rest upon her chest, her eyes closed. "You've been gone a long, long time, and now it's time to go home. . . ."

CHAPTER SIXTEEN

THE STORM HAD PASSED WITHIN THE HOUR, AND BY three-fifteen, after a minor delay, the plane took off. Miranda gazed out the window as the plane rose into the clouds, which had just started to lift, then closed her eyes. She hated takeoffs and landings. It wasn't so much that she knew the statistics, that most planes that crashed did so either while headed up or headed down. It was more the change in direction. She liked being on an even keel. Too much up or too much down disturbed her equilibrium and made her feel out of control somehow. And if there was one thing Miranda could not tolerate, it was the sense of not being in control.

She leaned back against the seat and feigned sleep. She didn't want to talk to anyone right now, particularly Will, who sat in the seat next to her, flipping through the latest *GQ* that he'd picked up at the airport's newsstand. She fully understood the similarities between her relationship with Will and her mother's relationship with her father. That on-again, off-again thing—no strings, no commitment—may have been fine for Nancy Cahill, back in the day, but it wasn't fine for her daughter. Not this day, not any day. Lucky for Miranda she'd figured it out in time. She could work with Will; she could socialize with Will; but they'd never be lovers again, because as far as she could see, they'd never be anything more than that.

But when she asked herself what more she wanted from him, she had no answer. None that she felt like dealing with, anyway.

She shifted uncomfortably in her seat, annoyed that she'd let Will draw her into a conversation about Jack. She refused to call him anything but that. Just Jack. As if by refusing to acknowledge him by anything other than his first name, she could disavow their blood relationship.

She'd always been better at that than Portia. She wondered if Jack had sent Portia a separate packet of photos. If he'd sent them to the house she and her sister shared, Miranda would have seen them. Maybe he'd intended for them to share the photos, though wouldn't he have addressed the envelope to both of them? Unless he knew that Portia wasn't there.

Of course Jack knew Portia wasn't there; Miranda mentally slapped herself on the forehead with an open palm. She'd been in London last month on a short leave. She must have called him.

I'll bet every dime I have that she called him.

The thought was so jarring that she sat straight up in her seat. Will looked over at her, one eyebrow raised in question.

"Just . . . dreaming, I guess." She muttered the first thing that came into her mind.

"You weren't sleeping," he noted, and went back to the article he was reading.

"I was almost asleep," she lied, and settled herself back into her seat again.

The more she thought about it, the more she knew that her sister had met with the enemy. Over the years, Portia had brought up contacting Jack many times, and Miranda had always blown her off. Well, Portia must have tired of waiting for her twin to come around, and had contacted him on her own. How else to explain the photos, the chatty letter, arriving out of the blue after all this time? To the best of her knowledge, he'd never shown much interest in either of his firstborns. Why now, unless Portia had pushed him?

She tried to move past the growing anger, but she found she could not. It was mixed too tightly with a lifetime of bad feelings and a sense of betrayal. She tried not to think about the photographs Jack had sent, but the scenes kept playing over and over in her mind. She'd lied to Will when she'd said she didn't remember. Of course she remembered.

They'd spent the day on the beach, she and Portia and their mother and Jack, whom Miranda remembered as being impossibly tall, to her eye, the tallest man in the world. And he was strong, strong enough to carry Miranda on one shoulder and Portia on the other. Nancy had stayed on the blanket and snapped that little camera of hers just about every time one of them moved, so that if you placed the pictures in order and fanned them slowly, it was almost like watching a film. Portia used to do that, stack them in order and then flip them, so that she could watch Jack pick her up and plunk her down on his shoulder, then lean over to pick up Miranda and do the same with her. Then he walked for what seemed like forever down the beach, his daughters on his shoulders, all the time talking to them in that deep Brit voice about a beach in England he used to go to as a child, and how he'd take them there sometime.

Of course, he never had. It was all just a game to Jack.

Miranda remembered, too, how her mother had cried herself to sleep the next night, after Jack left. How her face went pale a week later when a photo of him with another of his celebrity girlfriends appeared on the cover of a magazine. There was always someone new for Jack, some beautiful model or singer— or, yes, even a princess. In the magazines, there was always someone young and beautiful on his arm, but never Nancy, who was not beautiful nor particularly talented nor clever—nor was she royal. She was the daughter of two science teachers from a tiny town outside Omaha. Every time Nancy saw one of those photographs, she'd crumble, and she'd stay crumbled for days, leaving her daughters pretty much to fend for themselves until she snapped out of it.

When Miranda was old enough to understand the situation, she'd yelled at her mother for having gone into one of her funks after seeing Jack on some award show.

"Mom, would you look at yourself?" Miranda had lectured. "You're wasting your life waiting for a man whose greatest love is himself. He thinks he's done just swell by you. He's given you two kids and a steady income until we turn twenty-five, isn't that what you said the deal was? Why do you keep pining for him, for a man who doesn't love you? Every once in a while he drifts back into your life, and you let him."

"But he does love me," her mother had responded quietly, "and that's why he keeps coming back. That's why I let him."

Miranda had been so shocked that she hadn't known how to reply. So she'd simply left the room, and she never brought up the subject again. It had been years before she'd even repeated the conversation to Portia, who had her own ideas about the relationship between their mother and Jack.

"I do believe he loves her," Portia had told her. "I think she's probably the only bit of sanity in his entire life. She's his rock, and he keeps coming back to her to get the rest of it out of his system."

"Then he's just plain selfish," Miranda had snapped. "If he's just using her to make himself feel good, he doesn't care about her, and he certainly doesn't care about us."

"I don't know." Portia had been surprisingly kind in her judgment. "I don't know what he thinks or what he feels or what motivates him. But I do know that he must care about Mum, or he'd just forget about us."

"Don't say 'mum,' " Miranda had exploded. "It's too . . . *English*."

Portia had flounced off in a huff, and it had been a while before they'd talked about the relationship between Jack and their mother again.

She's seen him, Miranda told herself. *Portia has been to see Jack.*

"Damn her." She spoke aloud without realizing it.

"Damn who?" Will asked.

"No one," she grumbled.

"Hey, Cahill, you want to talk about anything, you know—"

"Yeah, yeah. I know. You're there if I need you."

He laughed.

"I'm sorry," she said. "That was rude. I know you're trying to be a friend, and I appreciate it."

"Sure," he said. "Buckle up. We're getting ready to land. Or did you miss the announcement while you were busy cursing out whoever it was who incurred your wrath?"

"I missed the announcement." She searched for her seat belt. "I must have dozed off."

"Uh-huh."

"Shut up and strap yourself in like a good boy."

Twenty-five minutes later they were picking up their rental car and heading toward Wynnefield on the Ohio-Kentucky border. Will drove while Miranda called the Wynnefield police and spoke with the sergeant, who gave her the good news. They'd located Ronald Johnson; he was working in a restaurant in Gilbert just ten miles away.

"We have a live one," Miranda told Will when she ended the call. "The sergeant said to take a left onto Essington Road just before we get into Wynnefield. It should be coming up in about a mile or so."

"What's the name of the restaurant?"

"Buckeye Bob's."

"Cute."

"I'm sure someone thought so."

"Did the sergeant say if Johnson remembered Channing?"

"I didn't get the impression that they questioned him. I think they just located him and confirmed that he's the same Ronald Johnson."

"Well, then, I guess he's all ours."

"Guess he is." Miranda stared out the window. Autumn had come and gone here, leaving the trees mostly bare.

"It's almost Halloween," she said. "Few more days . . ."

"What?"

"I said, it will be Halloween in a few days."

"I wondered why I keep having this sudden urge to rip the sheet off the bed and cut holes in it."

"I would have expected something more creative from you. Please don't disillusion me by telling me that the white sheet was your costume of choice."

"Actually, I didn't have a favorite costume. I mean, I didn't have costumes."

"They didn't trick-or-treat where you grew up?"

"Well, yeah, they did. At least, everyone else did."

"Are you saying you never trick-or-treated?" She frowned. "Every kid trick-or-treats on Halloween, Fletcher."

"Not quite everyone."

"So what was the deal? Chocolate allergy? Fear of rubber masks and fake teeth?"

"My parents wouldn't let us go." He glanced over

with an odd smile plastered on his face. "Halloween is the devil's holiday. Didn't you know that?"

"Huh?"

"Sure. It's all about devil worship. It's a celebration of the occult."

"You believe that?"

"No. But my parents did."

"Wow." She tried to think of something more intelligent to say, but could not.

"Yeah, wow. That pretty much sums it up."

"I'm . . . I'm sorry, Will."

"Thank you, Cahill. That's the nicest thing you've said to me in a long time." He continued staring straight ahead. "What was the name of that road again?"

"Essington."

They drove in silence for another minute, then Miranda said, "It's kind of sad, don't you think, that we know so little about each other? I mean, we've slept together a dozen or so times, and we don't really know each other very well at all."

"I think the times we slept together, we weren't concerned about how well we knew each other."

"That doesn't speak well for either of us." There was a hint of regret in her voice.

"It's not too late, you know."

"For what?"

"To get to know each other."

"Maybe," she said softly.

"I'll take that as a yes."

"There's Essington up there at the light." She pointed.

"Are you trying to change the subject?"

"You betcha. Take a left here."

"And then what?"

"Then you go about three hundred yards to . . . yes, there it is. Buckeye Bob's. Right where it's supposed to be. Pull in here. . . ."

He made a right into the parking lot and stopped the car.

"What are you doing?"

"Waiting for you to tell me where to park."

"Very funny. Move it."

He grinned and made a wide circle in the parking lot before parking the car in a space near the front door.

"Is this close enough for you?" he asked.

"You are pushing your luck today, Fletcher." She got out of the car, slammed the door, and walked up the wide concrete steps, then paused at the top to wait for Will.

"I trust you'd like to do most of the talking," he said as he came up the steps.

"Well, I am lead on the case, but you can feel free to chime in at any time."

"I'll do that." He held the door for her, then held it a moment longer for the three women who were leaving the restaurant.

"Table for two?" the hostess asked.

"Please," Miranda said with a nod.

"It will be about five minutes."

"That's fine," Will told her, then stepped back so as not to block the doorway.

"What exactly does Mr. Johnson do here?"

"I think he's the manager."

"And this is his shift, right?"

"The sergeant said Johnson would be working tonight."

A waitress appeared and motioned for them to follow her to a booth toward the back. Miranda slid into her seat and shrugged out of her jacket.

"Oh, look. There's a sign that says they make old-fashioned milk shakes here." She was grinning from ear to ear. "Yum."

When the waitress reappeared with menus, Miranda shook her head. "Don't need the menu. I'll have a black-and-white milk shake and a burger."

Will suppressed a smile and ordered the same.

"Copycat," she taunted.

"It sounded too good to miss out on."

"Portia and I used to go to this little place when we visited our grandmother in Nebraska. Dolan's. They made the most incredible milk shakes ever. We'd arrive at the house and make nice with Gramma for a while, then when she and Mom would hunker down on the back porch with tea, Portia and I would race down to Dolan's." A cloud passed over her face briefly.

"What?" he asked.

"What what?"

"What was that little bit of a frown for?"

"Mr. Dolan wasn't always very nice to us. He knew our mother in school, and sometimes, when we came in, he'd make a big deal out of us." She lowered her voice. " 'Well, well, what have we here? Looks like

Nancy Cahill's little girls. How's your mother doing, girls? She ever get married?' "

"Wow. That's ugly." Will frowned. "Those must have been some great milk shakes, for you to keep going back there."

"He wasn't always there. Most times, someone else was working the counter. We used to sort of tiptoe in. If he wasn't around, we'd feel like the gods were smiling on us that day." She shrugged. "Besides, there was no other place to go in town, and I should also add that by the time we were eight or nine years old, we were used to hearing that in Morningside. This was a real small town, and everyone knew my mother's family. Everyone knew the story of how Nancy Cahill had spurned the local lads to take up with a wild Brit. And just look at what happened to her."

"Didn't it upset your mother when people said unkind things to you like that?"

"It would have killed her if she'd known. We just never told her." Miranda chewed on the inside of her bottom lip.

He started to say something when the waitress appeared with their order.

"Can I get you something else?" she asked.

"Actually, yes." Miranda smiled up at her. "Is Ronald Johnson available?"

"He's here," the waitress replied, "but I'm not sure if he's busy. Are you friends of Ron's?"

"Sort of." Miranda slipped her ID out of her pocket and laid it on the table. The waitress's eyes widened slightly, then flickered from Miranda's face to Will's, then back again.

"Could you tell him that we're here, and that we need to speak with him about someone who used to work for him?"

"Sure." She nodded. "Sure . . ."

She disappeared into the back room.

Before three minutes had passed, Ron Johnson, a balding man in his mid-fifties, with acne-pocked skin and thick glasses, appeared at their table. "You the folks who wanted to speak with me?"

"We are if you're Ron Johnson," Will responded.

"I am. What's this about someone who used to work for me?"

"Curtis Channing." Miranda slid over on the wooden bench and patted the seat next to her. "Can you join us for a few minutes?"

"Curtis Channing." Johnson sat. "I should have known it would be him. I read all about him. The papers were full of stuff about how he killed those women back in Pennsylvania, and how they traced him to some murders out here. I should have figured someone would be asking about him one of these days."

"We understand that he used to work for you."

"Yeah, yeah. 'Bout five, six years ago. The Red Door in Wynnefield."

"We heard you fired him."

"Yeah, well, he wouldn't work the last shift. Midnight till seven in the morning." Johnson shrugged. "You work at the Red Door, you work all the shifts. The place is open twenty-four hours a day, seven days a week. You can't opt out of the last shift."

"How did he take getting fired?" Will asked.

"As I remember, he just sort of nodded his head. Said okay. Took his apron off, hung it up, and left."

"That's it? He just left? He didn't argue, plead for his job, threaten you?" Miranda frowned.

"Nah, that wouldn't have been like Curtis. He never reacted to much of anything. Everything sort of rolled off his back, you know what I'm saying? Never saw him get angry with anyone. Just did his job, kept to himself. He was a good employee, except he refused to work late shift, so I had to let him go."

"He never got into arguments with any of the other employees? No bad blood between him and any of the others?" Miranda persisted.

"Not that I was aware of. Honestly, a more laid-back guy you'll never meet. Just did his thing, and when it was time, he moved on."

"You ever see him after he left the Red Door?"

Johnson shook his head. "Not until they flashed his picture on television a few months back. You coulda knocked me over with a feather. I said, no way is that Curt Channing. No fucking way." He turned to Miranda somewhat sheepishly. "Sorry. Forgot for a minute I wasn't in the kitchen."

She waved it off. "Can you think of anyone Channing might have had a problem with back then? Anyone he might have wanted to hurt. Someone who'd gotten in his way outside of work, maybe."

"He never talked about himself. Now that I think about it, he didn't talk much at all. He'd just come in, do his job, leave. Next day, same thing."

"How about the women on the job? How did he act toward them, do you remember?" Will asked.

"Respectful. Pleasant. Never even cursed when one of the waitresses was in the kitchen." Johnson shook his head. "No complaints about him. Some of the other guys, yeah. But never Curt. It just doesn't make sense, you know?"

Miranda handed him a card. "Will you call me if you remember anything else about Channing? Or if you think of someone who might have been on his shit list?"

"Sure thing," he said as he stood up, "but I gotta tell you, as far as I knew, Curt Channing didn't have a shit list. He was just a real nice, quiet guy. Never bothered anyone. That's why when all this stuff came out, man, I just couldn't believe it, you know? Like, I even said to my wife, they must be talking about some other Curtis Channing, because the one I knew, he just couldn't have been what they said—a serial killer. I just can't see him killing all those women." He looked down at Miranda. "You're sure it was him? Him that killed all those women?"

"We are sure. Absolutely, positively sure."

He shook his head again. "Boy, you just never really know about people, do you?"

Archer sat on the edge of the bed and chewed his last fingernail down as far as he could go and not have a mouthful of skin, and he tried not to blubber like the baby he knew he was.

He'd spent all day out at the edge of Landry's woods, watching the man go about his business and writing down what he did and when, just like Burt insisted. He hadn't done it right on Monday, and Burt's eyes had gone all thin and dark. It scared Archer when he squinted like that.

"You need to write the times down." Burt had smacked Archer on top of the head with his open hand. "You're looking for a *pattern* here, asshole. How you gonna figure out a pattern if you don't write down the times?"

So on Tuesday, then yesterday, and again today, Archer had dutifully written down times. The time Landry came outside, the time he went into the barn, the time he came out. When he walked out to the pond, when he came back. When the other man came out to the field to call him back, when they both went inside. Archer thought it was all a waste of time, but he wasn't about to tell Burt that.

Today on the way home, Burt had made Archer read his notes aloud.

"Hmmm," he had said. "So the old man goes out in the morning, strolls around, then someone else comes out and makes him come back in. Wonder who that is?"

"Don't know." Archer had shrugged. "And then both days, a police car came up the drive around eleven, and again around one, and then around three."

"Wonder what that's all about." Burt had gone quiet for a long time. "Cops coming by every couple a hours."

"They don't stay long or nothing. They just turn around in the drive. This morning, one of them got out and went up to the door and knocked on it. When they came by later, Mr. Landry was already outside, and they stopped and talked for a while with him and the other man. Then when the police left, Mr. Landry went into the barn and came back out with something in his hand, I couldn't see what."

"Time them again tomorrow," Burt said, "then maybe we can probably nail it."

"Huh?"

"If the pattern holds, then the day after tomorrow will be the day for you to do Landry." Burt never turned his head; he just kept looking straight ahead, and talked as if they were planning a trip to the beach. "Once you have the pattern down, that's all you need to know. You hit between visits from the police. All you need to know now is how and when to hit. I have an idea about that. . . ."

Archer's palms sweated just remembering the conversation. He didn't want to kill Mr. Landry. He didn't want to kill anyone. He wanted to go home. That's all. He just wanted to go home.

He searched the pockets of his jeans for his wallet. In one of the small compartments was the card Miranda Cahill had given him. He'd folded it up so that Burt couldn't find it, if he decided to look through Archer's wallet, and who's to say he wouldn't do just that one of these days? Archer unfolded the card and studied the phone number, trying to memorize it. In his jacket pocket was the cell phone Burt had given him. Archer thought about getting the phone and calling the pretty FBI agent and just telling her everything. Everything about Curtis and Vince and him and the game. About getting out of High Meadow and planning on forgetting he'd ever met them, ever talked to them, ever played that stupid fucking game. Then Burt came along. Burt had made him kill Unger, was making him kill Landry. And if Archer didn't figure out a way out of it, that was exactly what he was going to have to do. The thought of taking another life sickened him.

The thought of defying Burt sickened him even more.

He got up and went into the bathroom and turned on the light, then stared at his reflection for a long time. He wasn't a killer. He'd never wanted to be a killer.

When he'd started this whole thing, he had no idea what it would be like. He wished he'd never had to go into that room with Curtis and Vince that day. Wished he'd never met either one of them. Wished he'd kept his damn big mouth shut.

It had sounded so tough, so cool. *Yeah, let's talk about who we'd do when we get out.*

God, he didn't know it would be like this.

Tears rolled down his face, and he didn't even bother to wipe them away. One way or another, no matter what he did now, he was fucked.

CHAPTER SEVENTEEN

ARCHER MADE HIS WAY THROUGH THE EARLY-MORNING mist and listened to the engine of Burt's truck fade into the distance. Today was the day, Burt had declared when he woke him up at four that morning.

"Today's the day," he'd growled as he shook Archer awake. "Get up and get moving. You have a job to do."

Archer had all but frozen to the bed. *I don't want to get up. I don't want to do this job,* he'd longed to protest. But the words stuck in his mouth, as words in defiance of Burt's orders always did. As terrified as Archer was of killing another man, the thought of what Burt would do to him if he refused terrified him even more.

So he had gotten up and gotten dressed and gotten into the pickup while it was still dark, and he rode with Burt in the silent truck through the dawn. When they came to the place where Burt always stopped to let Archer out, Burt asked, "You know what you're going to do, right?"

"Right." Archer's head nodded jerkily. "Sure. Right. I know what I'm going to do."

"You're going to hide in the barn. . . ."

"I said I know." Archer jumped out of the truck and slammed the door before Burt could reach across the seat and slam it in his face. He set off down the dark road in the direction of the woods he'd come to know well over the past week.

In his pocket was the cell phone and the tiny folded-up card with Miranda Cahill's phone number on it. All the way through the quiet woods he debated. What would happen to him if he called and told her everything? Would she send someone to get him, someone who could protect him from Burt? Maybe even arrest Burt?

"What could they arrest him for?" Archer mumbled aloud as he picked his way through the dark. Burt hadn't shot anyone. Was it a crime to make someone else do something like that? Archer wasn't sure, but he thought it might be. Then again, he had no proof. It would be his word against Burt's. Who would the law believe?

Probably not me, Archer lamented as he reached the edge of the field. No one ever had . . .

He leaned back against a tree and sighed deeply. He'd flip a coin. Heads, he'd call the FBI; tails, he wouldn't. He took a quarter from his pocket and flipped it into the air, but he couldn't see where it landed. He got down on his hands and knees and searched the ground, but the coin was nowhere to be found.

"It figures," he muttered as he walked the tree line down to the fallen log he'd used as a perch the previous days.

He took the cell phone from his pocket and turned

it on but did not dial. Instead he sat for a long while, staring at the farmhouse just a few hundred feet away, and thinking. The man who slept in there had only a few more hours to live, and it would be he, Archer Lowell, who would be pulling the trigger. Not Burt. Not Vince Giordano. Archer Lowell. He'd killed one man so far, and he'd hated it. He hated the thought of doing it again.

He took the card from his pocket and unfolded it slowly. He studied the number, then started to dial, and stopped. Started, then stopped. Finally, he made up his mind, and dialed.

If she answers, it means I have to tell her. If she doesn't . . .

The phone rang six times. Finally, on the sixth ring, he heard a click, then, "Hi, you've reached Miranda Cahill. I can't take your call right now, but if you'll—"

He turned off the phone and sat shaking, looking over his shoulder, expecting Burt to jump out at him, take the gun from Archer's own pocket, and shoot him with it.

Maybe the other number on the card . . .

He dialed the second number.

"This is Miranda Cahill. Please leave a message . . ."

Archer sighed heavily, wondering what message he could leave. By the time she got it, Burt would probably be back, looking for him. If he hadn't killed Mr. Landry by then, well, it wasn't much worth thinking about, was it?

There was no way out, Archer knew that now. Turning off the phone, he stuck it back in his pocket and started off across the field in the direction of the barn. Sick to his stomach, he stopped partway and lost the little bit of breakfast he'd had that morning.

At the back door of the barn, he paused and took the screwdriver and flashlight from his pocket. Holding the small light in his teeth, he carefully removed the screws that held the lock and bolt on the door. He slipped the three screws into his shirt pocket and opened the door slowly, quietly, though he knew no one was in there. No animals lived there, either. It was like the barn was just for show. Well, for show and for storing Mr. Landry's gardening tools. If today was to be like every other day this week, in a few hours from now, Mr. Landry would come out of the house and walk to the pond, where he'd watch the ducks for a while. Then he'd go into the barn and get a rake or some other garden thing. He'd rake leaves or something around the flower beds for about twenty minutes, then he'd put the rake or whatever away. At some point—usually while Mr. Landry was working in the garden—the other man would come out and talk to Mr. Landry, and pretty soon they'd go back into the house.

Archer climbed the ladder to the loft and settled himself down in a spot where he had a clear view of the door. If Mr. Landry was alone, he was supposed to shoot him then. If the other man was there, he'd have to wait until later in the day and hope that Mr. Landry came back out without the other man following right away.

He hunkered down on the hard wooden floor, the gun in his hand, and waited for the door to open. He would not permit himself to think any more about what he was going to do when Joshua Landry stepped through it.

Archer had all but fallen asleep waiting. His one arm had gone numb, and he'd just sat up and leaned back against the wall, shaking the arm to get the blood flowing again, when he heard the latch lift on the wide door below him. He rested his head on the wall behind him, shaking his head slowly and fighting back the tears. Then, knowing there was no use, there was no way out now, he stretched his neck to look down into the barn.

Now or never . . .

Josh Landry pushed the door open just enough to walk through it. He stood with his back to Archer and sorted through some garden implements as if searching for just the right one. He'd just reached out for one when the first bullet whizzed past him on the left. Landry jumped back, ducked, and looked around the barn.

"What the—"

The second bullet passed him on the right.

"Son of a bitch," Landry yelled.

The third bullet struck him in the chest, and he fell back, a surprised look on his face. The fourth and fifth bullets missed the mark, but the sixth hit near the third, taking him all the way down to the ground. As if in a daze, Archer came down the ladder holding on with one hand, the gun still in the other.

Just as he got to the bottom, the door was flung open, and the other man stood there, a gun held in front of him as he scanned the interior. Before he turned in Archer's direction, Archer fired twice. The man fell, his gun useless now.

A loud discordant hum in his brain, Archer Lowell ran out the back door and fled for the shelter of the woods.

"This is getting old," Miranda grumbled as she climbed into the passenger seat of Will's car the next morning. "Old, old, old . . ."

"Hey, you were the one who wanted to work on Saturday, remember? I was just as happy to work from home."

"Well, after losing half a day, yesterday, chasing our tails in Ohio . . ." She snapped her seat belt closed. "All that way just to find out that Curtis Channing had been a model employee. Who'd have thought that?"

"Yeah, the least he could have done was show a little hostility toward the waitresses. Give us something to work with."

"Shut up and drive." She sank into her seat.

"I see we're just a little ray of sunshine this morning."

She glared at him.

"No coffee this morning, Cahill?"

"I was out."

"Uh-oh. We all know what that means."

"I said shut up, Fletcher."

He chuckled, further incurring her wrath, but he redeemed himself when he pulled into the first convenience store they came to.

"No, no, you stay right there," he told her as he got out of the car. "I'll get your coffee."

"I'll come in." She opened the passenger door. "You don't have to go in for me."

"I do if I ever want to shop here again. God only knows what kind of damage you could do to my reputation, the mood you're in. . . ."

She slammed the door closed again and sat back in the seat.

Will was back in under five minutes, a cardboard carrier holding three cups of coffee in one hand, a bag in the other.

"I got you an extra cup. And look, Cahill. Doughnuts." He got into the car slowly, trying not to tip the cups. He tossed the bag in her general direction, then looked over at her when the bag hit the floor. "Hey, you were supposed to catch—"

Miranda sat stock-still, her phone up to her ear, her face white. "Fuck," she yelled. "Fuck!"

"What . . . ?"

She got out of the car and paced the parking lot wildly. She looked stricken, furious.

Will followed her, pinned her up against the car, and took the phone from her hand.

"What happened? What?"

"Landry is dead." She spat the words at him. "The Plainsville police found his body about forty minutes ago."

"Jesus." He appeared momentarily stunned. "What about Phillips?"

"He's in the emergency room at Princeton Hospital. He took one shot, but he'll survive." She pushed

Will away with a two-handed shove to the chest. "Son of a bitch! How the hell is this little wienie getting away with this shit?"

Before he could answer, she'd taken off around the car and was getting back in.

"Drive," she pleaded. "Get back in and drive."

All the way to Plainsville, she muttered curses under her breath, stopping only long enough to make those phone calls she knew she needed to make. The first was to John Mancini. The second was to the Plainsville police for an update.

"You were supposed to be watching this guy," she'd said in her most controlled voice. "Why weren't you watching him?"

"Hey, we don't have enough officers to have one stationed twenty-four hours a day watching any one individual, okay?" the chief of police had spat back. "And besides, since the FBI had a man there, we figured Mr. Landry was in good hands. So why don't you ask your own man what happened, Agent Cahill? Ask him what he was doing while Josh Landry was being shot and killed on *his* watch."

"I just can't believe this." She shook her head after she'd hung up the phone. "I can't believe that Archer Lowell has pulled this off. Where the hell was Art Phillips?"

She leaned forward and turned to Will. "How could he have outsmarted us, not once, but twice? How could he have shot not only Landry, but the agent who was supposed to be watching Landry? What is wrong with this picture?"

"All reasonable questions." Will accelerated as he

hit the highway. "Ones I intend to ask of Phillips, assuming he lives."

"He'll live. It didn't sound as if his injuries were that serious." She sat back in her seat and exhaled. "This is the damnedest case I ever worked, I swear it is."

"Drink your coffee, Cahill, and calm down a little."

"I don't want to calm down. I'm so pissed off right now—"

"I understand. I feel every bit as pissed off as you do. But save it for when it will do some good. Right now, drink your coffee."

She took one of the cups from the holder, peeled back a portion of the plastic lid, and passed it to Will, then fixed one for herself. She sipped at it for a few minutes, watching the highway fly by.

"I really liked him, Will," she said without turning her head from the window. "Landry. I really liked the man."

"So did I."

"And his daughter. I liked her, too. This is going to be just terrible for her." She looked at Will. "She trusted us. She knew that we knew her father could be in danger, and she trusted us to keep him safe."

"There has to be some reason why it was so easy for Lowell to get to Landry. Before we castigate ourselves or Phillips, let's find out what happened."

"I hate this case. It's been a total screwup right from the start."

"It happens sometimes. Sometimes, no matter how well you think you're doing the job, something, someone, screws up, and it's bad right on through to the end." His jaw set tightly. He didn't want to think about what might mark the end of Archer Lowell's run.

So far, it was bad guy 2, good guys 0. And the third and last name on the list might very well be Miranda's.

Well, he can't have her. I will personally rip his heart out before I let him have her. I will shove that gun of his so far up his—

"What's that for?" she was asking.

"What?"

"That look on your face. Jesus, Fletcher, you looked like you're going to rip someone's head off."

"Close enough," he muttered. "Close enough . . ."

The local crime scene techs were already at work in Landry's barn and in the fields when Miranda and Will arrived. The first person they saw when they got out of the car was Regan Landry. She stared at the two agents with red-rimmed eyes set in a face that was almost blank with disbelief. Miranda stopped to speak with her, but it was clear that the woman was in shock.

"Regan, is there someone I can call for you?" Miranda asked gently.

Regan shook her head no.

"A friend, maybe. A relative?"

Again, the blonde head moved slowly, side to side.

"I shouldn't have left him," she said. "I should have known he was going to play this his own way."

"I'm so sorry," Miranda told her. "I don't know what to say—"

"If I told him once, I told him fifty times this week. Agent Phillips is here for a reason, stop treating this like a game. He took every opportunity to slip away, outside, alone. He wanted to confront the killer," Regan said without taking her eyes from the open barn door. "He was fascinated by the thought that he was a potential victim. Can you believe it?"

She turned to Miranda and grabbed her arm.

"He thought it would make a wonderful book. He already had pages of notes . . . what he would write. He had it all planned. He thought he'd be able to talk the killer out of doing what he'd come to do. . . ."

"He thought he could talk Lowell out of killing him?" Miranda appeared stunned.

Tears welled in the corners of her eyes. "My father was such an arrogant man. He thought that because he wrote so intimately about death, he'd be able to talk his way around it. That because he studied the criminal mind, he could influence it."

"Regan, I'm so sorry." Miranda tried to comfort her. "I know we promised to protect him—"

"You don't understand," Regan said. "He didn't want to be protected, didn't believe he needed it. He truly and honestly wanted to handle this his own way. He was looking forward to confronting his would-be murderer."

She shook her head again, the tears falling freely. "Such arrogance. *Damn* him."

CHAPTER
EIGHTEEN

"So what do we do now?" Miranda stood with her hands on her hips, watching one pair of techs dust the back door of the barn for prints while another made a cast of several footprints leading from the barn to the woods beyond Landry's farm. The entire property was swarming with representatives of several law enforcement agencies, from the local Plainsville police officers, to the county detectives and crime scene investigators, to FBI.

"I think we put you in a locked room somewhere under heavy guard," Will replied.

She started to make a smart remark, but the look on his face assured her he wasn't kidding.

"What's your second choice?" she asked, hoping to take the tension down a notch.

"There is no second choice."

"Will, I think—"

"Hey, there's Mancini." Will nodded in the direction of the drive, where a black car had just emptied of its passengers. "John and someone else—looks like Lucy Martinez and Colin Moss. I'm impressed. They're bringing out the big guns for this one."

"I'm not surprised. The Bureau has serious egg on

its face right now. I'm sure they're going to do everything possible to keep the story from the press." Miranda watched John approach Plainsville's chief of police. The two other agents stood by, surveying the scene.

"You think anyone will put it together?" Will asked.

"Not without help from the inside, and that won't be coming from me."

"I worry about the locals, though. Once the bullet is tested, if it comes back a match to the one that took out Unger, there will be some who are going to want to talk about it."

"That's why the boss is here. He's going to schmooze the locals, look at him with the chief there. He'll have him eating out of his hand in no time."

"John's pretty smooth," she admitted, "but I don't know if he's smooth enough to keep this under wraps."

"Well, he's taking the chief off for a walk, just the two of them." Will watched for another moment, then said, "My money's on John. He is not going to want this all over the news."

"Well, I guess we'll see how good he is at keeping the lid on." She stepped out of the drive to permit a crime scene lab van to pull past them. "Of course, the press has been all over Landry's death since this morning. They are going to want some answers. Starting with cause of death and who pulled the trigger."

"Josh Landry was pretty famous," he reminded her. "And you're right. The media is all over the story.

I wouldn't be a bit surprised if John wasn't helping the chief there to compose his official statement."

"How long does it take to say 'no comment'?"

A helicopter hovered overhead.

"See what I mean?" He looked skyward. "Network news is already in on it."

"What do you suppose is going on out there?" She nodded to the tree line, where a number of officers had gathered.

"Let's go find out."

They trudged across the field to the edge of the woods.

"What do you have?" Will asked as they approached the small group.

"Looks like the killer had the house under watch for a few days. Lots of different prints out here in the field, but the ones around the trees there, they look like they might have been made with the same shoe, but on different days. See here." The tech knelt down and pointed to the ground. "There are several prints, some are deeper than others, but they're the same tread. It rained earlier in the week, the ground would have been soft, the impression would have been deeper than a print made yesterday would have been."

"Because yesterday the ground was dry." Miranda nodded.

"Right." The tech stood up and pointed along the edge of the field. "We're casting them just to make sure; could be some might have been made by kids, but I don't think so. Then there are the prints from the police officers who checked the woods the other day. And there are a number of deer prints; most of them are pretty much in a steady line. Creatures of habits, deer are. But the footprints, they go all the way back to the road on the other side of the woods."

"So someone might have parked a car over there and walked here?" Miranda thought aloud.

"Maybe. More likely he'd have left it down the road about a quarter mile. There's a little side road; someone could have left a car there. If he'd left it here, out in the open, someone would have reported a car parked there for too long at a time. We don't have any such reports." The young man removed his hat, smoothed back his hair, and replaced the hat. "There are tracks along the side of the road. Not sure it's worth casting them, too. There are cars going back and forth all the time."

"If he was walking a quarter mile back and forth on this road, maybe someone saw him," Will noted.

"Could be. We'll be stopping cars for the next few days, see if anyone remembers seeing someone walking along the road, or a vehicle parked up along that dirt road. This narrow old road is mostly used by the old-timers around here. Most of the new folks going between Plainsville and Route One will use the Plainsville–Junction Road. A guy travels this road every day for fifty years, he'll know when he sees something that's out of place. We're setting up an officer right now to stop cars and start asking questions. Best we can hope for is that someone will have seen something that struck him or her as being unusual. Maybe get a description we can go with."

"You'll keep our office apprised of your findings?"
Will asked.

"Sure thing." The tech nodded, then went back to
work.

"How did Lowell do this, Will? He doesn't drive,"
she reminded him as they walked back toward the
barn. "How did he get here? How did he go back and
forth from wherever he's staying? How is he getting
around?"

"Your guess is as good as mine." They walked
along, both thinking. Finally, Will said, "I think it's
time to put out an APB on Lowell."

"I totally agree. Let's see if we can flush him out. I
do think we should check in with the boss, though,
find out what his thoughts are. He still may not want
to publicly connect Lowell with Unger. The brass at
the Bureau has to be feeling real touchy about this."

"Well, there's John, at the back of the barn. Looks
like he finished his little chat with the chief."

"He's looking at us." Miranda waved, and John
lifted a hand in response.

"He's waiting for us," Will murmured.

"Sure looks like it. You think that's a good thing,
or a bad thing?"

"Only one way to find out." He quickened his
stride, and she moved a little faster to keep up with
him.

"Hey," she called as they drew nearer.

"Anything interesting out there?" John nodded in
the direction of the trees.

"Lots of footprints. Looks like the killer—whom
we presume to be Archer—spent a lot of time out

there, just watching the farm. Of course, it would have been nice if the police had been watching him as carefully, but I guess that's something that you'll have to take up with their chief, seeing as how you're his new best friend," Will said dryly.

Before John could react to that, Miranda jumped in. "The techs have tracked the footprints back and forth through the woods. They think he might have parked whatever he was driving on a small access road off the county road that runs parallel to the one we drove in on." She paused long enough for John to notice.

"What?" he asked.

"Archer Lowell doesn't drive," she told him.

"Archer Lowell doesn't have a driver's license," Will corrected her. "People get stopped driving without a license every day. You think he cares about that?"

"He would know that if he got caught driving, he'd be pulled in, which will violate his probation."

"Do you honestly think he cares about that now?" Will laughed out loud. "He's just *killed* two people."

"I think he believes he'll get away with the killings. But he won't be able to find a way around the probation violations once they go on his record."

"You have to be kidding." Will stared at her.

"Look, we're talking about a really unsophisticated kid here. He thinks he's already gotten away with murder, Will. I really think he believes if he can avoid drawing attention to himself, he'll be fine."

"Well, there is one other possibility," Will said.

"What's that?"

"Maybe someone's helping him."

"Someone?" Miranda frowned. "Someone like who? You think there was a fourth person involved?"

"I think we were right all along about Lowell not being smart enough to pull all this off on his own. I think someone's been giving him a little guidance. And that same person may be acting as his chauffeur."

"You could be right, Will." John nodded. "We're putting out an all points for Lowell. As a 'person of interest.' If we can bag him, maybe we'll bag our mystery man at the same time."

"Are you going to publicly connect the Landry murder to Al Unger's?" Miranda asked.

"Not yet." He shook his head. "Hey, not my decision. I don't think it matters, but there are those who think it will make the Bureau look really stupid. And we all know how much the higher-ups at the Bureau like to avoid looking stupid at all costs."

"But his picture is going out, right? So that people in Ohio will see it . . ." Miranda grabbed his arm.

"There's going to be a press conference at seven tonight, then again at nine in the morning. We're going to have Archer Lowell's picture in every newspaper on the East Coast," John assured her. "Someone has to have seen him."

"Ohio is not on the East Coast," Miranda reminded him.

"Figure of speech. Don't worry, Archer Lowell's picture will be every place you want it to be."

"Great. Things should start to heat up real soon."

Miranda nodded. "Maybe, with luck, we'll be able to track him down and—"

"Not we." John shook his head.

"What do you mean, 'not we'?" She frowned.

"I'm taking you off the case," he told her.

"What?" she said, stricken.

"Too dangerous," John said.

"John, if you're thinking about what Josh Landry said, about me possibly being the third victim, I appreciate that you're concerned—"

"Don't even try to talk me out of it. I want you as far from the action here as I can get you. This guy has turned out to be so much smarter than anyone gave him credit for. He got to Unger; he got to Landry. I can't take the chance that he'll find a way to get to you, too." He set his jaw. "I'm sorry, Miranda. You're off the case."

She opened her mouth to protest, and he said, "Besides, I need you someplace else right now."

"Sure you do," she said dryly. "Counting incoming flights at Reagan International, no doubt."

Ignoring her sarcasm, he continued, "I just heard from Genna."

Her head shot up.

"Is she out of the compound?"

"Yes. She should be leaving Wyoming as we speak." He paused for a moment, then added, "With the Douglas girl. This is going to be really hard on everyone. Annie, her sister, and even harder on the child. For seven years, this girl has been told that her mother was dead. This isn't going to be a pretty reunion."

"What do you want me to do?"

"Jules Douglas has gone to great pains over the past seven years to hide that girl. He's not going to give her up now without a fight." John's voice was tight. "I want you and Will on Mara and her daughter like white on rice. Aidan's already on the scene. Douglas will be coming after her, and I want him taken down and brought in. Preferably alive. But if not, well, do what you have to do."

Will's phone rang, and he pulled it from his pocket to check the caller ID.

"Excuse me," he said to John, "but I need to take this. . . ."

He held the phone to his ear, listening to the caller, then paced five or six steps off to the right, then back again. After he'd disconnected the call, he turned to Miranda and John.

"That was Evan Crosby," he told them.

"He's figured out where Channing, Giordano, and Lowell hatched their plan?" Miranda asked.

"He found the deputy who put them all in the same room while the courthouse was on lockdown. He told Evan that the men were in there for hours, alone. Plenty of time to work out a plan like theirs."

"Did he mention a fourth man?" Miranda looked hopeful.

"No. He was adamant there were just the three of them. Later that day, the charges against Channing were dismissed and he was released."

"He was brought in on a warrant that turned out to be a different Curtis Channing, if I recall correctly?" John asked.

"Right. But Evan had other news for us as well." Will paused. "The bullet used to kill Unger had a match in DRUGFIRE."

"To . . . ?" Miranda asked curiously.

"To the bullets that killed Vince Giordano's wife and sons." Will nodded slowly. "Think about that for a long minute."

"I am." Miranda crossed her arms over her chest. "How the hell could that be . . . ?"

"I think we need to ask Vince Giordano that question." Will turned to John. "That is, if you think there's time before Genna arrives with Mara's daughter."

"There's time." John nodded. "I'm still not sure where the reunion is going to take place. I'm leaving that up to Annie. She may be the girl's aunt, but she also has a background in psychology. I'm sure she'll know what's best under the circumstances. You go ahead and talk to Giordano. And let me know what he has to say. I'm as curious as you are. . . ."

"So, Archie, you sure you don't want none of this?" Burt sat at the desk in the small motel room, the open pizza box in front of him.

"No. You eat it." The thought of food made Archer want to hurl. Everything about this entire day, from the minute he'd opened his eyes till now, seeing the pizza in front of him, had made him want to hurl.

"Put the television back on," Burt told him. "The news oughta be coming on again soon."

"I don't wanna see it again," Archer all but moaned. "I saw it twice already."

"Put it on anyway."

Archer found the remote and turned on the television. The tape taken from a helicopter that hovered over Landry's barn and fields was on again. The same tape the networks had been running over and over all afternoon.

". . . though police are still not giving any information as to motive," the anchor's voice spoke above the sound of the helicopter's blades.

A shot from a handheld camera on ground level showed numerous law enforcement agencies on the scene.

"Hey, look at that, Archie. You got 'em all running around like chickens with their heads cut off, damned if you don't." Burt's laugh was raw and loud. "This was one important dude you wasted, man. I had no idea he was such a big shot."

"Yeah. He was famous." Sicker still, Archer went into the bathroom and closed the door.

Burt took the slice of pizza he was chewing and moved to the end of the bed closest to the TV. He turned the sound up, clearly enjoying the play-by-play. The police think the killer waited in the barn, yada yada yada.

He moved back slightly on the bed and, in doing so, knocked Archer's jacket to the floor. He glanced down and saw the cell phone he'd loaned Lowell the week before slide out from the pocket. When he leaned over to pick it up, he noticed it was turned on. He held the phone in his hand for a long minute, thinking.

Then he hit the scroll button, looking for the last number dialed.

Cahill, M. 410-555-1143.

Burt stared at the phone.

Cahill, M.

As in Cahill, Miranda. Special agent, FBI.

What the fuck . . . ?

He continued to stare, thinking carefully.

Behind the closed bathroom door, the toilet flushed. Burt heard the sound of running water. He slid the phone back into Archer's jacket pocket and took another bite of pizza, chewing slowing, still thinking.

What had Archer told her?

The son of a bitch had called *her*. He had called the FBI, for chrissake. What the hell kind of moron had he gotten mixed up with?

Archer had called the fucking FBI.

The bathroom door opened, and a white-faced Archer stepped in the room, then all but fell upon his bed. An attack of conscience, or anxiety because he was waiting for something to happen? Had he told her where they were?

Archer lay quietly on the bed, his head on the pillow. Burt watched him until the soft rise and fall of his chest assured him that Archer slept. Burt dug into the pocket for the cell phone and pulled up the last call. The call had been connected for less than thirty seconds. Long enough to leave a very short message. Or not.

Maybe that's all that had happened. Maybe there was just a brief message.

Yeah, real brief, like we're in the Park Motel on Route 1 outside of New Brunswick.

Burt tossed the phone from one open palm to the other, then tossed it onto the room's other bed. He piled the pillows up against the headboard and sat back against them, watching the news coverage of the murder of Joshua Landry and considering his next move.

If Archer had told Cahill where they were holed up, the FBI would have been there already, wouldn't they? So Burt felt he could reasonably assume that no one knew where they were. At least, not now. Who knew how many ways they might have to trace a call from a cell phone. Burt didn't know of any, but then again, he wasn't with the FB-fucking-I, and you never knew what the feds could do.

So even if he assumed that while the FBI didn't know where he and Archer were *now,* it didn't mean that Cahill couldn't find them *soon.*

Which meant it was time to leave and go someplace else.

But where? Burt bit his nails and thought it through.

He could go anyplace. No one even knew he was involved in this mess. Archer, however, wasn't going anywhere. Not anymore. He was a liability with a capital *L.* The sooner Burt got rid of him, the better things would be.

Burt closed his eyes and considered several scenarios. Once he'd made up his mind, he got off the bed and poked at Archer.

"Come on, man, it's time to go. Wake up, Archie."

"Go where?" Archer mumbled.

"Someplace else. We gotta get rid of the gun." Burt began to gather his things. They wouldn't be coming back tonight, or any night.

"Get your shit together, man. I want to leave now. I'm getting restless. I spent enough time working this all out for you. I'm done, and I'm moving on. We'll get rid of the gun, then I'm going my way, you're going yours."

"But what about the last one? The lady FBI agent?" Archer, sleepy-eyed, sat up.

"What about her?" Burt kept his voice steady even though, for two cents, he'd have beaten Archer's head in. Stupid fuck.

"I'm supposed to, you know . . ." Archer was awake now. "You said you'd help me."

"Yeah, well, that was then. Before I knew how much trouble this whole thing was going to be." Burt stuffed his belongings into a black-and-gray gym bag.

"You're not gonna help me no more?"

"No, I'm not gonna help you no more." Burt mimicked Archer's whine. "You're on your own. So get up, get your shit together, and we're outta here."

Archer began to do as he was told, whining the entire time.

"Why aren't you gonna help me? If you throw the gun away, I won't have anything to . . . to do that lady agent with."

"You should have thought of that before you called her." Burt spun around, his index finger pointed at Archer.

"Wh-what?" Archer went white. "Called who? I didn't talk to no one—"

"Don't make it worse by lying about it, asshole. You called her. The number is right there on the phone I gave you to call me with." Burt got right into Archer's face. He towered over him by more than half a foot.

Archer's eyes went wild with fright.

"I didn't talk to her, I didn't talk to no one, I swear—"

"Only because she didn't pick up, right? If she'd a picked up, what would you have said?" Burt grabbed Archer by the throat. "What were you going to say, huh? What were you going to tell her?"

"I . . . I . . ." Archer began to tremble all over.

"Were you going to tell her what you did, or what you were going to do? Is that it? You were going to call her and taunt her, hey, you're next, FBI lady?"

"N-n-no. I mean yes. Yes. I mean, no . . ."

"Bullshit." Burt threw Archer nearly across the room. "Get your stuff, and get it now. We are outta here. Now."

Hands shaking, his head pounding with terror, Archer picked up his belongings and threw them into the brown paper bag he'd brought them in. Burt opened the door, and Archer went through it, headed toward the truck.

"You get in, and you don't say a word, understand?" Burt growled.

"Yes. Yes. I understand." Archer climbed into the passenger side of the pickup and watched Burt walk around the front toward the driver's door. For a minute, Archer was tempted to lock the doors and lean on the horn until someone from one of the other rooms came out to see what the problem was. But he didn't think of it fast enough, and before he could blink, Burt was in the cab, tossing his gym bag into the space behind the seats and jamming the key in the ignition.

"Where . . . where are we going?" Archer asked.

No response from the driver.

"I didn't mean no harm. I wasn't gonna tell her anything. Honest. I don't know why I called her. I don't know why. . . ."

No response.

"But I wasn't gonna tell her about . . . about none of this. I swear, I wouldn't have told her. . . ."

They drove in silence for another fifteen minutes.

"This is the road that goes to Landry's," Archer said, confused. "Why are we going there?"

No response.

The pickup drove a mile past the Landry farm, where police cars and media vans still congregated, before turning into the small county park that sat between a pond and a wide field, the crop of which had recently been cut. There were no other cars in the lot, nor had they passed any on the road. All the local folks were home right about now, watching the news reports of the drama that had unfolded right down the road, or so Burt suspected. The truck drew to a stop all the way at the end, and Burt cut the ignition. This being farm country, no one would think twice about seeing a pickup truck parked near the pond.

"Out." Burt gestured to Archer. "Out of the truck."

"You're gonna leave me here?" Archer looked out the window. "With all those cops down the road? They're gonna find me."

"That's the idea, asshole." Burt pointed to the door and said, "Don't make me say it again, Archer."

Archer sighed and jumped out of the truck and stood next to the door, as if waiting for instructions.

"Walk," Burt told him, pointing toward the play equipment near the pond.

"Wait." Archer took a few steps toward the truck. "I forgot my stuff."

"Don't bother." Burt pulled the gun from his belt. "There's nothing in that bag you're gonna need."

It took a moment for Archer to realize what was about to happen.

"No, you can't. You . . . can't." He shook all over, and he looked around frantically for an escape route. There was none.

"Tell you what I'm gonna do, Archie. I'm gonna count to five. I'm firing on five. So when I say *one,* you make a run for it. Five seconds, give you time to run into the woods, find a place to hide. Maybe I won't find you."

"B . . . but . . ."

"That's your choice, Archie. You can run when I say *one,* or I can shoot you where you stand. It's up to you." Burt spoke softly, enjoying himself. "I'm gonna start counting now, Archie, so you turn around and get ready to run. One . . ."

"But—"

"You're wasting time, asshole. Two . . ."

Archer turned and ran toward the trees.

"Three." Burt fired and hit his target square in the back. Archer fell face forward onto the stones that covered the parking lot. "I was only kidding about giving you till five."

He walked over and put a second bullet in the back of Archer Lowell's head.

Tucking the gun into his belt, Burt walked back to his truck and drove from the parking lot, careful not to kick up stones that might further mar his paint job. He'd noticed a few pockmarks on his rear fender that morning, and he was determined to avoid adding to them. He took his time as he drove back the way he had come, easing on the gas as he passed the Landry farm. Laughing to himself, he sped up. The sooner he left the fields of New Jersey behind him, the better.

CHAPTER
NINETEEN

"WHERE ARE WE?" JULIANNE STIRRED IN HER SEAT IN
the small plane, then sat up and rubbed her eyes as if
it were a huge effort.

"We're on an airplane, sweetie." Genna leaned forward and tucked back the hair that had fallen over
Julianne's face.

"A plane?" The girl sat up groggily. "Why are we
on a plane?"

"Because we're taking you home," Genna replied,
dreading what came next.

She'd been coached by Anne Marie, who, as a psychologist, had stressed the importance of answering
truthfully any questions Julianne might ask. But Anne
Marie wasn't here, looking into those blue eyes, anxious even through the residual effects of the sleep
she'd been coaxed into by Jayne Young, the agent
who'd been sent to assist with Genna's flight from the
Valley of the Angels with Julianne. A little sleeping
aid into the hot chocolate had been all it had taken to
rock Julianne gently to sleep.

Just as well, Genna thought, since the ride to the
airport over treacherous roads had been anything but
smooth. When they'd finally reached a stretch of

highway that was all but closed due to drifting snow, Jayne had called for assistance, which had arrived in the form of a road crew and several agents who'd blocked the way from Linden with a mock accident that prevented the inevitable caravan that had been sent to find and return Julianne to the compound. By keeping her car directly behind the snowplow, Jayne made it to the airstrip in time for the small jet to take off before the worst of the storm hit. All in all, it had been a hair-raising trip, and Genna wasn't sorry that Julianne had missed the worst of it. No doubt the drama of the ride would have scared her half to death.

All behind us now, Genna reminded herself.

Then again, for Julianne, perhaps the worst still lay ahead. How to convince this child that her beloved father was a kidnapper and a liar, not to mention a conspirator in a scheme that sent her friends into slavery of the most debauched sort? That he'd told his worst lie to her?

And why now, Genna wondered, would Julianne believe the truth, told to her by a stranger?

"Why are we on a plane to go home? We can go in the car. . . ." Julianne sat all the way up and looked out the window. "Where is my daddy?"

Genna exchanged an anxious glance with Jayne, then said, "Julianne, there's something we need to talk about. . . ."

The girl's head turned toward her.

"Why did you call me that?" The look on her face was total shock. "My name is Rebecca. Rebecca West."

"No, honey, I think you know that's not true," Genna said in her softest voice. "Think. Think hard . . ."

"My name is Rebecca. I don't know why you called me . . . that other name. I'm Rebecca," she insisted, her face white, her fingers clutching the arms of her seat.

"Do you remember when your father first started calling you Rebecca?" Jayne asked gently.

Julianne stared at her.

"It was when you were five, do you remember?" Genna tried to take one of the girl's trembling hands, but Julianne pulled them out of reach.

Genna looked up at Jayne, who understood. The girl felt double-teamed. Without another word, Jayne walked to the front of the cabin.

"Do you remember when your father first told you that he wanted to call you Rebecca?" Genna asked again.

Slowly, Julianne nodded her head.

"Did he tell you why?"

She nodded again. "Because my mommy had named me . . . the other name. And my mommy died and went to heaven and took my name with her. So I had to have a new name."

Genna closed her eyes and squeezed them tightly shut to close out the girl's pain.

"Do you remember when you were called Julianne?"

She stared at Genna, then out the window. When her eyes returned to Genna's face, she whispered in the voice of a very small child, "I'm not supposed to.

Daddy said it would make us both too sad to think about Mommy, so I'm not supposed to remember her. I'm not supposed to remember being . . ." She could not bring herself to speak the name.

"Do you remember your mother, Julianne?" Genna asked.

Another nod of the head. "Don't tell my father."

"I won't, sweetheart." Genna turned her seat around to face Julianne, wondering how she would get out the words she knew she had to say. She wished this hadn't come up until they'd landed. Surely Annie would know the best thing to say. Genna had only her instincts to guide her, and she wasn't sure how good they were. "But there is something I need to tell you."

Looking wounded and scared, Julianne waited.

"Your mother . . ."

Tell her the truth, Annie's words rang in Genna's ears. *Don't make the situation worse by telling her more lies. Whatever she asks, you must tell her the truth.*

Easy for you to say, McCall, since you're not the one who has to break the news.

"Your mother didn't die, Julianne."

The girl made no reply, but simply stared as if Genna spoke in a foreign tongue.

"Julianne, did you understand what I said?"

"Why are you lying, Miss Ruth?" Julianne's eyes narrowed. "Why are you lying to me?"

"I'm not lying, honey. And my name isn't really Miss Ruth. It's Genna. Genna Snow. I'm with the Federal Bureau of Investigation, and I was sent to

Reverend Prescott's compound to find you, and to bring you back to your mother."

"NO!" Julianne's hands slammed into Genna's chest. "You're making this up! Why are you making this up?"

She began to cry, punching out at Genna, then at Jayne, who rushed to help subdue the young girl.

"You are lying! My mother is dead! She is dead!" She sobbed. "My father told me! He told me . . . he wouldn't lie to me."

They let Julianne sob and rail against them until she simply went slack, like a doll. Genna moved back into the seat next to her and cradled her in her arms until the girl could cry no more.

"We're taking you to your mother, Julianne. I'm sorry we had to do it this way. I'm so sorry." Genna rocked her gently. "But your mother has waited seven years to have you back, and it's our job to take you there, do you understand?"

"Why would he do that?" Julianne's whisper was almost inaudible. "Why would he lie about her? If she didn't die, why would he take me away?"

Genna looked over Julianne's head to Jayne and grimaced. She didn't want to answer these questions, didn't feel it was her job to tell the daughter that the father was an egotistic fool who'd kidnapped her rather than permit her mother the joy of watching her grow up. She wasn't sure how best to phrase it.

Oh, hell, let the psychologists explain that part. I might end up doing more harm than good, Genna rationalized. "I'm not exactly sure."

"I don't believe you." Julianne grew restless and

pushed Genna away. "I don't believe you. If my mother was alive, why wasn't she with us?"

"Your parents divorced, Julianne. Didn't you know that?"

"No, they didn't." Julianne's face went dark. "They weren't divorced. That's how much you know. They loved each other. My daddy was so sad when she died. That's why he took me away. That's why he called me Rebecca. . . ."

Genna sighed deeply. She was in over her head, and she knew it. She looked to Jayne for help, but instead of words of wisdom, she got only a helpless shrug of the shoulders from her companion.

"Tell me what you remember about your mother." Genna thought perhaps the best thing to do at this point might be to take the focus off Jules, for now. There was nothing she could say about the man that would help the situation now. Perhaps getting Julianne to talk about Mara might be the better path.

Julianne's trembling hands lay in her lap, her fingers intertwined.

"She was pretty. She had long dark hair and a soft voice. She laughed a lot," she said tentatively.

"What else?" Genna encouraged her.

"She sang to me. Played with me. She took me to school in the morning. When I came home we had lunch outside every day when it didn't rain. I had a swing in the tree, and she pushed me. . . ." Her eyes shifted to one side, then appeared to focus on something Genna could not see. "Sometimes she sat on the swing and I sat on her lap and we swang together. We sang songs. . . ."

Genna watched Julianne's eyes flicker, then fill with tears.

"I always missed her," Julianne confided. "Daddy told me not to think about her, but I always did. . . ."

"You'll see her soon," Genna told her. "She'll be waiting for you at the airport."

Julianne gave her that look again, that look of not understanding what was said to her. She gazed out the window but did not speak again until the plane touched down at the small airport in Bucks County. A long black car waited just off the runway, and when Julianne was led off the plane by Genna, the back door opened and a pretty dark-haired woman stepped out.

Julianne stood on the third step from the bottom of the portable stairway and stared as the woman approached her. She walked slowly toward the plane, her face a study in joyful disbelief. As the tears began to roll down her cheeks, she opened her arms wordlessly, and Julianne hesitated for several very long moments before walking into the circle of her mother's embrace.

Genna Snow blew out a long-held breath and looked over her shoulder at Jayne, whose eyes were wet. The hands of the two women touched briefly, then Jayne said, "Hey, we must be really important. We scored brass for a driver. . . ."

The driver's door opened, and John Mancini emerged. He patiently waited for his wife at the side of the car, and Genna stepped up her pace.

"Nice boots," he said as she drew near.

"Like these?" She grinned, never taking her eyes from his face. "I had to trade my shoes for these babies."

"Ahhh, the person you traded with . . . was she dead?"

"Dead? No. She was in the infirmary, though."

"That would explain why your signal hasn't moved for over a week."

"Sorry about that." She smiled. Just looking at him made her smile. Every time. "Were you worried?"

"Yeah, I was. I was worried about you." He held her as she slipped into his arms. "Welcome home, Gen."

"Good to be home." She rested her head on his chest. "You don't know how good it is to be home."

"You did a great job, getting Julianne out. You know we're going to have to pick your brain now about the operation out there, about Reverend Prescott's doings, so we can go back in and shut him down."

She nodded. "Pick away tomorrow. I'm taking the rest of the day off. Let's go home."

He tossed the keys to the driver of a second car that had pulled up, and caught a set of keys in return.

"Hey, I don't get to ride in the limo?" Genna pretended to be offended.

"You're not going where that limo is going," he said as he led her to the passenger side. "That limo is headed for Linden. This car is headed home. Still want the limo?"

"Nah. I want the driver, though." She leaned over and kissed his mouth after he'd gotten into the car.

The limo pulled past them.

"How do you think that's going to go?" John rubbed his cheek against Genna's.

"I don't know. Julianne is going to be one very confused little girl. She wants her mother, but she won't want to believe what her father did. She won't want to believe he lied about everything. I feel so sorry for her. For her and for Mara." She sighed, her heart heavy again. The past weeks had worn her out more completely than even she had realized.

"Can we go home now, John? I just want to go home. . . ."

Miranda had been watching Will's face for much of their drive to the prison from Landry's farm. It had been a quiet drive. Very quiet. Miranda couldn't remember the last time Will had had so little to say. So a few miles back, she began to study his expression. When she realized that merely staring was not going to shed any light on his silence, she decided to resort to interrogation.

"So, I guess you're thinking about what you're going to say to Giordano."

"No. I figured you'd do most of the talking," he said without looking at her.

"Why would you figure that?"

"Because you usually do." He pulled into the left lane. "Most of the talking, that is."

"Should I be insulted by that?"

"Does the truth hurt?"

Miranda watched for the sly smile that generally

accompanied such a remark. When no smile tugged at the corners of his mouth, she tried another tactic.

"Wonder how Genna's doing. Wonder if they've landed yet."

"I guess we'll find out soon enough."

"Aren't you at all concerned about how all this is going to play out? I mean, with Julianne having been gone for seven years, thinking her mother was dead. . . ."

Will shrugged. "I have no clue what's going to happen. The only thing I know for certain is that Annie will be there to help keep things from getting out of hand. Hopefully she can keep things on the right track."

"That's all you have to say on the subject?"

"Why speculate? We'll find out soon enough what's going on, since we'll head to Mara's right from the prison."

"Do you think John's right?"

"He usually is."

"So you think Jules is going to come for Julianne?"

"I think someone is. We can only hope it's Jules."

"You think Prescott would send someone else for her?"

"I think Prescott has got to be feeling a bit tense right about now. As far as we know, no one has left the Valley of the Angels who didn't leave at the reverend's command to go into a situation he controlled. Now, he has to be worried about where Julianne might be, just what she knows about his operation, and who she might be talking to."

"You don't think old nutbar Jules would let anyone do his work for him, do you?"

She waited for him to respond. When he did not, she leaned over and grabbed her bag from the floor. She rummaged around for a minute, then held up a tin of mints.

"Want one?" She offered the box to him.

"No, thanks."

She dropped the box back into her bag, then took out her cell phone. She checked for messages.

"Message from John, Jayne is on her way to Mara's, with Mara and Julianne . . . she and Aidan will be there until we arrive." Miranda paraphrased John's message. "How do you think Julianne will react when she realizes that her mother is involved with another man? Mara and Aidan are inseparable."

"Guess we'll find out soon enough."

"And a message from . . . huh, no message." She hit a button on the phone and scrolled for the number of the caller who had declined to leave a message. Finding it, she hit the return call button, then held the phone up to her ear. The number rang and rang, and finally, she heard the message prompt.

"This is Miranda Cahill, FBI, returning a call from this number. The caller didn't leave a name, but if there's someone there who still wants to speak with me, please call me back. You obviously have the number. . . ."

She disconnected and dropped the phone into its designated spot in her bag, then opened the box of mints and popped one into her mouth.

Finally, she asked, "So, are you going to tell me what's eating you?"

He appeared to be debating a response, but when a

full minute had passed, and he hadn't replied, she said, "Nod if you can hear me, Fletcher."

"I'm thinking," he said, and moved to the right to allow a large truck to pass. "It's hard to think when I have a headache."

"You have a headache? Why didn't you say something? Pull over and I'll take the wheel. I just realized, you've been driving all day. I'll drive the rest of the way, and you can relax."

"It's not the driving that's making my head hurt."

"What is?"

"You are."

"I make your head hurt?" She sat straight up in her seat, offended.

"Among other things, yes."

"I hope you're going to explain that, and not sink back into silence again."

"I'm thinking, Cahill, okay? Just stop talking for a minute and let me think, will you?"

She grew quiet then, and waited, hurt, wondering what she'd done to cause him to react to her in such a manner. They'd always gone round and round with each other, but it had always been mostly in fun, hadn't it? And she couldn't recall that there had been one of their usual go-rounds today. Or maybe even yesterday, for that matter. She looked over at him, confused, and felt the slightest stirring of apprehension, and thought back several days to having watched him and Annie walking across the parking lot, their heads close together, chatting like conspirators.

Miranda swallowed hard. Well, she hadn't given

him much encouragement, had she? She had no one to blame but herself if he had found someone else.

Which wasn't to say that she wanted him, of course. Did she?

"That lightbulb go on yet?" she prodded, suddenly impatient.

"Okay," he said, still looking straight out through the windshield. "I guess the best way to say it is like this: I just don't want to go on like this anymore."

"Like what?" she asked cautiously.

"Like, friends. I don't want to be your friend anymore."

"You don't want to be my friend?" She felt as if he'd struck her.

"Well, of course, I want to be your friend." He exhaled sharply. "I just don't want to be *just* your friend, okay, Miranda? We're a little old for this shit."

"But you were the one who brought up the friends thing. You said you wanted to be friends, Will."

"I said what I thought you wanted to hear, okay?"

She blinked, not expecting him to sound so . . . vehement.

"Will—"

"Let me finish, will you? You wanted to hear this, you listen."

"Okay." She shifted in her seat so that she could watch his face, give him her full attention.

"I understand that the way things have been between us hasn't been especially . . . stable. I don't know if that's the right word, but it will have to do for now. I know it's no one's fault more than the other. I mean, look at the way it's always been for you and me. We've always had this great chemical thing going for us. Attraction." The smile finally appeared, but barely. "An understatement, I know, but let's just call it that for now."

"You used to call it hot monkey sex."

"That was when I was immature. Before . . ."

"Before what?"

"Before I realized I was starting to fall in love with you." He never took his eyes from the road.

"Oh." The tiny word escaped from her mouth without her even being aware of it. She couldn't think of a single word to say, he'd taken her so off guard. So she simply repeated, "Oh."

"Now, I've come to realize that you don't understand what love is . . . no, don't interrupt me." He held up a hand when she appeared about to rebut. "You don't, Miranda. You understand great sex, and you understand friendship, but you don't understand the rest of it. The heart stuff."

"That's the stupidest thing anyone ever said to me," she blurted out.

"Oh, speaking of maturity—"

"If you weren't driving, I'd—"

"Spare me. You're only trying to change the subject."

"You think I'm not capable of loving someone?"

"That is not what I said. I think you're more than capable. I just think you don't want to."

When she didn't respond, he said, "You look at what went on between your mother and your father, and you think, Who needs that? Who needs a man who comes and goes, in and out of your life, the way Jack came and went in and out of your mother's. You saw what that did to her, so you want none of it. I can respect that."

She looked at him, her eyes dark, unreadable.

"But I am not Jack, Miranda. I won't love you and leave you, and I'm tired as hell of coming in and out of your life. If you'd let me, I'd stay, for as long as you wanted me." He took a deep breath. "If you'd let me, I'd take this as far as it could go, wherever it leads. If you'd let me."

"It seems like you're always leaving me." The words were so soft, he wasn't certain at first that she'd spoken at all.

"Sometimes you're the one who leaves," he reminded her. "Assignments sometimes come in the middle of the night; we both know that. It isn't always me leaving you, babe."

"It feels like you're always the one to go. It hurts, Will. It hurts when I wake up in the morning and you're gone. I never know if it's been just a good time, or if it meant something more to you. You never told me how you felt." She could have added, *And I knew just how my mother must have felt,* but she couldn't bring herself to say it.

"Neither did you."

"Everyone knows the man is supposed to say it first."

"I just did," he reminded her.

Miranda put her face in her hands, and he reached over and gently pulled them away.

"Let's start by not hiding anymore, okay? Over the

past few years, we've each found a hundred ways to hide from each other." His voice grew soft. "Let's stop doing that, okay?"

Will drove with both hands on the wheel, as if needing something sure to hold on to. He'd put his heart on the line. He was so afraid of what might come next.

"So, what do you say, Cahill?" he asked, trying to infuse his voice with a lightness he did not feel.

"I don't know what to say. I think I'm terrified."

"Oh, that's encouraging," he muttered dryly.

Feeling rebuffed, he fell back into silence.

A few miles down the road, she said, "Are you saying you don't want to sleep with me unless there's something more than friendship between us?"

"I didn't say that exactly, but that pretty much sums it up. Strange as it may sound, sex just isn't enough for me anymore. I want it all, but I want it all at the same time. Body, mind, heart."

"You left out soul."

"Everyone's entitled to keep a little something for themselves."

"You realize you've rendered me pretty much speechless, don't you?"

"That's a first."

"Will . . ."

"Hmmm?"

"That was our exit."

"Swell." He glanced in the rearview mirror in time to see the sign fade around the bend.

"The next one is just around that next curve, if I remember correctly." She pointed ahead.

The exit was there, and he eased into the lane. Once off the expressway, they were only a few miles from the prison.

"What if we can't . . . you know, make it as anything other than friends?" she asked.

"You really think that's going to happen?"

"I don't know what will happen. I've never seen this type of thing work out."

"Of course you have. Look at Genna and John. You don't have to look far to find relationships that work when both people want them to work. Stop looking so hard for a reason not to . . ." He paused, then said, "Unless, of course, you don't feel that way toward me. If that's the case, then—"

"I don't know what to call what I feel for you. I can tell you very honestly that I've never felt that way about anyone else, though." She leaned back into her seat, her blue eyes focused on his face. "Do you really think that things would have been the way they were between us if I hadn't felt something really strong for you?"

"A guy can hope."

"It's hard to put a name to something you've tried to avoid thinking about for so long."

"Well, I think that's my point. We've both been avoiding this whole relationship thing for years." He pulled to the side of the road and stopped the car. "We never talked about it, but we're talking now."

"I'll give you this much"—she unsnapped her seat belt and leaned over and took his face in her hands— "there's never been anyone but you. I've never known what to call what I feel for you, but the whole time

since we've known each other, there's never been anyone else."

"I can live with that, for today. For now." He drew
her close and kissed her, almost weak with relief. He
held on to her as if to a lifeline, his heart pounding.
He wondered if he'd ever tell her how the thought of
this conversation had struck terror in his gut. He'd
been so afraid she'd shoot him down.

"I think we can work this out somehow," she whispered, returning his kiss and running her top teeth
along his bottom lip, because she knew it made him a
little crazy.

"We'll work on it."

"Day and night until we get it right."

He laughed and kissed her again, wanting to feel
her pressed against him, but there was the console,
and the steering wheel. So he kissed her one last time
and said, "We can do this. No more joking around.
We can do this."

"I've missed you, Will. Missed the closeness. Missed
this." She was as close to him as she could be, and still
be in her own seat. "Maybe you're right, maybe it's
time to . . . like you said . . ."

"Take it to the next level."

"Right."

"Move the relationship ahead."

"That, too."

"See where the road leads."

She began to laugh softly. "See how many more
really tired clichés you can come up with."

"I got a million of them." He rubbed the back of
her neck gently.

"Save a few for after we chat with Vince."

"Don't worry, babe. There are plenty more cheesy lines where those came from." He turned the key in the ignition. "But you know, I'm thinking maybe we don't need to be at Mara's until tomorrow. Maybe if Jayne and Aidan are there to keep an eye on things . . ."

"There's always the Fleming Inn. Just about forty minutes from the prison." She grinned as she leaned back into her seat. "Less, of course, if I'm driving . . ."

CHAPTER TWENTY

"So, do I get to ask him anything?" Will asked as he and Miranda made their way across the parking lot toward the entrance to the prison. "Or are you really planning on doing all the talking?"

"Hey, Vince and I are old buddies. This will be like a reunion." She grinned, ignoring the look on the face of the guard when he saw her come through the door. She pulled her credentials out of her bag and smiled. "Agents Cahill and Fletcher. We're here to see Vince Giordano."

The guard glanced from her badge to Will's, then at the visitor's log for the day.

"You're not on the sheet," he told them. "You weren't expected?"

"When did 'not on the sheet' ever keep a federal agent out of a prison?" Miranda narrowed her eyes and stared the guard down.

"I was just saying . . ." the guard mumbled, then grabbed the phone. He turned away for a minute or so, then turned back and told them, "Warden said to put you in the room down the hall, not in the visitors' area. He's sending someone up for you, and he'll have the prisoner brought down."

"That's better." Miranda flashed a million-dollar smile and paced the reception area until the guard arrived to take them through the building.

Their escort arrived within minutes, and they followed him down a short hall to a small room.

"In here." The guard unlocked the door. "The prisoner will be down in a minute."

"Thanks," Will said as they entered the room.

"I'll bet I've been in a hundred nasty little rooms, just like this, over the past six years, but I never get used to the way they look or feel."

"Or smell," Will noted.

"That, too." She wrinkled her nose.

The door on the back wall opened, and Vince Giordano shuffled in, his ankles in chains.

His eyes lit up when he saw Miranda.

"Hey! When they said there was a babe here, wanted to see me, I thought they were kidding. Agent Cahill," he said as he sat down clumsily in the yellow chair. "Last time I saw you, you were holding a gun on me."

"Hey, don't thank me. It was my pleasure," she told him.

"No hard feelings. If it hadn't been you, it woulda been someone else. At least I got to feast my eyes on the finest the Feds got to offer."

"That's a disgusting thought, Vinnie. The thought of you feasting on any part of me in any way makes me want to throw up."

"So, I see you still care for me as much as I care for you."

"Vinnie, my feelings for you have never changed."

He laughed again.

"So, what sends you and . . . who is this guy?" Giordano pointed to Will.

"Oh, pardon my manners. You haven't met Agent Fletcher before. Agent Fletcher, this is the infamous Vincent Giordano. I get to call him Vinnie 'cause we go way back."

"Not back far enough," Giordano said, still appearing to size up Will.

"Heard a lot about you, Vince." Will sat on the edge of the table.

"Yeah, like what did you hear?"

"I heard you were the mastermind behind that whole 'Let's do some good deeds for each other when we get out' thing."

Giordano looked up at Miranda, his face blank.

"What's this guy talking about, Cahill?"

"Vinnie, we already know about the game," she replied.

"Game, what game? Someone betting on a game? Hey, gambling's illegal here," he deadpanned.

"Stop it." She slammed her fist down on the table unexpectedly, and he jumped. "Just . . . stop it, okay? We know. We know how you and Channing and Lowell were shoved into a room together last February and passed the time away with a little game of hit list. You do mine, I'll do yours."

She rested her arms on the table and looked him straight in the eye. "Did you know that Channing was going to do it when he got out, or did that come as a big surprise to you? When did you know for sure that the game had really begun, Vince? Was it when they found your mother-in-law with a bullet between her eyes? Or when they found Judge Styler raped and murdered, just like the Mary Douglases were?"

"I remember reading something about that judge. Shame, wasn't it?" He shrugged, but did not blink. "And Diane's mother, well, hey, guess that was one of them wrong-place, wrong-time things, huh?"

"Eight o'clock at night, in her own house sound like the wrong place, wrong time?" Miranda met his stare.

"Hey, just goes to show—"

"Enough, okay?" She looked up at Will and said, "He's not going to tell us a damned thing."

"I got nothing to say." Giordano shook his head.

"So I guess if we were to ask you to tell us who Lowell's third victim was going to be, you'd just tell us to go to hell."

"I prefer kiss my ass."

"Well, I guess since you're not talking," Miranda pretended to study her nails, "you're not going to want to talk about how it is that the bullets from the gun that killed your family match the bullet that killed Albert Unger."

"Who?" Vince's expression never changed, but there had been a definite spark in his eyes.

"The man who murdered Curt Channing's mother."

"Never heard of him." Vince began to chuckle. "But I guess it just goes to prove what I been saying all along. Guess it proves that someone else killed my family. Just like I told you."

"Or maybe you told someone else where to find the gun. Or maybe you gave the gun away. But it doesn't prove that anyone other than you killed your wife and kids."

Ignoring Will's comment, Vince asked, "Aren't you wasting time sitting here talking to me? Shouldn't you be out looking for the guy who killed my wife and kids?"

"Waste of time, Cahill." Will shook his head. "I told you he was a waste of time."

"Hey, sorry I couldn't be of any assistance." Vince made no effort to hide his smirk.

"Vinnie, your sincerity is choking me up."

"And your interest is touching, you know? I don't get much company. A guy can get pretty lonely in here."

"Sooner or later, we all get what we deserve, I guess." She stood up to leave.

"I guess we do." Giordano stared at her, then grinned broadly. "Sooner or later, you're gonna get what you deserve, too, Agent Cahill. Wish I could be around to see it all go down."

Miranda looked at Will and smiled.

"I'd take that as a confirmation, wouldn't you?"

"I would."

"Thanks, Vinnie."

"For what?"

"For saving us the time we would have spent looking for that third victim."

"I don't know nothing about no victims." Giordano smiled back at her. "Except my own, of course."

"You know, you never did say how you came to choose those individuals to murder, Vinnie."

"They were in my way."

"Right. And I'm the Lone Ranger."

"You lonely, Cahill, I got something for you. Pretty lady like you should never be alone."

"Ugh, I'm gagging now." Miranda signaled to the guard. "Get him out of here."

"You want to talk, Giordano, you just give a holler," Will said.

"Cold day in hell, Fletcher." Giordano headed back to the door, calling over his shoulder, "Be seeing you, Cahill."

"Not if I can help it." She tapped Will on the arm to let him know she was leaving, and he followed her through the door.

Well, then. Wasn't that interesting?

Vince couldn't help but grin all the way back to his cell. Well, of course, that Cahill was always something to look at. And if things went the way they were supposed to go, he probably wouldn't get another chance just to sit and stare at that face, that body. Those legs . . .

Damn shame, take out a looker like that. But, hey, a deal's a deal, and Channing wanted her out, so she's out. Assuming that Archer was on the ball, and that was assuming a lot, Vince knew. Archer hadn't been the brightest bulb in the room that day back in February.

But he'd apparently been true to his word, Vince reminded himself. Faithful to his promise. Vince had seen the press conference on television, had seen the photograph of Archer they'd shown. Had caught the New Jersey cop's comments about how Lowell was wanted for questioning in connection with the Josh Landry murder as well as a murder in Ohio, and Cahill had just confirmed that Unger had been taken out. That meant that Archer Lowell had already gotten two out of his three. As many as Channing had gotten, as many as Vince himself.

Vince shook his head slightly as the guard opened the cell door and stepped to the side to permit Vince to enter. Hard to believe that Archer Lowell might even best what the other two had done. Boy, that would be something, wouldn't it? If dumb-ass Archer managed to do what neither Vince nor Curtis Channing had been able to do: hit all his targets.

There was still Cahill, though, and she was not going to be an easy target to hit.

Vince sat down on the edge of his cot, still thinking about the irony of Lowell besting the other two.

Lowell had had help, though, hadn't he? Didn't that give him an advantage? Then again, dumb as Archer was, he deserved the handicap. Assuming that Burt had been true to his word and ridden herd on Archer the way Vince had asked him to. And Burt had been paid handsomely for his trouble, hadn't he?

If in fact he'd gone to the trouble . . .

Rubbing his chin, Vince thought about the possibility that maybe Burt had simply taken the money and said the hell with any deal he might have made with Vince.

Not a chance, Vince reassured himself. He'd had Burt pegged as a greedy son of a bitch from day one. No way he'd have walked off with half if he thought he'd end up with twice as much.

Of course, there was no other half, Burt had gotten it all on the first round, but he wouldn't find that out until he came back to tell Vince that all the deeds were done. And what was he going to do, once he found out that Vince had duped him, go to the police? Call the FBI?

Vince stood up on the end of his bed and tried to look out the narrow window. He had a view of the parking lot, though not a very good one, since the parking lot was so far away. In the distance he could see two figures walking. It could be Cahill and Fletcher, though they were too far away for him to be sure.

His chin resting on the windowsill, he watched until the figures faded completely, then jumped down off the bed.

That Cahill was real fine. It was a shame Channing had put her name on his list.

CHAPTER
TWENTY-ONE

•

THE FIRST THING BURT DID WHEN HE RETURNED TO
the motel was to flop onto the bed, the TV remote in
hand. He was more than a bit spooked when, while
channel surfing, he found Archer Lowell's mug front
and center on the screen.

That sure got his attention.

He turned up the volume in time to hear the earnest
and excited young reporter describe how Archer
Lowell was wanted for questioning in the death of
Joshua Landry as well as for the murder of an Ohio
man.

Burt sat up and rubbed his chin thoughtfully.
Damned good thing I dumped him when I did.

"According to the FBI," the reporter continued, "the
suspect should be considered armed and dangerous—"

"Not anymore." Burt chuckled.

A sobering thought then occurred to him. Should
he worry that the desk clerk or the cleaning people
might recognize Archer as one of the inhabitants of
Room 109? He tried to remember if Archer had actually been in the office. Burt didn't think he had. Didn't
think he'd been out of the room much at all, except
for the trips down to Landry's farm in Plainsville, and

those trips had been made pretty early in the morning. Burt had brought in takeout for their meals, so it wasn't likely that any well-meaning waitress was going to call the cops and say she'd seen Archer Lowell and he'd been with a tall guy with dark hair who drove a black pickup with tinted windows.

Now that he thought about it, they hadn't really run into too many people at all since they'd been staying here. Burt mentally reviewed all the places they'd gone and things they'd done over the past week and decided that he was probably okay. But all the same, it was time for him to be moving on.

Besides, they'd be finding Lowell's body pretty soon, wouldn't they? He wondered if anyone had seen his truck there in the park, but thought he was probably okay there, too. He'd pulled all the way to the back of the lot, and hadn't stayed for more than a few minutes. He didn't even recall passing many cars on the road.

He searched the room to make sure there was nothing of his or Archer's remaining, then wiped down all the surfaces with bath towels to remove any fingerprints Archer may have left behind. It probably wasn't necessary, but still, why take chances? Besides, it gave him time to think about what he was going to do next.

By the time he returned the towels to the bathroom, he'd figured out his next moves. He wanted the rest of the money. He'd promised Vince three dead bodies; he got three dead bodies. Of course, one of those bodies was Archer's instead of that hot FBI agent, but how the hell was he supposed to find her now? He'd been given half the money for making sure Archer killed Unger and Landry. Well, he'd done that, hadn't he?

But would Vince think that killing Archer was a fair trade for doing Cahill?

Burt gathered up the remains of the pizza and tossed it into the box. He stood in the doorway and looked around. The room was clean. There was no trace of him—or, more important, of Archer Lowell—left behind. Satisfied, Burt turned off the light and went outside. He tossed the pizza box and the empty soda cups into the Dumpster, then headed for his truck.

He'd be able to make it to the prison before visiting hours were over if he hurried. Along the way, he'd rehearse what he was going to say to Vince Giordano when he got there.

Burt sat in the pickup truck, the driver's window down, and tried to get his thoughts in order. The longer he sat, the less hope he had that Vince would just hand over the location of the rest of the cash in exchange for a, *Well, I wasted Lowell, but I won't be able to do Cahill. Can't we just call it even all the same?*

Who was he kidding? Vince wasn't going to give a shit about Lowell. It was Cahill who was supposed to be the victim here.

And wasn't it more likely that Vince was going to be royally pissed when he told him he'd gotten rid of Lowell before he'd been able to finish the job Vince had wanted him to do?

Might as well save myself the trouble, Burt told himself. There was no point in even getting out of the truck. He'd just have to make do with what he had left of the first half of the money. There was still plenty left, but shit, he really wanted that franchise. . . .

The doors to the main section of the prison opened, and a man and a woman stepped out into the autumn sun. The man was big, big as Burt himself, and the woman was tall with the most incredible legs he'd seen since . . .

Burt sat and stared at the woman with the dark hair and the incredible legs. He actually pinched himself to see if he was awake and not just dreaming that it was really Miranda Cahill walking toward him. For a second, he almost ducked before she got close enough to the truck to see him, but then he remembered. He'd seen her at the bar back in Fleming, but she had not seen him. He unfolded the map that lay on the seat next to him and pretended to study it.

His heart began to pound as he pondered the possibilities.

The couple drew closer to the truck, and Burt, still pretending to study the map, leaned slightly to the open window to see if he could catch some of their conversation.

"We're not really going to the Fleming Inn now, are we?" Miranda Cahill was saying as they briskly approached the truck, oblivious to the fact that they were being watched.

"That was just a lot of wishful thinking on our part, wasn't it? A little bit of fantasy to keep us going."

" 'Fraid so." The big guy took her hand. "Besides, if John is right, looks like we're going to have to—"

The words were lost on Burt as the couple passed by.

Son of a bitch! He shook his head and started his engine, marveling at his good fortune. It had been her. It had really been her. Was there a luckier guy on the face of the earth?

All he had to do was follow them, Cahill and the guy. He watched in his rearview mirror as the two got into a car thirty feet away.

I'll bet they were in there talking to Vince. Wonder what they asked. Wonder what he'd told them.

Maybe they'd found Lowell's body. Maybe they'd put it all together. Maybe they think it's over.

Had his name come up? Had Vince told them about his deal with Burt?

Nah. Vince wouldn't give him up. He'd bet his life on it.

He eased out of the parking lot and drove slowly to the end of the row, giving the driver of Cahill's car a wave, letting him pull in front of the pickup. He was good at tailing without being detected, and the couple in the car seemed to be in a serious discussion. They'd never make his tail to wherever they were going. He'd be able to take her out, then come back and tell Vince he'd taken care of all his business. There would be no loose ends left, no reason for Vince not to tell him where the rest of the money was. Cheered, he cautiously followed the car ahead of him, thinking about the condo he was going to buy when he got to Florida.

CHAPTER
TWENTY-TWO

MARA SAT ON THE OTTOMAN IN FRONT OF THE WING chair and studied her daughter's face. Julianne had barely moved since their arrival. Wide-eyed and confused, she had stood at the end of the cobbled walk for a long time, staring at the house. The only spark of life she'd shown during her homecoming was when Spike, Mara's Jack Russell terrier, had danced around her feet, greeting her wildly.

"You have a dog," Julianne had said, even as she avoided looking at Mara.

"His name is Spike," Mara told her, forcing a steady note into her voice. "I bought him after you . . . went away. You always wanted a dog, and I wanted him to be here for you when you came back."

Julianne had merely nodded, sitting down on a chair to allow Spike onto her lap. He lavished her with dog kisses, bringing the first true smile to her face.

"He likes me," Julianne said softly.

"He does," Mara had agreed.

Mara sat quietly and watched as her dog won over her daughter, knowing that she, as Julianne's mother, would need to take things a little more slowly than Spike did. She wished she could hug her daughter again, wished she could gather her back into her arms as she had at the airport, but after that first connection, Julianne had begun to withdraw. She'd barely spoken in the car on the way home, and once at Mara's house, she had said nothing until Spike had welcomed her home.

The front door opened cautiously, and Mara's sister stepped inside.

"Hi," she said. "May I come in?"

She addressed the question to Julianne, who openly studied her face, then nodded slowly.

"I'm your aunt Anne Marie," Annie told her as she closed the door behind her.

Julianne nodded slowly. "Ammy."

"You remember me?" Annie dropped her briefcase and overnight bag near the door and exchanged a fleeting glance with Mara. As a child who had found "Aunt Anne Marie" too much of a mouthful, Julianne had called her Ammy.

The girl nodded again.

"Do you remember this house, Julianne?" Mara asked.

Another nod.

"There were plants there." She pointed to the wide windowsill behind the sofa. "And a picture of a lighthouse there." She pointed to a space near the stairwell that now held photographs of Julianne as a baby.

She stared at the photographs for a long moment, then turned to Mara for confirmation.

"Yes," Mara told her, "that's you."

Julianne got off the chair, Spike still in her arms,

and stood on the bottom step to more clearly see the photographs.

"Do you want me to take them down?" Mara started to get up.

"No. I can see them." She touched first one, then the next, then turned to Mara and said, "There's you and Ammy, but not Daddy."

"No," Mara answered, not wanting to look at Annie, afraid to risk finding approval or disapproval in her psychologist's eyes. "No. There are no pictures of you with your father in this house."

"You're really angry with him," Julianne stated matter-of-factly.

"Yes. I am still angry with him."

"I'm angry, too." Julianne turned to her, that anger burning in her eyes. "You must have done something really bad for him to take me away."

Shocked, Mara sat back as if she'd been shot.

"You must have been a really bad mother." Julianne aimed at her heart again.

"Julianne, sometimes people do things for their own reasons, reasons that have nothing to do with what someone else might have done or might not have done." Anne Marie stepped in immediately. "Do you remember when you lived here? Do you remember when you were little?'

Julianne's face hardened.

"Do you, Julianne?" Annie pressed her.

"Yes. I remember."

"What is it that you think of when you remember living here?" Annie walked toward the stairs.

"I want to go to my room. Do I still have a room?"

"First door on the left," Annie told her.

Julianne ran up the steps and, seconds later, slammed the bedroom door.

"That went well." Mara grimaced.

"Actually, it didn't go badly at all." Annie sat down behind her sister on the chair that Julianne had vacated. "Julianne remembers you, she remembers the house—"

"She hates me." Mara covered her face with her hands. "She blames me for all this. She thinks it was my fault that Jules ran away with her. You heard her—"

"It's not an unexpected reaction, honey. She's a very, very confused little girl. You're just back from the dead, as far as she's concerned, remember? She's been with Jules all these years, and regardless of what else he has done, she loves him. He's her father. She's feeling betrayed by him right now, and finding it really, really difficult to understand how her loving, wonderful father could have done something so terrible. So instead of blaming him, she has to blame you."

Mara broke into tears.

"Sweetie, I'm sorry. I told you this was going to be very hard for both of you."

"I know, but I want so much for her to love me again. I want her to know how much I love her, how I never gave up hope—"

"That much, I'm sure she knows. After all, you did send someone to find her. She'll think of that, by and by. But for now, her life is a huge jumble, a huge mess of a puzzle. She's been totally upended. You need to give her time to think things through."

"I don't want her to hate me."

"She doesn't. She's just afraid and confused. It's normal. It's exactly what I expected her to do."

"You could have warned me."

"I thought I had." Annie massaged her sister's shoulders for a few minutes, then told her, "By the way, Aidan is here."

"Where?"

"Right out front."

"What should I do? What should I tell him? Should he be here?"

"It's up to you," Annie said. "What do you think?"

"I think I'm glad he's here, but I don't think he should stay overnight right now."

"I agree. Tell him that."

"I will."

Mara opened the door and stepped outside. Aidan was leaning against his car, which was parked in the driveway.

"How's it going?" he asked when he saw her.

"I don't think it's going so well, but Annie thinks it's all as she expected."

"That bad, eh?"

He walked to her and took her into his arms.

"Julianne thinks that her father took her away because I was such a bad mother, he had to save her from me," she whispered.

"She didn't say that." Aidan rocked her slowly, side to side.

"That's what she meant."

"She has a lot to think about right now. The changes in her life over the past twenty-four hours must be terrifying her."

"That's pretty much what Annie said."

"Annie knows what she's talking about."

"I'm scared," Mara cried into his chest. "I'm afraid she won't love me, won't let me love her. That she wants to go back to her father . . ."

"Well, since he's going to be facing federal charges, there's not a snowball's chance in hell of that happening. The minute he shows up, he's going to be arrested."

"No shooting, Aidan." She tilted her head back and looked up into his eyes. "Don't shoot him."

"It isn't anyone's intent to shoot him. The government wants him alive and well and singing like a bird."

"You mean, about Prescott's camp or school or whatever it is he has going with these young girls. . . ."

"Right. There's lots of money floating in and out of that organization. They want to know where it's coming from and where it's going."

"Did you know?" Her eyes narrowed as she studied his face. "When we were there, in Wyoming, when Miranda came for us. Did she know? Did you?"

"Yes," he said without hesitation. "Not until she told me, but yes, she told me that Julianne was in there."

"Why didn't you tell me? Why did you let me believe that we'd failed?"

"Because I knew that if anyone had a chance of getting Julianne out safely and bringing her home, it was Genna Snow. And there was no way I could risk Genna's life—and Julianne's—by telling you what Miranda had told me. I'm sorry, but I had to back away quietly."

"And if Genna had failed?"

"Failure wasn't an option."

"You really believed that?"

"I did."

"You wouldn't have let anything happen to her. If you'd thought something might happen to her . . ."

"I'd have gone in myself to get her."

"I believe you would have." Mara reached up to touch the side of his face, and he turned his head to kiss her hand.

"It's not always going to be like this, you know." He answered her unspoken fears. "She's going to be okay with you. When all of the truth comes out, she'll understand."

"I wish I was as confident as you and Annie are. That I could believe it would be all right. Until then . . ."

"Until then, you'll be there for her and answer her questions honestly and let her know that you love her, that you never gave up, that you never would have given up."

"It's not easy."

"No one thought it would be."

"Which reminds me . . ." She stepped back and held him at arm's length. "I don't think you should stay here until—"

"Until Julianne's settled?" He finished the sentence for her. "I hadn't planned on it. I figured this was all going to be hard enough without her finding out that, on top of everything else, there's another man in your life. Especially since there's a pretty good chance her father will turn up pretty soon. Mrs. West next door has gone to stay with her sister until this is over. She left the key with me so that we can use her house if any of us need to grab catnaps, so I'll be getting what sleep I can on her sofa."

"That was really sweet of her. But you don't mind, until things settle down here?"

"You waited for Julianne for seven years." He raised her hand to his lips and kissed the tips of her fingers. "I can wait for as long as it takes."

"I really love you, you know that?"

"Actually, I do know that." He kissed her. "I love you, too. Now, go on back inside and get on with the business of getting to know your daughter again."

Mara stretched up to kiss him one more time, then started across the lawn toward the house. Just before she reached the front porch, she turned back to him.

"Don't forget. Please, Aidan. Don't shoot him."

"I won't forget," he promised her. "Don't worry. I won't shoot him."

But not because I won't be tempted to.

Aidan went back to the car and reached in through the driver's-side window to retrieve his ringing cell phone from the console.

"Shields here." He listened for a long moment. "They lost him where? How long ago was that? Great. Swell."

He began to pace slowly, still listening.

"Tell Fletcher and Cahill I'm already at the scene.

I'll be here when they get here. No, Jayne's gone. She's been reassigned. Sure. I'll keep in touch. . . ."

He disconnected the call and tossed the phone back onto the car seat. Then he walked to the end of the driveway and stood in the halo of the streetlamp, wondering who would arrive first, his backup, or Jules Douglas.

CHAPTER
TWENTY-THREE

It was just barely dusk when Will stopped in front of the driveway at 1733 Hillcrest Road and turned off the engine.

"This is the house?" he asked, leaning forward slightly to take a look.

"Yes. And there's Aidan, back near the garage. Doesn't look as if much is happening right now," Miranda observed. "At least not outside. Inside, I'll bet there's plenty going on. I wonder how Mara's doing with Julianne."

"I'll bet it's pretty tense all the way around. And on top of everything, here come the Feds to lay a trap for her daddy. I hate using a kid for bait." He shook his head as he pocketed the keys.

"So does everyone else, but no one could come up with a better way to lure Jules close enough to pick him up. Besides, those were the orders." Miranda unsnapped her seat belt and opened her car door. "Let's hope this goes quickly and quietly."

"Hey, guys." Aidan walked down the drive to meet them.

"What's going on?" Will asked.

"Nothing yet. Rob Flynn got here just before you

did. He's next door changing into what he calls his nighttime surveillance attire. He takes that all-black thing real seriously. The old lady there has offered us the use of her house for as long as we're camped out here. She's real close to Mara, and she has had nothing good to say about Jules, so she's been great about letting us set up in there." Aidan turned to Will. "Go ahead and pull your car in the drive there behind Flynn's. That way, if—when—Jules shows up, there won't be this cluster of vehicles around Mara's house. We don't want to scare him away."

"Won't he expect to find someone watching the house?" Mara asked. "He can't possibly be stupid enough to think that we'd leave Julianne here without a watchdog."

"Tough to know what he's thinking. Keep in mind, he doesn't know who was sent in to bring her out. For all he knows, it could have been a private investigator, someone hired by Mara. I don't know what he'll expect to find when he gets here. But I do expect him to get here as quickly as he can."

"Do you think he'll have help from some of the reverend's security staff?" Mara wondered.

"He's traveling alone. We already know that much," Aidan told them. "He was tracked to the airport, but he managed to slip past our guy out there. Looks like Prescott loaned him one of his private planes for the trip. What's that tell you?"

"That Prescott wants the girl back pronto, before she gets to talk too much about what's going on out there." Will nodded.

"That's my feeling, too. Now, we know he'll be

headed this way, but there are so many airports within a few hours' drive of here, it's tough to know where he'll be landing. We're trying to determine where the plane will have clearance to land. We just don't have as many agents available for this job as we could use, so we're going to have to be ready for just about anything at any time."

Will started toward the car to move it into the driveway next door, pausing near the back of the sedan as a black pickup passed by. He watched it speed up, then proceeded to pull the car into the drive. He was on the phone when he returned to where Aidan and Miranda were still in conversation. He snapped the phone closed and dropped it into his pocket.

"So what's the plan here, Aidan?" he asked as he joined them.

"During the day, two outside. Once Julianne goes to bed at night, there will be two agents inside, two outside. During the day, we'll be taking turns grabbing what sleep we can on the sofa next door at Mrs. West's. She also has one of those air mattress things that she made up in her den for someone to catch a few winks on."

"Nice of her," Miranda said, recalling the small, white-haired woman she'd met on previous visits to Mara's house.

"Very," Aidan agreed. "Sleeping in the car gets real old real fast."

"I hope we can wrap this up before Halloween." Miranda watched several children run up the front walk of the house across the street. "I'd hate to see this play out with the sidewalks filled with little trick-or-treaters."

"Not to mention big trick-or-treaters," Aidan said thoughtfully. "You never know who's behind those masks. You could have someone like Jules slip right in with a crowd of teenage boys, and who'd know the difference if everyone was wearing a mask."

"Great. Something else to worry about." Will grimaced.

"Just hope Jules moves tonight or tomorrow night, then we won't have to deal with the Halloween crowd. That could be really dicey." Aidan didn't really want to think about just how dicey things could get if Mara opened the door to a masked Jules.

"So, I take it Julianne doesn't know any of this is going on?" Miranda nodded in the direction of the house.

"Annie thought it would be a good idea if she didn't. Her bedroom is on the other side of the house, so she won't see us if she looks out the window," Aidan explained.

"Doesn't that leave the other side of the house unguarded?" Will walked toward the back gate to look over the yard.

"Only during the day, but there are no doors on that side of the house, and few windows, all of which are locked and alarmed," Aidan pointed out. "Plus, keep in mind that because of the fence across there, anyone wanting to approach the house from the back has to go through Mrs. West's backyard. There's no way to sneak across the yard without being seen during the day. At night, we'll be keeping an eye on the house from inside and out. I don't think Jules will be able to get too close."

"Let's hope you're right." Miranda glanced at her watch. "Who will Julianne think we are if she sees us during the day? And hasn't she seen you out here? Who does she think you are?"

"She'll be told that you and Will are new neighbors, if she asks," Aidan said. "She already knows that I'm a friend of her mother's."

"Does she know how good a friend?" Miranda asked.

"Not yet. We thought we needed to go real slow on that. Let her get used to the idea that her mother is still alive, that she's back home, all that."

"That going to be hard on you?" Will asked.

"Not as hard as it will be on Mara and Julianne," Aidan told him.

"It's starting to get dark," Miranda noted. "Where do you suppose Flynn is?"

"He mentioned something about throwing a frozen pizza in the oven. Have you ever known him to show up for a stakeout without enough food to take him— and the rest of us—through a long siege?" Will said. "He arrived with a couple of grocery bags under his arm, so I'm guessing he stocked up."

"Ah, that Rob. Always plans ahead." Miranda turned to Aidan. "Is the house next door open? I'd like to change my clothes and be ready to take my place once it's dark."

"The back door is open; you can go right on in," Aidan told her. "Annie's supposed to let us know when Julianne has gone to bed for the night, then we'll move you and Will inside until dawn. One of you will watch the front of the house, one the back. Rob will be in Mrs. West's backyard, I'll take the outside of Mara's house, side and front."

"Will, I need to open the trunk to get my bag out." Miranda held up her hand, and Will tossed the keys. She snatched them out of the air.

"I won't be more than five, ten minutes," she told him as she started off toward the trunk of the car. "With any luck, Rob has a couple of greasy pepperoni pizzas in the oven and some strawberry ice cream in the freezer."

"The pizza's a definite, but I wouldn't count on the ice cream," Aidan called to her.

"Oh, I've worked with Rob before," Miranda called back over her shoulder. "He knows how to keep a girl happy."

Rob Flynn did, indeed, know how to keep Miranda Cahill happy. He brought enough strawberry ice cream, frozen pizza, diet Pepsi, and black licorice to keep a smile on her face for the next week. At ten-thirty that night, she was sitting on the floor outside Mara's den, her Sig Sauer on one hip, her walkie-talkie on the other, and a strand of licorice dangling from the corner of her mouth. She propped her back against the wall and twirled the licorice between her lips. She had a clear view of the back door, the deck, and, if she stood, the area around the garage, though that was in shadow now. She wondered how long it would be before Jules Douglas showed up.

She was in complete agreement with Aidan and

whoever else had orchestrated this stakeout—probably John, she thought idly. John liked tidy, and this particular scene was tidy. No superfluous personnel. Not that they had agents to spare these days. More and more of the new agents, and plenty of the established ones, were signing up for the terrorist division, like Portia had.

Portia had tried to talk Miranda into joining with her, but Miranda had never had a feel for the work. This was what she knew, what she liked. She did best in situations where she knew the players, knew what the stakes were. Those tracking the terrorists played a different game, one Miranda wasn't sure she understood. Portia, however, loved the excitement, the intrigue, the whole chasing-across-continents thing as much as she loved hunkering down in dusty caves with her brothers in arms. Miranda shook her head. For identical twins, they couldn't be less alike.

She chewed up the last of the licorice and thought about Portia meeting up with Jack in England. She was certain they had. She just couldn't decide how she felt about it.

And then there was Will. She was pretty sure she knew how she felt about him. As soon as this watch was over, as soon as they had Jules Douglas behind bars, she and Will were going to take a long weekend. Maybe at the Fleming Inn, maybe at the beach someplace. Aidan lived near the beach. Maybe he could suggest an inn. Then again, it was pretty cold for the beach.

Will had been quick to see the parallels between their relationship and that of her mother and father.

She'd recognized the similarities herself, of course, but had refused to acknowledge them. Once she had acknowledged them, she'd have to deal with them. In order to do that, she'd have to put a name to her feelings. She'd never been able to do that.

Will, however, had been far less reluctant.

"I'm falling in love with you."

Yes, well, that certainly put a name to it. How like him to just throw it out there.

How like her to wish he hadn't.

Well, it was there now, like it or not, and she'd have to deal with it. With Will.

Static crackled from the walkie-talkie.

"All quiet back there?" Will asked from his post in the living room.

"All quiet."

"So, whatcha doing?"

"Thinking about what we're going to be doing when this is over."

"Can you be more specific?"

Static crackled at her again.

"Will?" she asked.

"Hold up."

"Will?" she repeated after several minutes had passed.

"False alarm. I think. I thought I saw something . . . never mind, it's Rob."

"The static is about to make me deaf," she complained. "I'm turning this damn thing off now. I'll check back with you in a few, see if it's any better."

She slipped the walkie-talkie back onto her belt, then stood up and walked to the back door. She peered out across the deck. There was a scant slice of moonlight that fell across one side of the yard. She looked skyward and saw clouds move across the face of the moon. Nothing else moved. For now, all was quiet.

The clock on the mantel in the living room chimed four. A few more hours and she'd be able to catch a little sleep. She went back to her post outside the door to Mara's den and slid down the wall until she was seated again. She knew it was unlikely that Jules would have shown up so soon. Tomorrow would be the more likely night for him to make his move. Even if he had managed to make it into the area tonight, he'd be studying the lay of the land. Looking for security. Trying to figure out the best way to strike.

No, it would be tomorrow night at the earliest, the next night at the latest. It hardly mattered which. Either way, they'd still be waiting for him.

She pulled another piece of licorice out of her back pocket and began to chew on it, wondering why she felt less afraid of facing Jules than she did of loving Will.

Burt Connolly lay on his stomach in the damp, cold grass under Helene West's grapevine and tried to figure out what was going on.

He'd been watching for the past few hours, and couldn't figure out which of the two houses Miranda Cahill was in. He'd thought it was the little bungalow there across the yard, but then he'd seen her come out of the house next door and go inside here with the other agent, the big guy. Then some other guy showed up, and the big one left for a while, then came back. Burt had meanwhile backed into the shelter of the grape arbor to hide himself, and he wasn't certain that she hadn't come back out again.

What the fuck was going on around here? What's up with the house next door, anyway?

Well, it was a riddle he wasn't going to be solving for a while, since the sun would be up in another few minutes and he couldn't very well be caught in the yard there. He eased himself out from under the thick woody vines, using his elbows to propel himself backward to the end of the garage. He raised himself to his knees and crawled along the fence to the place where he'd cut an opening a few hours earlier. He'd found a motel about four blocks away, one street in from the highway, and he'd left the truck there. He hadn't liked the way the big guy had stopped to stare at the truck when he'd driven past earlier. Probably hadn't meant much of anything, but still, you never knew with these FBI types. For all Burt knew, the big guy had already called in the license plate. Not that that would tell him anything. He wouldn't know Burt from Adam. He certainly would never be able to put Burt together with Archer.

In the shadows of early morning, he brushed off the dirt as best he could, then crept across another yard, wondering if Archer's body had been found yet. He knew a momentary bit of uncertainty, then shook it off. No one knew he had been with Archer, with the exception of Vince Giordano. And there wasn't much he was going to say about it, since this whole killing thing was his idea. No one could connect him to any of the murders, except Vince. That would implicate Vince, too, wouldn't it? Sure it would. Conspiracy and all that. Nah, he needn't worry about Vince.

Those FBI types, though, they worried him. There were at least two men with Cahill. Were they guarding her, or someone else? And were there more than two? He couldn't see what was going on in the front of the house.

He walked along through the frosty dawn, wondering if maybe he shouldn't just drop it, walk away with what he had. He'd already come to the conclusion that Vince wasn't going to hand over the rest of the money unless Cahill was a done deal.

The questions were, What were the risks of doing Cahill, and was the money worth it? Worth it to go ahead and do her, or worth it to walk away?

He'd have to sleep on it. Rest for a few hours, have a nice big breakfast, then reevaluate the situation with a clear head and a full stomach. All those FBI agents around the house had made him nervous.

Then again, the thought of all that money, just waiting for him someplace, pricked at his streak of greed. All that cash, just waiting for him . . .

It would be a toss-up which would win out in the end: fear or greed.

CHAPTER
TWENTY-FOUR

MARA PACED ANXIOUSLY IN THE KITCHEN, WONDER-
ing when her daughter would come downstairs for
breakfast—if she'd come downstairs—and if so, if
she'd have what Julianne wanted to eat. Was she a cereal eater? If so, what kind?

For the tenth time that morning, Mara opened the
cabinets and checked the cereal boxes.

"I'll bet they're the same boxes that were in there
ten minutes ago," Annie said from the doorway.

"I don't know what she eats." Mara turned to her
sister. "She's my child, and I don't even know what
she eats for breakfast."

"And until yesterday, you didn't know what she
looked like after seven years. Now you do. Take it
easy, Mara. It will all work out. Just stop being so
anxious about everything. You're going to make
yourself crazy."

"I'm afraid I'm already a little bit crazy." Mara
closed the cupboard door. "I think I need coffee."

"Let me make it." Annie smiled and came the rest
of the way into the kitchen. "Your coffee is atro-
cious."

"You sound like Aidan."

"Hey, those Shields boys know their coffee." Annie's smile still dimmed a little when she spoke of her late fiancé, Aidan's brother, taken out by a drug dealer's bullet over a year ago. "Dylan made a mean pot of coffee in the morning. He liked it strong enough to walk on, but it was still pretty damned good."

"I don't recall that I ever had the pleasure," Mara said.

"Hey, you'd remember. Trust me. Dylan's coffee was potent enough to put hair on your chest."

"Now that I would remember." Mara nodded, a weak smile on her face. Then, a moment later, she said, "I wonder if she slept all right."

"I'm sure she was fine."

"Spike stayed in her room all night. He hasn't even been outside yet."

"Want me to try to get him? I'll take him for a walk," Annie offered.

"Let's wait until he shows himself. I'd hate to wake her if she's still . . ."

Mara's attention was drawn to the doorway, where Julianne stood, holding Spike in her arms like a shield.

"I'm awake," Julianne announced flatly. "You don't have to worry about waking me."

"Did you sleep well?" Mara asked, trying her best to sound calm, *normal*.

"I didn't sleep much."

"Oh. I'm sorry—"

"You should have thought of that before you had me kidnapped," Julianne said flatly.

"Julianne, I did not have you kidnapped," Mara protested.

"What would you call it?"

Mara thought it over, then looked to Annie for help.

Annie had gone upstairs.

Coward, Mara thought.

"I don't know what they call it. A rescue—"

"I didn't need to be rescued. I was with my *father*."

"Your father who stole you from me seven years ago, changed your name, and hid you away so that no one could find you."

"That's not why he changed my name," Julianne shot back.

"Oh? Why did he change your name?" Mara felt her patience slipping in spite of her best efforts to hang on, to be nonconfrontational.

"Because he said . . . he said . . ." For the first time, Julianne faltered.

"He said what?"

"He said that when you died, you took my name to heaven with you."

"What is that supposed to mean?" Mara asked gently. "I don't understand."

"I guess he meant . . . well, that it was a name that you chose." Julianne's face clouded. "That you wanted to keep it close to you . . . ?"

"Does that make sense to you?"

"It sort of did when I was little," Julianne said uncertainly.

"You're not a little girl anymore. You're almost

a teenager. A very smart teenager. Think about the things he's said to you. Do they make sense?"

Julianne made a circle on the tile floor with her bare toes, but did not respond.

"What do you like for breakfast?" Mara asked, deciding that she'd do well to take the pressure off Julianne for a bit. She'd given her something important to think about. She didn't want to burden her with too much at once.

"Just juice is okay."

"Maybe some toast with it?"

"Okay."

Annie called the dog from the living room.

"Walk, Spike. Let's go."

She didn't have to call him twice. Spike ran to Annie, his tale wagging a mile a minute, eager for his morning excursion.

"Can I go, too?" Julianne asked.

Mara felt the panic rise within her. Jules could be out there, anywhere, waiting.

"Not this time," Annie told her as she snapped Spike's lead to his collar. "He wants to go out now, and you're not dressed yet. Next time, maybe."

"Okay." Julianne nodded and reached for the glass of orange juice Mara held out in trembling hands.

Julianne watched her with wary eyes.

"What would you like to do after breakfast?" Mara asked.

"I don't know. I can't go anyplace. I don't have any clothes." She took a sip of juice. "If you're going to make me stay here, you're going to have to get me some clothes to wear."

"I'll ask Annie when she gets back," Mara told her.

"Why do you have to ask her?" Julianne frowned. "Can't you take me?"

"I've been having problems with my car. She'd have to drive." Mara averted her eyes. She couldn't bring herself to tell her daughter that she was afraid to let her leave the house.

Maybe we can get Miranda to come along. She has a gun. Annie doesn't carry a gun. . . .

"Do you work?" Julianne asked.

"Yes."

"What do you do?"

"I'm a lawyer. I work with the courts. I'm what they call a child advocate. When there are custody disputes in families, I represent the child or children."

Julianne stared at her, then said, "So if my dad came for me and went to court with you, they'd give you custody because they know you. That won't be fair."

Mara bit her lip. She wasn't going to get into what could be an ugly discussion with Julianne. She wanted to tell her daughter that the courts would give her, Mara, custody because her father had broken the law, but she couldn't let her feelings for Jules surface to sour this time with Julianne. So she said nothing. She poured herself another cup of coffee and sank into a chair at the table.

"Does she work?" Julianne pointed out the window to where Anne Marie stood chatting with Aidan.

"Yes."

"What does she do?"

"She works for the FBI."

"Oh." Julianne watched Annie for a few minutes, then asked, "Who is that man?"

"His name is Aidan Shields. He's a friend of mine."

"Why is he here?"

"He works with Annie."

"He's an FBI man?"

"Yes."

"He's waiting for my father to come for me, isn't he? He's going to arrest my father, and they'll let you keep me because you work with those people." Julianne threw the glass of juice across the room. It hit the cabinet above the stove and shattered.

"Julianne . . ." Mara jumped out of her chair.

"I'll tell them I want to be with my father. I'll tell them how you had those people steal me away. How my father had to keep me away from you because you were a bad—"

"Stop it," Mara said softly. "You know that isn't true. I have never stopped loving you. I never stopped praying that you'd come home."

"Then why did it take you so long to find me? If you were looking so hard, why did it take you so long?" Julianne sobbed and rushed from the room.

Mara followed her daughter to her room and opened the door that had just been slammed in her face. She leaned against the doorjamb and watched as Julianne threw herself facedown onto her bed. Hesitating for just an instant, Mara went to her, sat down on the side of the bed, and gently rubbed her daughter's back, trying to think of the right thing to say.

Hell, how could anyone know the right thing to say?

When no words came, she lay down next to the sobbing girl and held her. Brushing Julianne's blonde hair back from her face, Mara cried tears of her own.

"Why are you crying?" Julianne demanded.

"Because I don't know what else to do," a weary Mara told her, her emotions worn to the quick. "I don't know what to say to you, or what to do for you. I want to tell you that everything your father told you about me was a lie, but I know I'm not supposed to say that, because it would make you feel conflicted. But obviously he didn't tell you the truth about things. Look at me. Certainly I'm not dead. And I was a good mother—I was a very good mother—but if I start telling you all the ways in which I was a good mother, then I'll be wrong for showing your father up as a liar. I am damned if I do, and I'm damned if I don't."

Mara sat up and exhaled. "I'm sorry, Julianne. I shouldn't have said that. Not any of it."

She rubbed her temples, tried to rub away the throbbing pain that had settled in and kept announcing itself, over and over and over. Neither she nor Julianne seemed able to look at the other. The storm of emotions had been so swift and so strong.

"My room is the same," Julianne said after a few very long minutes. "I remember a lot of the dolls. And the stuffed animals there on the shelves."

She got up and went to the bookshelves and touched the spines of several books.

"I looked at a lot of these last night. I remember some of them. I remember you reading to me at night."

"We always read together at night."

"*Mr. Willoughby's Christmas Tree.*" Julianne took one from the top shelf. "I liked this one. The rhymes. I liked the way the tree kept getting smaller and smaller."

She smiled as she flipped through the pages. "I liked how the mice had the tiniest tree at the end. . . ."

"You used to make me crazy, wanting me to read that over and over and over." Mara managed a smile.

"I remember." Julianne skimmed the last page of the book, then slid it back onto the shelf.

"Why didn't you get rid of my stuff?" she asked. "You didn't change anything."

"I wanted your things to be here for you when you came home."

"What if I was twenty when I came back? What if I was in college?"

"It would still all be here."

"What if I never came back?"

"It never occurred to me that you wouldn't come back someday. I wasn't sure how old you'd be, but I knew one day, I'd find you and you'd come home."

Julianne picked up a music box and brought it to the bed and sat down next to her mother. She opened the lid, and watched the tiny skaters whirl stiffly across the ice in time with "The Skater's Waltz."

"It still works." She closed the lid and the music stopped.

"I kept replacing the batteries."

"How many times?" Julianne looked up at her. "How many times did you have to do that?"

"Lots, I guess. I didn't keep count."

Julianne leaned back against her mother, her head resting on Mara's chest, and raised the lid again. She hummed along with the tinny music as the skaters resumed their dance. Mara put an arm around her child and closed her eyes tightly, giving silent thanks, no longer concerned about what came next. She allowed this first bit of closeness to fill her, every lonely corner, and knew that for now, it was enough.

"So what do you think, Cahill? Same places as last night?" Will asked as they left the house next door to Mara's and headed across the drive.

"Sure." She shrugged. "Makes no difference to me, either way."

"Maybe we'll have a bit of action tonight, what do you think?" Keeping to the shadows, he took her hand for just a minute.

"I don't know. What if we're wrong and this is all a waste of time? What if Jules decides it isn't worth it to him to take the risk to get Julianne back? I mean, he has to know that Mara isn't going to give her up without a fight."

"You're right. And I don't think he's the type to back off without fighting back. I think the thought of displeasing his boss will urge him on, even if his paternal instincts do not. He'll be here, maybe tonight. I doubt he's going to want Julianne to spend a minute longer with her mother than she has to."

"Afraid she'll find out just how much he's lied?"

"Afraid that mother-child bond will take over and she won't come willingly. It would be interesting to see how he's going to explain to his daughter that her mother has been alive all these years."

"Like that's going to be an issue. He's not going to get close enough to Julianne to have that conversation."

"How's that going, by the way? What did Annie say about how Mara and her daughter are getting along?"

"She said it goes back and forth. One minute Julianne seems happy to be home, talking to Mara about things she remembers. Then the next minute, she's angry at her mother for taking her from her father. She said it's like a seesaw that's totally out of control."

"It's probably going to be like that for a while," Will said. "Julianne has gone through a lot. I'm sure her loyalties are being severely tested right now."

"Annie said it was to be expected. But it sounded as if it's starting to wear on both of them."

"It's going to wear even more when Jules shows up and we have to take him in," Will reminded her. "That's not going to be a pretty scene."

"Well, maybe we'll get lucky and we'll be able to get our hands on him before Julianne even knows he's been here."

"That's the plan." They reached the backyard, and Will knocked softly on the door. He stepped back when Annie appeared and opened it.

"Sorry," she said softly, "but Julianne just went up to bed. It isn't so easy to talk a twelve-year-old into going to bed early, you know? I told them that I'd be right up, that I needed something from my car. We're going to watch a movie on the TV in Mara's room."

The three stepped into the back hall and Annie closed the door behind them, then locked the dead bolt.

"Got your walkie-talkie?" Will whispered.

"Got the walkie-talkie, got the gun." Miranda patted first one hip, then the other. "And got the all-important licorice."

"Guess you're all set, then. See you later." Will followed Annie down the hall.

"See you." Miranda leaned back against the wall. "Hey, keep in touch, okay? Feel free to call if anything exciting happens."

She slid down the wall, watching Will disappear into the darkness.

Her walkie-talkie buzzed softly against her hip ten minutes later.

"I just heard from John," Will told her.

"And . . . ?"

"And guess whose body was just found facedown in the mud with a couple of bullet holes?"

"I have no clue." Miranda sat up straight, intrigued.

"Maybe it would help if I told you where it was found."

"Go on."

"In a park down the road from Landry's farm."

She processed the information. "Down the road from . . . I don't know. Tell me . . . oh, no, please don't say Regan Landry—"

"No, no. Archer Lowell."

"Lowell? You're kidding, right?"

"Nope. No gun found, they're rushing the testing on the bullets they recovered, see if they're a match to anything we already have. They're hoping that once the story breaks, someone will come forward, have a description of a car or an individual who might have been seen with him. Right now, they have nothing but the body and the bullets."

"Holy shit." She was still in shock. "Poor, stupid Archer . . ."

"Poor Archer was going to plant a bullet between those baby blues of yours. Save the sympathy."

"I can't help it. He was so . . . pathetic." Miranda shook her head.

"Pathetic enough to have killed two men and walked away unseen both times."

"Well, I guess that's good for me, though, right? At least I don't have to worry about him trying to cross me off his hit list," she said. "But who would have wanted him dead?"

"Your mind does sort of wander back to that fourth-man theory now, doesn't it? Someone had to have pulled the trigger."

"But we know there were only three men in that room, Will. Evan confirmed through the deputy sheriff's office that there were only Channing, Giordano, and Lowell. When would they have added a fourth? And why? Doesn't it seem that the more people who knew what they were planning, the more likely it would be that, sooner or later, someone would slip up and tell someone else?"

"Unless one of the three arranged for a fourth to

sort of oversee the game, make sure it was played out."

"But who could have done that? Channing had already played out his piece before Giordano was released from prison, and Archer was still behind bars when Vince was doing his thing," Miranda reminded him.

"Good point. Think there's any chance we can get Vince to fill in the blanks?"

"Yeah, fat chance. Same as they always are with him."

"Well, right now we've got the Plainsville police canvassing the area; we've got tests being run on the bullets. Guess we'll have to wait and see what turns up from either source."

"Let me know what you hear." She sighed. "This is really crazy, isn't it? For just a split second, I felt relieved. Like I can stop looking over my shoulder. Archer's not coming after me. Then up pops the specter of some unknown someone who might be keeping the game going."

"Let's see what ballistics comes back with."

"Right. Thanks. Keep in touch."

Will slid his walkie-talkie into his hip pocket and walked to the kitchen. He stood at the window and slowly pulled the curtain back enough to allow him to look outside. Nothing out of the ordinary. Just another cold fall night. Leaves lay scattered across the lawn and part of the sidewalk. A car door slammed across the street, and a young couple got out and walked to a front porch. At the bottom of the steps, the boy waited while the girl searched her pockets for keys. Feeling a bit like a voyeur, Will watched them kiss hastily, then the girl ran up the steps and unlocked the door. She turned back toward the street and waved before going into the house and closing the door behind her. The boy gunned the engine before he pulled away from the curb, then disappeared around the first bend in the road.

A few more moments of silence, then a car or two passed. Someone out for a walk strolled by, then crossed the street and disappeared down the driveway of the house at the end of the block. Silence again.

Will opened his cell phone and checked his messages. He returned one call immediately, listened to the information he was given, voiced his thanks, and hung up.

He began pacing again, not sure what to do with the information he'd just been given, or what it meant. He'd only known that all of his senses had gone on alert when he'd seen that black truck drive past Mara's house two days ago. There'd been a truck just like it parked outside the prison when he and Miranda had come out after visiting Giordano. The driver's face had been hidden behind a map, which in itself had aroused Will's interest. Who could read something that was right in their face like that?

No one he knew.

And when an identical truck passed by shortly after he and Miranda had arrived here in Lyndon, Will's keen eye had picked up the license plate number and called it in to Evan at the county detectives' bureau and asked him to run a trace.

Now he had a name, but it wasn't one he recognized.

Burton Connolly. Who the hell was he?

Will was counting on Evan to find out.

CHAPTER
TWENTY-FIVE

HE WALKED ALONG THE BACK OF THE PROPERTIES, counting over four from the end, observing the changes that had been made while he was gone. He stared at the fence that carved out the backyard of number 1733. Seven years ago, there had been no fence. From the other side, he heard a long low growl.

Seven years ago, there had been no dog.

It occurred to Jules Douglas that perhaps she'd moved, but then, he knew better. Mara would never leave this house. She'd stay here, weeping and mourning her loss, until the day she died. He'd bet she'd made a shrine out of Julianne's room.

He paused. Odd, how quickly he'd lapsed back into thinking of his daughter as Julianne. After seven years of being so strict with himself, of never permitting himself ever to refer to her as anyone other than Rebecca, now that he was here, she was Julianne once again. Strange.

On the other side of the fence, the dog continued to growl. Damn nuisance. He never did like dogs.

He stepped back into the shadows and moved along the outside of the fence, walked cautiously behind first his old garage—noting that it sported a new coat of paint—then slunk behind the garage belonging to the next-door neighbor. He was met by a fence there, too. What was it with all these fences?

He poked around and was surprised to find that a portion of the fence closest to the garage could be moved aside quite easily. Poor construction, or had someone deliberately snipped the wire that held the end piece to the corner post?

He shrugged, not one to look a gift horse in the mouth, so to speak, and slipped between the post and the garage, then paused to review his surroundings. The grape arbor the old lady had planted years before had really taken off since he'd been gone. The vines were a thick tangle, and the last of the brown and yellow leaves clung halfheartedly to the branches.

"Great shelter," he murmured as he eased between the arbor and the side of the garage. A man could hide here for hours and never be seen from the house.

Or, he realized, from the house next door.

He worked his way to the front of the arbor, then studied the house he'd shared with Mara for eight years. It seemed like a lifetime ago. He barely remembered what it had been like, living there. Over the past few years, he realized how totally unimportant his life with Mara had been. Teaching advanced math at Miller College there in town—now that had been a plum gig, he snorted. He wondered how he'd ever tolerated it. Mundane students, mundane salary, mundane life. And a wife who just couldn't hold his attention for all that long.

The only thing that had made that time in his life

tolerable was that endless line of ladies, all who were willing to play with a handsome professor. Of course, once Mara caught on to that and demanded a divorce, his hand had been pretty much forced.

It still rankled that she had told him how it was going to be. That she had called the shots.

She'd never cheated on him, she'd told him, and she wasn't going to accept his cheating on her. The fact that she'd accidentally run into him while he was in the middle of romancing a fellow professor had made it pretty difficult to deny. Still, all in all, he was supporting her, wasn't he? He was the one who went to work every day so that she could have the luxury of being a stay-at-home mom. You'd have thought she'd have shown a little more gratitude.

But no. It was, "Jules, it's over. I've already talked to a lawyer. He's filing the papers on Monday. . . ."

He'd begged and pleaded, of course he had. Who wanted to get booted out of the house he'd worked so hard to buy? But in the end, it had turned out to be a blessing in disguise.

The best day of his life had been the one on which he'd decided to walk away from it all. He'd gone along with Mara's request that the divorce be amicable, agreeing to share custody of Julianne, agreeing that the best thing for her would be to have both parents in her life, parents who were friendly and respectful of each other.

Like *that* was going to happen.

He'd had his game plan completely laid out right from the start. Phony identifications, in a multitude of names. Phony credentials. Stock certificates cashed in. Bags packed. A car purchased in the name of one of his new aliases, credit cards in the same name. He'd been planning for months to leave Mara and take Julianne with him, knowing there was nothing, nothing, he could do to Mara that could possibly hurt more than taking her daughter from her.

So that was what he did.

The hardest part had been the tears he'd felt obligated to make himself shed when he told his daughter about how her mommy had died and gone to heaven.

The easiest part was hitting the open road with his adoring daughter and traveling around, seeing the country.

Stumbling onto the Valley of the Angels five years ago had been the icing on the cake. The reverend had needed a man who was very adept with numbers. Jules had needed a place to lay low. It had been a marriage made in heaven. He'd been permitted to try out the ladies who'd flocked to the reverend's side, but he'd never touched the underage ones. Uh-uh. Personally, he'd thought that whole thing was sick, but as long as they kept their hands off his daughter and paid him as handsomely as they did, well, he didn't really give a damn. Most of those girls were on the skids when they were brought in anyway, hooking and using drugs and putting their lives in danger every day. At least the reverend offered them a safe haven, one where they could get themselves cleaned up and off drugs, get fed and clothed. Okay, so after a while they were turned over to some old geezer with money to burn and a desire for sex with a girl young enough to be his granddaughter. They were still off the streets, weren't they?

Frankly, Jules didn't give a damn about any of it. He was getting his. Money and a fine young new wife who never questioned him, who never seemed to care how often he spread his handsome talents around. It had been one sweet life, until Mara had pushed herself into it, sent whoever it was she'd sent to grab Julianne and split.

He shook his head. That was all Prescott needed to hear, that Jules didn't know who had spirited her away. When the reverend had asked, Jules had told him it had been a private detective hired by Mara. Prescott hadn't pressed it, but in his heart, Jules wasn't 100 percent certain himself. He assumed Mara was behind it. Who else would care enough to go to all the trouble of getting someone into the compound, waiting patiently while the whole scheme was set up? It had to be Mara. Jules had known better than to show any sign of doubt when discussing it with Prescott. The reverend had been incensed that he'd been duped by Miss Ruth—whoever she really was—and that there was now someone on the outside who knew what really was going on inside the Valley of the Angels.

Thinking about Prescott made Jules feel just a little bit edgy. He knew that the reverend would make good on his threat to come after the girl himself if he had to. If it came to that—if it looked as if Jules couldn't control his own child, his own life—well, just where would that leave Jules?

No one who'd ever left the compound had surfaced to talk about what had gone on there. Prescott wasn't about to take the chance that Julianne would be the first. That she was the daughter of one of his most trusted financial counselors meant nothing at all. Jules knew that, and it bothered him, but it merely strengthened his resolve to find Julianne and take her back himself.

Then there was the question of Miss Ruth. Jules knew that Prescott would go to the ends of the earth to track her down. He didn't want to be around when Prescott found her.

Mara, of course, was the key to finding Ruth. It was Jules's plan to take Mara with them in order to turn her over to the reverend. He might as well make points where and when he could. He figured Prescott would have his men take Mara to one of his many homes that were scattered throughout the country, and would, more likely than not, send Jules and Julianne to a different location.

Assuming, of course, that Prescott didn't have other plans for the two of them. Jules's mouth went dry at the thought of what Prescott could do to them, if he wanted. He could easily kill Jules, and send Julianne to one of his clients. Handing over Mara, which hopefully would lead to finding Ruth—if in fact that was her name—would go a long way toward rectifying the problem. A speedy return of Jules and his daughter would further placate Prescott.

So, if he was to survive, he was going to have to take care of business now. They would have to leave, the three of them, and they would have to leave soon. Prescott had lent him his private plane, and he'd had someone meet him at the airport with a car and a .38.

But he'd also only given Jules forty-eight hours before he sent in someone to finish the job for him, and those forty-eight hours were almost gone. Jules got sick to his stomach every time he thought about what finishing the job might mean.

From his shelter beneath the arbor, Jules kept his eyes on the house. Mara would have someone keeping watch, wouldn't she? Surely she couldn't possibly think that he'd let her get away with a stunt like this, could she? She couldn't possibly be that stupid.

He was just beginning to think that perhaps she was indeed that stupid when the back door of the neighbor's house opened and a figure emerged. He stood for a long time on the top step, his arms folded across his chest. Finally, he raised one hand and gave some kind of a sign. Jules's eyes followed the gesture. It took him a while, but finally he saw the second figure, also dressed in black, near the corner of Mara's garage.

More than one private investigator?

Cops?

Nah, he mentally smacked himself on the forehead. FBI.

That would explain all those Virginia "Friends of the Chesapeake" license plates he'd seen when he'd driven past the house earlier.

Sure. Annie. FBI Annie, he used to call her. She'd have brought in the troops for this, wouldn't she?

And wasn't that just dandy, he thought sourly. Just what the Right Reverend Prescott was going to want to hear.

He watched the man on the porch finish smoking

his cigarette, then toss it onto the grass. He stepped on it and the small dot of red disappeared.

Next door, the kitchen lights were turned out. The first floor of the house lay in darkness now. If he was going to make his move, he couldn't wait much longer. The sooner he got in and out of there and away, the better off he'd be. He started to sweat just thinking about how Prescott was going to react to hearing that the FBI had been behind Julianne's disappearance from the compound.

He'd worry about what to say to Prescott later.

Right now he had two FBI agents to deal with—at least two.

He paused. Could there be more? Inside, maybe, might be another. Three cars with Virginia plates, three agents?

He watched for another half hour but saw no one, other than the two agents he'd previously spotted. The one on the porch never ventured farther than the end of the house, while the agent closest to Mara's house wandered toward the front every fifteen minutes or so, blending into the shadows.

Jules patted his leg for the knife he had strapped there. He could take out the agent on the porch silently the next time the agent closest to the house made his round out front. Then, when the second agent returned to that spot near the garage he seemed to like so much, Jules would be waiting for him. He could get into the house through the window in the den. He could cut out the glass, slice through the screen. . . .

Yeah. That would have to be the plan. He was way

too close to being out of time . . . this would be his best chance. His last chance.

Then the agent on Mrs. West's porch went inside the house. Jules froze. Should he wait for the man to return, or should he go in after him?

Several minutes passed before he realized he would have to make a move. He'd have to go inside, hope that with the element of surprise on his side, he would be able to overtake his quarry. He was trying to recall the layout of Mrs. West's house—was there a laundry room off the back hall, or a door to the basement?—when he heard a distinct rustle from the open end of the arbor. Flattening himself to the wall, he watched as a tall figure eased backward into the cover of the thicket. Silently Jules drew his gun and extended his arm so that the newcomer backed into the muzzle.

"Not a sound," Jules whispered over the taller man's shoulder. "Don't say a word."

The man froze.

"Now, how many?" Jules demanded.

"Wh-what?" the man stuttered.

"How many more of you are there?" Jules whispered.

"It's just me."

"Liar. I know you've got one man in the house here, and one man outside next door. How many more?"

"I don't know what you're talking about. I don't know who is inside that house or who is outside over there. I swear. . . ."

"Shhhh. Keep it down. Turn around and face the garage and put your hands on your head." Jules continued to hold the gun to the middle of the stranger's back. "Hands on your head. Come on, you've arrested how many people, you don't know where to put your hands when you're going to be frisked?"

"Arrested . . . ? Hey, I ain't no cop—"

"No. You're no cop. You're FBI."

"FBI?" Burt Connolly was incredulous. "Buddy, I don't know what the fuck is going on here, or why you think I'm FBI—"

"Shut up."

"Listen, you've got me confused with someone else. I swear. . . ."

"Oh, right, you were just passing through the neighborhood and decided to take a shortcut through the grape arbor." Jules sneered softly and jabbed the gun into the middle of the man's back. "And keep your voice down. Don't make me tell you again."

"Listen, I can explain—"

"Where's your ID?" Jules demanded.

"Only ID I got is my driver's license."

"That in your wallet?" Jules asked after he'd finished patting down his captive and finding only one weapon, which he confiscated and stuck down his belt.

"Yeah. Left back pocket."

Jules retrieved it, but he couldn't see the name on the license. It was too dark. There was nothing there that even vaguely resembled an FBI identification, though. He'd seen a few of those over the years, when they first started looking at Prescott for tax evasion. He knew that no agent would go on a job without his ID.

"If you're not FBI, and you're not a cop, you must be private security or private investigation. Which is it?"

"Neither."

"Who do you work for?"

"I don't work for anyone." The man started to turn and Jules jammed the butt of the gun into his back again.

"Then what are you doing here? The truth."

"I'm watching the house next door."

"Why?"

"Because I think there's someone in there I want to see."

"Who?"

"Woman named Miranda Cahill."

"Never heard of her." Jules frowned. Had he underestimated Mara? Had she sold the house in his absence?

"She live there?" he asked.

"I have no idea. I followed her here." Burt paused. "If you're looking for FBI, though, maybe you're looking for her. She is an FBI agent. And I suspect the guy who came with her is FBI, too."

"So you're telling me there are two in there?" Jules nodded in the direction of Mara's house.

"Two that I know of."

"How about this other house? How many?" He tilted his head toward Mrs. West's.

"I don't know about that house. I don't know who's there."

"Who else is over there? With the two agents?"

"Some blonde woman, pretty. Mid-thirties, maybe.

Another woman, dark. Small. I saw them yesterday, but I didn't see them today."

Annie. Mara. No surprise there, Jules thought.

"A girl? Blonde girl, about twelve, maybe looks a little younger?" Jules asked.

"Didn't see a kid." Burt shook his head.

"She's got to be in there," Jules muttered, more to himself than to his unwanted companion. "Where else could she be?"

They stood in the same place for another few minutes, the gun still solid in the middle of Burt's back. Finally, Burt said, "Look, my arms are really starting to hurt. I don't know what you're doing here, or what you want with those people, and frankly, I don't give a fuck. Let me just turn and leave. I haven't even seen your face; I can't identify you even if I wanted to. Not that I want to. The last people I need to see right now are the cops. . . ."

"What do you want her for?" Jules asked. "The woman you followed here."

Burt took too long to come up with a good answer.

"Don't bother trying to think up a story. Just tell me the truth, goddamn it. What do you want with the woman? She your ex or something?"

"Someone paid me to follow her."

"For what purpose?" Jules poked him again with the gun. "Turn around. I want to see your face."

Reluctantly, Burt did as he was told. "I'm supposed to take her out."

Jules stared at the man for a long moment.

"By take her out, I assume you don't mean on a

date," Jules said dryly. "You mean, you're supposed to—"

"Get rid of her, yeah." Burt slumped back against the garage.

"Well, that would certainly create a lively diversion, wouldn't it?" Jules said thoughtfully.

"What?"

"Maybe we could help each other." Jules lowered the gun, but only slightly.

"Maybe. What is it you want?"

"I want my daughter. And my wife. They're in that house." He nodded in the direction of the house across the drive. "But you're telling me there are two FBI agents in there. One is the woman you're after. . . ." Jules scratched his head and continued to think through the situation.

"You know, maybe we can help each other." The other man nodded. "I want the woman to come out; you want to get in."

"We need to draw both agents outside," Jules observed.

"Then you can slip inside, do whatever it is you came to do, and we both go on about our business."

"There are two agents outside," Jules told him. "We need to get rid of both of them. How are you with a knife?"

Burt shook his head. "Never used one. Gun is my weapon of choice, and right now, you're holding mine."

"So I am." Jules pondered the situation, trying to figure out how best to utilize this strange turn of events.

When it came to him, he thought himself quite brilliant.

"I have an idea," he whispered.

"Great."

"We're going to have to work together on this."

"Whatever." Burt's eyes were still on the stranger's gun.

"This is how I see it." Jules leaned closer, and laid out his plan.

"Hey, that could work." Burt nodded with a little more enthusiasm, now that he hadn't been shot in the back. "I can see that working."

"You get what you want; I get what I want. Then we both go on our way."

"Sounds good to me."

"The timing is important, though. We have to wait until the guy there by the end of the garage makes his move toward the front of the house. Should be in about another—" Jules looked at his watch and pushed in the pin on the side that illuminated the face. "—four minutes or so. He'll start over to the house, keep to the shadows, walk all the way around to the front. I'm thinking he might go around to the other side before he starts back."

"He does." Burt nodded. "At least, he did last night. There's that hedge over there, he walks along it as far as the back fence, then he comes back around again. Sometimes he stands in the doorway and just watches the street. There's a small porch out there, and it's dark without the lights on. He sometimes hangs out there a little. I was behind the hedge last night and watched him."

"Good, good to know." Jules smiled. "Now, all we need is for the agent in this house to come out. I don't know what's taking him so long. . . ."

"Oh, him? Last night he was mostly out by the front. There are some shrubs around the front steps."

"Yes, yes, I know them."

"Well, he stays mostly around the shrubs. Sits on the step, sometimes smokes a cigarette."

"Great. I've got that covered. Give me five minutes." Jules slipped out through the vines. "Then watch for me to come back around the corner of the house. We'll give the guy there by the garage about three minutes, then you'll make your move."

"And you'll take care of him?"

"I'll take care of everything."

"Great. Great." Burt nodded. "It could work. It could be dicey, there's some room for error, but not bad for impromptu."

"Thanks." Jules patted Burt on the back and started out of the shelter. "Good luck."

Burt grabbed him by the back of the shirt and held him motionless.

"My gun," Burt reminded him. "You've still got my gun."

Jules pulled it from inside his belt and handed it over.

"Sorry."

"No harm, no foul," Burt assured him.

What a rube. Jules shook his head as he slipped through the shadows toward the back of Mrs. West's house and around the far side. *But that rube is the best shot I have to make this work. . . .*

Jules stood in the midst of the shrubs that Helene West had long ago planted along the front of her house. There was just enough cover for him to blend in long enough for him to get his bearings and to plan his course. The agent he stalked was leaning on the opposite corner of the house, well in the shadows himself. Jules watched him for a full ten minutes, but the man never seemed to have moved a muscle. He unsnapped the sheath, then slowly removed the knife. Keeping to the mulched beds, he crept along the porch, then around it. Knowing he must keep the element of surprise on his side, he made a sudden rush and slammed the knife into the back of his unsuspecting target. A whoosh of surprise escaped the lips of his victim, and Jules pulled the knife out, then reached over the slumping figure to slice the man's throat from one side to the other. He let the body down easy, the rest of the way to the ground, and watched the mulch grow soggy and red. Wiping first the knife, then his hands, on the back of the dying man's shirt, he dropped the knife back into its holder and stepped around the corner of the house, searching in the dark for his new best buddy.

He spotted him there, at the arbor, gesturing for Jules to stay put. Sinking back into the shrubs, Jules watched for the agent across the way to make his move. After a long seven minutes, he finally did. As soon as the agent disappeared around the side of the house, Jules's new friend emerged from the shadows. Burt ran toward the back gate of the house next door, waving in Jules's direction so that he would know it was clear for him, too, to move.

But instead of following the agent to the front of the house, where he was expected to surprise and overtake him, Jules kept to the shadows that surrounded Mrs. West's house and, standing in the middle of the driveway, fired two shots straight through Burt Connolly's back.

The shots echoed through the backyard, and just as Jules had anticipated, the back door of Mara's house flew open. He watched a woman emerge and fly off the deck as two men ran from the front. As they gathered around the fallen stranger, Jules ducked behind the cars and made his move toward the open front door. He figured he'd have, at best, a scant few minutes before his window of opportunity closed. He couldn't afford to be on the wrong side of it when it did.

CHAPTER
TWENTY-SIX

MIRANDA WAS THE FIRST TO REACH THE FALLEN MAN. After checking and determining there was no pulse, she looked up at Aidan and Will, who'd run down the drive from the front after hearing the shot.

"Nice aim, Cahill," Will noted. "But we need to talk about the fact that you left the house alone and without telling me you were going."

"I didn't shoot him." She frowned. "I thought Aidan got him."

"I was on the other side of the house," Aidan told them.

"Which leaves Rob," Will said. He cupped his hands and called across the drive. "Hey, Rob. Great shot. You got him."

When there was no answer, Aidan called out, "Rob? You out there, man?"

Aidan and Will exchanged a worried glance.

"Something is not right," Aidan said under his breath. "Rob should be out there. . . ."

Aidan crept along the garage and headed for the West house next door.

Moments later, he'd made his way around to the front, where he found what he'd feared.

"Will," he called across the drive.

"You found him?" Will called back.

"Yeah. Yeah, I found him."

"He hurt? Need an ambulance?"

"Too late for an ambulance. But put a call in for the local police. We're going to need them. . . ."

"My God, what happened?" Miranda asked anxiously as Aidan trotted back toward them. "What's happened to Rob?"

Before he could answer, Annie ran onto the deck and down the steps.

"What's going on?" She grabbed Miranda's arm. "We heard a shot."

"Looks like your ex-brother-in-law showed up right on schedule. We think Rob Flynn took him out," Miranda said.

"Good thing I made Mara stay inside. I told her if Julianne woke up, she needed to be in there with her, in case she had heard the shot, too." Annie bent down and peered at the body. She stared for a long minute, then looked up at Miranda and asked, "Who is this?"

"Isn't it Jules?"

"No." Annie shook her head.

"Are you certain?" Miranda bent down next to Annie to get a closer look.

"Positive. I don't know who it is, but it isn't Jules Douglas."

"You're kidding." Will leaned forward as well, but the face wasn't familiar to him, either. He reached down and patted the man's pockets until he found a wallet, then carefully removed it, opened it, and took out the driver's license.

"Burton J. Connolly," Miranda read over Will's shoulder. "Who is he? I don't know that name."

"I do," Will told her. "Burton Connolly is the name of the owner of the black pickup that followed us from the prison."

"What black pickup? What are you talking about?" Miranda stared at him.

"When we were leaving the prison—after we spoke with Vince the other day—there was a black pickup parked in the lot. Whoever was behind the wheel picked up a map and held it in front of his face just as we were walking past. Well, naturally, it drew my attention."

"Naturally," Miranda said dryly. "I don't remember seeing him or the truck."

"Well, it was there. I didn't catch the plate at the time, but I did notice some dings on the rear fender. The day we arrived here, when I went to move the car, the same truck passed by."

"How did you know it was the same truck?" she asked.

"The dings in the back fender. Too much of a coincidence. So I called Evan Crosby and asked him to run the tags for me. The truck is registered to Burton Connolly. How likely do you think it is that there's another Burton Connolly in the neighborhood this week?"

"So what do you think happened here?" Annie asked. "You think he knifed Rob, left him for dead, then Rob got a shot or two off before he died?"

"No way." Aidan shook his head. "Rob was dead before he hit the ground."

He bent over Burt's body, inspected it, then stood up and said, "I can tell you this much, our friend here didn't kill Rob." Aidan stood with his hands on his hips. "Rob's throat was cut, one fast clean cut, side to side. Whoever killed him would have been sprayed with blood. Even if he'd come at Rob from behind, there's going to be blood on his hands and arms, at the very least. This guy's hands, shirt, they're clean."

"Then he was working with someone else," Annie said, and at that moment, the three agents turned to look at the house.

"Dear God, Mara . . ." Miranda took off toward the front of the house. "Will . . . the back . . ."

When Aidan started behind them, Annie grabbed his shirt and held on.

"No, no," she told him fiercely. "If Jules is in there, you cannot be a part of this. If you're planning on marrying my sister, you cannot be the man who brings down her daughter's father, understand? If Miranda or Will needs help, that will be a different situation. But right now, leave it to them. Get on the phone and get the Lyndon police on their way, but stay out of the house unless they need you in there. If you plan on being that girl's stepfather, you cannot be involved in Jules's arrest. . . ."

"Turn around, Mara, and go on back up the stairs." Jules stood inside the open front door, his gun pointed at the heart of his ex-wife. "Quietly, but quickly, we're going to get Julianne, and then the three of us are leaving. Together. That should make you happy."

"No," Mara said softly. "I've waited seven years for her to come back. I'm not giving her up. And neither of us is going with you."

"She isn't yours to give or to keep. She's mine," Jules sneered. "I'm out of time and well out of patience, Mara. Get her. *Now.* I don't have time to discuss this, and I don't have time to argue."

"I can't let you take her back there, Jules. Please. You've had her all these years. . . ."

"Don't waste your time begging, Mara. And don't bother to turn on the tears. It's not going to make a damned bit of difference."

"Jules, listen—"

"I'm out of time, you stupid cow. Move. Get her and bring her down here now, or I'll shoot you where you stand. I should have done it years ago."

"Daddy?" The small voice from the top of the steps floated uncertainly to the room below. "Daddy?"

"Get your things, and hurry, baby. Daddy's come to take you back. You and Mommy are coming with me."

Julianne, still in her nightgown, started down the steps, her eyes on her father.

"You said she was dead. You told me she died. Why did you lie to me?"

"I'll explain it all later, honey. Just leave your things and come on now, Julianne, we're out of time. Come with Daddy . . ." Jules held a hand out to her. "Mara, move."

"She's not a bad person. You lied about that, too. Why did you do that? Why did you have to lie?"

"Sweetheart, I'll explain everything to you later." Jules was starting to sweat profusely. "But right now, *we have to go.*"

"Why do you have a gun?" Julianne stood next to her mother.

"Julianne, we're going now. Do you hear me? Now. Right now." Jules's voice rose shrilly. The gun waved shakily in his hand.

"Jules, put the gun away. You're frightening Julianne," Mara pleaded.

"Out the door. Now." He reached out for his daughter with his free hand. Julianne took several more steps away from Jules, then her eyes widened with surprise.

Looking beyond him, an "Oh" escaped her lips.

Miranda Cahill had two more steps before she'd have reached Jules, but Julianne's inadvertent warning had removed the element of surprise. He spun around, his finger on the trigger, and the best Miranda could do was to swing one leg in the direction of his gun hand. That one long leg was all it took.

Jules's .38 flew across the room. He grabbed Miranda's leg in midair and flipped her onto her back before diving for his gun at the same time Will came at him from the back hall. Even with his adrenaline in high gear, Jules was no match for Will. Within seconds, Jules was facedown on the living room floor, both hands held behind his back in Will's strong grip.

"Cahill, you okay?"

"I will be in a minute."

"Have you got a pair of handcuffs on you?"

"No." She lay on her back, trying to regulate her breathing. "Guess you're just going to have to sit on him until the police get here."

"Are you going to arrest my father?" A shaken Julianne stood behind Mara, anxiously holding on to her mother.

"I'm afraid the police are going to have to take him in, yes," Miranda told her. To Mara, she said, "Maybe you'll want to take Julianne upstairs until we're finished here."

"Come on, sweetie." Mara turned her daughter toward the steps.

"You won't keep her, you know. They can't hold me. I'll be back, Mara," Jules snarled as Mara and Julianne climbed the steps. "Don't think for a minute that you're going to keep her. Julianne! Come back here!"

Julianne stared straight ahead until she reached her bedroom door. She went in, still holding her mother's hand, and closed the door.

"Bitch," Jules spat. "You won't be able to lock me up. I'll be out by morning. Reverend Prescott will be on the next plane to bail me out."

"I doubt it," Will told him calmly. "There are two dead bodies out there, one of whom is a federal agent. I'm betting the bullet in the other matches that .38 of yours. Besides, something tells me Reverend Prescott has his hands full right now."

"What are you talking about?" Jules looked up, his eyes red with fury.

"I'm talking about the fact that at eight o'clock

tonight, a team of federal agents paid a visit to Reverend Prescott. Seems they have some questions for him to answer. I think he's going to be way too busy to worry about you, Jules. I'm willing to bet he's not going to give you a second thought. . . ."

"I want a lawyer," Jules growled. "You call the compound and tell them I want Robert Springer out here right now."

"Springer, eh?" Will grinned and looked up at Miranda. "You hear that, Cahill? Nothing but the best for Prescott and his merry band of pedophiles, I guess."

Jules bucked wildly.

"I'm not a pedophile," he shouted. "I've never . . . I would never . . . you're disgusting. . . ."

"Yeah, yeah. You're pure as the driven snow. Only cooked the books, figured out how Prescott could hide the money he made off those poor young girls." Will, who still sat astride Jules, leaned over and said, "You're going to prison along with the rest of them, Douglas. I'm only sorry your daughter had to be here to see you go down like this."

Flashing lights in the street heralded the arrival of several Lyndon police cruisers and an ambulance.

"Hey, Jules, looks like your ride is here." Will stood as three uniformed police officers rushed through the front door. "Here's your man, fellas. He's all yours. . . ."

It was almost three in the morning by the time the last patrol car left Hillside Avenue in peace once again. Inside the house at 1733, Mara Douglas lay awake beside her sleeping daughter, praying that the nightmare was just about over.

Downstairs, Anne Marie McCall lay awake on the sofa in her sister's living room and wept for yet another dead agent, wept for his wife, who had yet to be told that she was now a widow, and remembered what it had felt like to get the call that the man she'd loved—the man who held her heart and her dreams—was gone.

Downtown, in the morgue, Aidan Shields sat beside the body of his friend, and waited for Rob's younger brother to arrive. The scene was achingly familiar to him, and he wondered if he would ever get used to the feeling of helplessness, of wasted life, useless loss. In the quiet antiseptic room, Aidan wondered if Mara was all right. It had damn near killed him to not rush into her house and take out that son of a bitch ex-husband of hers. But Annie had been right: If he and Mara were ever to build a life together, Aidan could not have been the one to have taken down Julianne's father.

In the room next door, on another slab, lay the other body they'd brought in that night. The M.E. had arrived and had already taken fingerprints. The prints and the gun they'd found in his hand had been turned over to the Lyndon police, who would run the prints through NCIC. They'd fire the gun, then test the bullets against those on file. Aidan couldn't help but wonder what they'd find.

In Helene West's living room, Miranda Cahill all but collapsed on the sofa, and rubbed the heels of her hands against her eyes, hoping to rub away the fatigue.

"How's your back?" Will asked from the doorway.

"Hurts."

"Want me to rub it?"

"Uh-huh. Just don't rub anything else, okay?" She turned over and fell facedown on the cushions. "I'm too tired to fight you off."

"That would be good news, if I wasn't too tired to take advantage of you." He sat on the edge of the sofa and began to knead her shoulders.

"Ouch. Not so hard."

"Better?" He eased up.

"Ummmm. Much better."

He continued to massage her back.

"So what do you think about taking that little side trip to the inn tomorrow?" he asked.

"I think yes. We're due for some R and R." She tried to nod, but her head barely moved. "Fleming Inn, *si*. Mrs. West's sofa, no."

He laughed, moving his hands farther down her back.

"You've got great hands, Fletcher. I ever tell you that?"

Her words were slurred with fatigue.

"Yes, actually, you have told me that. On several occasions, as a matter of fact. Want me to remind you of specifics?"

"No need. I remember." She fought the sleep that threatened to claim her.

"Maybe in the morning, I should call Mrs. Duffy and reserve her best suite."

"Good idea. Reserve it for a couple of days, can you?"

"Whatever the lady wants." He smiled in the dark, listening as her breath grew more and more shallow. He knew she was ready to drop off, overwhelmed by the lack of sleep over the past two days and the adrenaline rush of the evening's events. He was tired enough to sleep standing up.

"We'll have to stop at a store first," she told him groggily, just when he thought she'd fallen asleep. "There's a nice mall on the way out of town; I should be able to find what I want at one of the stores in there."

"What do you want?" He took a pillow from the end of the sofa and tossed it on the floor. He lay down, his head on the pillow, his arms folded under his head.

"Some pretty little silk scarves. Four should do nicely, I think." She yawned and turned over.

"What do you need scarves for?" he asked.

"Well, you said you couldn't find your hand-cuffs. . . ." She paused for effect, encircling one of her wrists with the fingers of the other hand, then whispered, "But I've always preferred scarves anyway. I seem to remember you do, too. . . ."

"Jesus, Cahill," he groaned, "you're killing me."

"Maybe so, but at least you'll die with a smile on your face. . . ."

He could feel her smile through the dark, and he laughed, then sat up and grabbed her around the waist, pulling her onto the floor next to him.

"Pillow," she muttered.

He reached for the one she'd been using and slid it under her head, then pulled her closer.

"Is the floor too hard for your back?" he asked.

"It's okay." She snuggled into him.

For a moment, he just enjoyed the sensation of having her this close again.

"Stay," she whispered. "Stay this time."

"This time and every time," he told her.

She was reaching her arms up to draw him close when his phone began to ring.

"Don't answer it," she protested. "Any time the phone rings at two o'clock in the morning, it's not going to be good news."

"It's three," he said as he rolled onto one side to retrieve his phone from his pocket and checked the incoming call. "It's John."

"Even worse," she groaned.

"Hey, John," Will said. "Yeah, you heard right . . . yeah, here's what happened. . . ."

Will proceeded to walk John through the night's events. When he finished the call a long twelve minutes later, he turned off the phone and tossed it onto the sofa.

"We have to be in the office tomorrow for a meeting around four to wrap this Douglas thing up, then we'll be briefed on the Prescott case. John wants us to fly out to Wyoming day after tomorrow and help track down the girls who have gone missing from the compound over the past few years. Looks like there have been dozens of them, John thinks maybe even hundreds. Genna's going to be lead on this; we're going to be working with her."

He lay beside Miranda, stroking her hair lightly with his fingers. "Looks like those pretty silk scarves are going to have to wait, babe. But maybe we can leave for Wyoming ahead of the others so that we can have a little time to ourselves. Won't be the Fleming Inn, but I'm sure we'll find someplace nice. What do you think? Miranda?"

He glanced down and realized that she was sound asleep.

"Well, that's okay," he whispered. "God knows you earned it."

Will lay awake in the still house, the only sound Miranda's gentle breathing, thinking that of all the nights they'd spent together over the past few years, he'd never felt closer to her than he did right at that moment.

He thought about where they'd been and where they were headed, about the things that had gone wrong between them in the past, and he promised himself that the road ahead would be different from the road they were leaving behind. He whispered that promise to her in the dark, then closed his eyes and joined her in sleep.

_____ EPILOGUE _____
•

VINCE WAS IN THE INFIRMARY, WAITING FOR HIS TURN
to see the nurse about an annoying rash he had developed over much of his body.

"Gotta be the lousy crap they wash our clothes with," he'd grumbled to the guard who'd brought him up.

The door to the nurse's office stood open, and Vince could see straight inside to the TV where the noon news was just coming on. He amused himself for a few minutes, listening to the political bullshit that passed for commentary on the elections that would be held in several days. When the anchor moved back to local headlines, Vince almost fell off his chair.

". . . body of suspected killer Archer Lowell was found down the road from the farm where true-crime writer Joshua Landry had been killed just days earlier. In an exclusive interview with the local chief of police, this station has learned that the bullets that killed both men were fired from the same gun. In an even more bizarre twist, that gun was found on the body of Burton Connolly, an ex-con who was shot and killed outside a house in Lyndon where the chief financial officer for Reverend Prescott was arrested two nights ago. . . ."

What the fuck . . . ?

Vince leaned as close to the open door as he could get when the tape of the arrest in Lyndon began to roll.

Wow, he thought as he watched the tape. Archer's dead. Burt-man, too. What the fuck was going on?

And hey, there's Blondie, the profiler. What the hell?

It occurred to him that apparently neither Archer nor Burt had survived long enough to talk to the FBI and bring up his name or they'd have been in his face by now. Thank heaven for small favors, eh?

"No word yet from the FBI as to how these cases are connected, but it's believed that the FBI is as baffled as the Lyndon police over the possible relationships among Lowell and Landry and this latest victim, Connolly, and what, if any, is the connection among those three and Reverend Prescott's Valley of the Angels. In a related story, Prescott's compound was the scene of a dawn raid by FBI agents this morning, and for more on that, we go to our affiliate in Wyoming. . . ."

Vince was filled with a perverse pleasure to hear that the FBI was stymied. Not that he had it figured out yet, but what the fuck, *they* cared. He didn't. Not really.

The taped interviews continued, and Vince found himself grinning broadly when Miranda Cahill come to the mike, her face filling the screen.

Her hair was tousled and she wore no makeup, but even so, she was some looker.

Vince realized he was almost relieved to see that Archer hadn't killed her. It would have been a waste. She was probably the most beautiful woman who'd ever spoken to him, and Vince took a twisted sort of pride in that, and in the fact that she'd managed to dodge the bullet, so to speak. That she'd outplayed him in the game.

He couldn't begrudge her her life. Especially when she filled out that shirt the way she did . . .

Nah, he wasn't sorry that Archer hadn't been able to get to her. He had even started to grow a little fond of her, in an odd sort of way. She was all right, that Cahill.

He stared into space, thinking about the morning he'd met the other two. A chance meeting, and an unholy alliance had been forged. Men with murder in their hearts and revenge on their minds, playing a game. *Pretending* to play a game. It was only supposed to be a game.

And then Curtis Channing had decided to play for real.

That Curt, he'd been a real card, all right.

Somehow, Vince hadn't been at all surprised to find out that the man was a serial killer. He'd read in the paper last week the cops were still trying to add up the body count.

Who woulda thought that?

And Archer, from all he'd heard over the past few days, was just some dumb-shit kid who'd liked to talk big. Well, he'd talked himself right into one hell of a mess, hadn't he?

One hell of a big mess. And if memory served, the whole game, this whole hit list thing, had been Archer's idea in the first place. It had been a game no one had won.

Well, that's not quite true, he smiled wryly, *at least I'm alive. More than Channing or Archer could say, right?*

Guess that makes me the winner after all. Last man standing, and all that.

It was one hell of a story, though. And wouldn't it make one hell of a book?

Shit, he nodded to himself, *this would be a blockbuster. It has bestseller written all over it.* All he needed was someone to work with him. Collaborate, that's what they called it. Someone who'd know how to put the words together to make them sound good.

Suddenly the thoughts began to gather and swirl around and around in his head.

Oh, but it was brilliant. Perfect.

By the time he got back to his cell, he was in need of a pen and paper, quickly, before he forgot what he wanted to say.

Using his best Palmer method handwriting, he began:

Dear Miss Landry:

Please accept my condolences—he paused, then erased and started again—*my most heartfelt condolences on the loss of your father. . . .*

She had nothing left to lose . . . except her life.

DEAD WRONG

by Mariah Stewart

It was inescapably chilling, as if the murderer was methodically working his way down a page torn from the phone book. The three victims brutally killed in their own homes had one thing in common: they were all listed as M. Douglas. The fact that Mara Douglas is next on the list has her jumping at shadows, until FBI agent Aidan Shields shows up to make sure she doesn't become the fourth victim.

Aidan has been out of commission since an undercover operation went bad more than a year ago. Back on the job, his razor-sharp instincts are returning. But it will take all of Aidan's wits to stay one step ahead of the elusive killer who has engaged him in a deadly game—a game in which Mara's life is the prize. A game only one can win . . .

Published by Ballantine Books
Available wherever books are sold

*She thought the terror was be-
hind her. She was right.*

DEAD CERTAIN

by Mariah Stewart

With her stalker captured, antiques dealer Amanda
Crosby can finally sleep at night. Having worked hard to
put the nightmare behind her, Amanda has vowed to
never be a victim again. But when her business partner,
Derek England, is found with a bullet through the back
of his head just hours after she left an incriminating message on his voice mail, Amanda finds herself in danger of
becoming a victim of another sort.

All the evidence points to Amanda as Derek's killer, and
Chief of Police Sean Mercer is building the case against
her. But when another of her colleagues is found brutally
murdered, it's obvious that someone other than Amanda
is behind the killings. Suddenly Amanda is a target once
again, as a diabolical killer circles ever closer—and the
only thing that stands between her and becoming the
third and final victim is the man who had tried to put her
behind bars. . . .

Published by Ballantine Books
Available wherever books are sold